LONDON ASSAULT

ALSO BY BRIAN DRAKE

Team Reaper Series

Steve Dane Thrillers

Scott Stiletto Series

Sam Raven Series

LONDON ASSAULT

A SAM RAVEN THRILLER

BRIAN DRAKE

London Assault
Paperback Edition
Copyright © 2024 Brian Drake

Wolfpack Publishing
701 S. Howard Ave. 106-324
Tampa, Florida 33609

www.wolfpackpublishing.com

This book is a work of fiction. Any references to historical events, real people or real places are used fictitiously. Other names, characters, places and events are products of the author's imagination, and any resemblance to actual events, places or persons, living or dead, is entirely coincidental.

All rights reserved. No part of this book may be reproduced by any means without the prior written consent of the publisher, other than brief quotes for reviews.

Paperback ISBN: 978-1-63977-706-8
eBook ISBN: 978-1-63977-707-5
LCCN 2024930714

LONDON ASSAULT

PROLOGUE

Ten Years Ago

SHANNON WARD ONLY WANTED A NORMAL DAY.

And normal meant not traveling with armed military security for a simple grocery run. Unfortunately, she had no such luck. Her husband's work meant the armed driver and passenger had to ride with her even for the most basic trips. Worse, she had no idea what he did—his job was classified. She knew Adam was an Army colonel attached to the Allied Joint Force Command at the giant NATO facility. They'd been in Naples for six years, longer than any other posting in Adam's long career. But this post was different. He assured her the work was important, and she also wasn't the only wife kept in the dark. None of the other officers in Adam's unit told their families anything, either. It was, the wives joked, an exclusive club. The women met now and again to let off steam over the secrecy governing their lives. And drink wine. Always wine.

But if she couldn't have a *normal* day by traditional standards, she at least had her daughter with her. Shannon had her five-year-old beside her. Faith's attention was on the tablet computer resting on her lap, and the matching game she played. The little girl had dark hair, which contrasted with the blonde hair both her parents had. She had her father's blue eyes, and her mother's bony chin and knobby knees. Shannon looked out the window at the passing buildings. The population in Naples was highly concentrated, and the architecture curious. The buildings on either side seemed to close in like the walls of a trash compactor, she often thought. The narrow streets didn't help the illusion. She and Adam lucked out with an apartment overlooking the ocean. It was a nice touch. The winding streets leading to their apartment? She didn't appreciate those much, but Naples was full of such roads.

The driver never took the same route from the apartment to any regular destination. It was a habit she understood. Adam explained they didn't want any "bad guys" predicting their travel routes. She didn't like the idea of any outstanding threats against them; he assured her it was only a precaution. But nobody took precautions unless they believed there was a reason.

A traffic jam put them behind ten minutes, but it was an unintended consequence of how the city planners organized Naples years and years ago. Narrow streets weren't made for as many cars the city had to support, and Naples had *too many cars*. At least most of those cars were compact, or people rode scooters. The NATO car wasn't huge by comparison, but it was larger, and sometimes tough to maneuver, which made Shannon glad she didn't have to drive. The man in the passenger seat, wearing military operational combat pattern fatigues, appeared more alert as they waited. The driver wore OCPs, too, as if they were soldiers standing by for orders to go to war. Well, they were—in a sense. All military personnel understood their superiors might order them into combat at any time. But Shannon didn't like thinking "bad guys" might force them into battle while she and Faith sat in the back seat.

Settle down. Why are you nervous?

Because, today, she carried a sense of dread with her. She'd felt the sixth sense as soon as they left the apartment. A bad gut feeling. They needed supplies, she wanted to get what they required, and then she wanted to go home and lock the doors until Adam returned. She kept her hands on her lap so Faith wouldn't see them shaking, and wished she knew how to steady her nerves. The armed men up front did nothing to make her feel less "off."

Get what we need, get home.

Her husband would call the declaration a "mission goal" —she wanted nothing more than to stamp *mission accomplished* on the statement.

Presently, and with great relief on Shannon's part, the driver pulled into the Carrefour Express grocery store. She loaded Faith into the shopping cart's child seat and hurried through the store. Faith didn't notice, she remained engrossed in her matching game on the tablet computer. Shannon hoped it didn't slip from her hands. It was a long way from the top of the cart to the polished tiled floor.

Her bodyguards stayed with her, at a discreet distance, as she gathered her purchases. Nobody paid attention. The NATO presence in the city meant everybody saw men and women in uniform throughout the city. The two men did not help her load the car when she finally finished. She understood. They needed their hands free to grab for the guns under their OCPs should anything happen.

Should anything…

It wasn't the 1970s or '80s any more. There hadn't been any brazen terrorist attacks in public for as long as she could remember. The days of the Red Brigade and Ordine Nuovo were long gone; Italian politics was no longer punctuated with bursts of gunfire, bombs, hijackings, or hostage crises. The Years of Lead, they were called, when far-left and far-right guerrilla groups ran rampant, leaving a mass of casualties behind. No. It was better now. At least, Shannon told herself it was better now.

It felt good to be back in the car, back on the road, and on the way home with the groceries in the trunk.

Always change the route…

One problem. There was only one way back to their apartment.

The driver made a turn up the curving road, homes and apartments pressed close together on either side, vehicles lining the curbs.

A left turn.

A right.

A small white coupe lurched from the curb and stopped in the road with a screech of tires, the driver's side facing the NATO car. The driver stomped the brakes and hit the horn. Shannon grabbed Faith.

The passenger jerked his head around, looking past Shannon out the back window. He yelled an alarm.

"Another one behind us!"

And they were stopped mid-turn. Shannon's pulse quickened.

She didn't have to look back to know what was happening. She clutched her little girl to her. Two men with stubby submachine guns jumped out of the car in front of them. The weapons chattered, flashing flame. A salvo shattered the glass and tore into the guard on the passenger side as he exited with a drawn pistol. Shannon screamed; Faith screamed because her mother screamed.

The driver shoved the gear lever into reverse, and stomped the accelerator. He slammed the rear end into the car blocking them, moving the vehicle a few inches, but then both cars stopped. The enemy car didn't budge any longer, and Shannon didn't know why. All she knew was the men who exited the second car approached with submachine guns, too. The NATO car wasn't bulletproof. Families of staffers didn't warrant such protection. The next salvo shattered more glass and punctured metal and ripped into the driver with such ferocity Shannon froze as his body jerked from the impacts. Bits of debris—glass and metal—flew at her. The firing stopped. The driver, dead, slumped against his seat belt.

Shannon's ears rang from the gunfire and Faith's crying, and she sat powerless as the gunmen approached her side. They didn't shoot. One opened the door and demanded they both get out. Shannon didn't see any choice. She followed instructions, holding on to her little girl, and let the gunmen usher her to the car up front. The other two went back to the second car. Shannon wanted to look around for help, but she registered nothing other than what lay in front of her. The car. Another back seat. Sweaty men with weapons crowding her. Nobody was coming to save her and she had no idea what to do.

A MAN SAT UP FRONT BESIDE THE DRIVER. HE TURNED TO look at Shannon as the gunners piled in on either side, smashing the woman and child between them. The man exuded strength. Muscular frame, prominent jawline, cheekbones, and trimmed hair. His dark eyes bored into her. The driver sped off.

Shannon stared back at the man. He might have been a bank manager, engineer, anything other than the leader of the gunmen.

"Be calm," he told her. He smiled. His smile did nothing to ease the fear brimming in Shannon Ward's green eyes. "We are not going to hurt you. My name is Rahmil, and I am in charge. We will treat you well. I am a man of my word."

Shannon only stared while trying to pat her daughter into quieting down. But none of the men appeared bothered by the little girl's crying. They appeared not to notice it at all.

THE MAN WHO INTRODUCED HIMSELF AS RAHMIL APPRECIATED Shannon Ward not launching into a "you'll never get away with this" routine. But he knew better than she what awaited them over the next forty-eight hours. Because forty-eight hours was all Rahmil planned to give her husband, the Colonel, to do what they asked, or he'd get his family back in pieces.

He told the driver to watch his speed as they drove. They didn't want any attention from police. He didn't think Shannon Ward would be silly enough to try and signal an officer should they see one. But one never knew. If she did, Rahmil didn't want to think about what he'd have to do to ensure her compliance.

THE DOOR SHUT WITH A THUD. THE LOCK CLICKED. SHANNON Ward swore she heard an echo as the lock slammed home.

Still clutching Faith, who clung to her, Shannon found a corner. She slid down the wall to the floor. Faith said, "What's going on? Where's Daddy?"

At least she'd stopped crying.

"Daddy will be here soon," Shannon said. The walls were bare, the room cold, the floor solid concrete. They'd not provided a chair or a bucket. She hoped they didn't expect— *what was she thinking?* All she had to do was keep Faith protected, even at the risk of sacrificing herself.

What did they want? They'd said nothing to her after Rahmil, the man in the car, spoke.

The lock clicked back and the door opened. Rahmil entered. He left the door open. Shannon caught a glimpse of an armed man standing outside. What did they expect from her? She had no weapons and held onto a child. What threat did she pose?

"These conditions are terrible," Rahmil began. He eased onto the floor and sat with crossed legs. His suit and tie looked out of place. But he didn't seem bothered by sitting on the dirty concrete. The suit looked expensive, and his shoes showed a bright shine.

"What do you want with us?" Shannon said.

Rahmil produced a cell phone from the inside pocket of his suit jacket. "Right now, I want you to phone your husband, and tell him about the day's turn of events. I'm sorry about your groceries, by the way."

"Gee. Thanks."

"This will soon be an unpleasant memory. If you remember at all. As long as you do what we say, you will be—"

"You made your point in the car."

"Of course." He smiled without humor. His dark eyes seemed darker.

"Who are you?"

"My name is Rahmil."

"No, who—what—is your group?"

"Our name will not mean anything to you."

"ISIS?" she said. "Al-Qaeda?"

Rahmil shook his head. "We are neither. Here. Use this phone. Call your husband and tell him and we will move this along to get you back home."

He was playing "good cop" but Shannon didn't trust him for one second. But she did take the phone with her right hand. Dialing Adam's number, she put the phone to her ear. She started to cry. She didn't want to, but emotion overwhelmed her. She had to be strong for Faith and let her daughter see how upset she was. But she couldn't stop. She wasn't sure she was up to the task ahead of her.

"Colonel Ward's office."

"It's Shannon Ward. Put my husband on," she said, urgently, choking on a sob, and the secretary didn't argue.

"One moment."

The moment felt like an hour.

"Honey?"

"Adam!" she screamed. Before she said anything more, Rahmil wrenched the phone from her hands. She screamed, startled, and heard Adam yell her name through the speaker.

Rahmil spoke into the phone.

"Silence, Colonel Ward. That's better. My name is Rahmil. Yes, you know me. We have your wife and child." A pause. He listened, his expression flat. "Spare me the boasts, Colonel. We both know what's at stake. You will do nothing but listen to me very carefully. Very carefully, Colonel Ward. Your wife and child are unharmed, and they will remain unharmed as long as you do what I ask. And I'm not asking for much. We will give you forty-eight hours to turn over the current list of NATO undercover spies operating against the jihad. All of them, Colonel Ward. We want names and locations. Is that clear? I can't hear you, Colonel. Am I clear? I thought so. Forty-eight hours, no more. Thank you, Colonel."

Rahmil ended the call.

He smiled at Shannon. She'd stopped crying, but tear streaks remained on her cheeks.

"See?" he said. "No reason for anybody to get upset. Your husband will deliver what we ask, and you go home."

He rose, straightened his suit, and left the room. The lock snapped once again.

Faith finally shifted, letting go over her mother's neck. Shannon let her settle on her lap. She stared at the floor with unblinking eyes. Adam would never—*never*—betray NATO, his country, or sacrifice an allied soldier. A list of spies? *Was Adam a spy?* It made the secrecy and security make sense, but this was a lousy way to learn the truth about his work.

Forty-eight hours.

Rahmil left out, on purpose, no doubt, the consequences if Adam failed to meet the deadline.

ALLIED JOINT COMMAND, NAPLES, OCCUPIED FORTY ACRES of land. NATO didn't pay rent on the property because of a deal with the Italian government, but NATO nations funded the upkeep and interior infrastructure needs. The six separate buildings provided work space for the command staff to handle NATO matters in Western Europe. In the main building, in an office on the top floor, the Admiral in charge faced Colonel Adam Ward across his desk.

Admiral Michael Leonard wore a look of concern as he listened to an even more worried Ward relate the tale.

Leonard's gray hair matched his weathered face. He was a man with a long record of experience, and his eyes displayed a wariness never missed by his subordinates. He'd joined the United States Navy as soon as he was old enough. He'd seen combat; ship-to-ship combat as deadly as any ground battle. He knew what NATO prepared for even if nobody often admitted what the training meant to teach. He feared the day the world required the full might of NATO, because it meant only one thing. It meant the world would be at war one last time.

But right now, they had more immediate matters to deal with.

"Who is Rahmil?" Leonard said.

"We don't know much," Ward admitted, shifting, clearing his throat. "He's a lone wolf. Not affiliated with any terrorist organization."

"Like Carlos?"

"Sort of. But more concerned with money than ideology. For now. We suspect he'll eventually pull off a mass casualty attack, either for himself or another organization."

"Well, we can't hand over the list. It's not a consideration. What we need to do is figure out how to get your family back. I've sent for help from home. I did so as soon as you alerted me. I don't like the idea of asking for covert assets. If they're caught, the locals will make a fuss. But I also don't see an alternative."

"Forty-eight hours isn't a long time, sir."

"They're on the way. Should be here within two hours. Coming from Germany. They're not far. And they're rescue specialists, Colonel. They'll know what to do."

Ward barely nodded. Admiral Leonard couldn't tell if the news gave the Army colonel any boost in confidence.

———

"WHAT HAPPENED?"

The question was one CIA officer Sam Raven often asked when presented with a new assignment. He was one to always cut to the chase, avoid needless talk.

His chiseled face and blue eyes faced a computer screen placed on the narrow table in front of him. He had a lean but muscular frame, and a close-cropped haircut. No facial hair. He was one of the few operators who didn't sport a beard. He looked eager, alert, showing no sign of the cynicism to later color his life.

The cabin of the CIA jet was quiet, the engine noise muted. The computer speaker relayed loud and clear the voice of the man on the monitor.

Raven's boss at CIA Special Activities, Christopher Fisher, answered with his usual matter-of-factness.

"Somebody kidnapped the family of Colonel Adam Ward less than three hours ago."

Fisher's well-groomed appearance and suit-and-tie uniform set the two men apart. But they worked and thought as one, with Raven in the field and Fisher coordinating at HQ.

Raven led Stalker Team Charlie, a specialized unit tasked with tracking terror suspects. The job called for watching, identifying, tracing. Assignments upgraded to kill missions once they found a suspect about to carry out an attack. They also served as a rescue unit when required.

"Who took them?" Raven asked.

"The caller referred to himself as 'Rahmil' and said Ward would know him. All we know at this point is he's an independent. He might be somebody Ward's people have investigated in the past, but he hasn't crossed our radar yet."

"What does he want?"

"He's demanding Colonel Ward hand over data on NATO undercover agents and informants."

"Are they looking for a specific spy," Raven said, "or to sell the information?"

"One or the other or both, Sam," Fisher said. "Rahmil didn't tell us his intentions."

"Does Ward have access to those names?"

"He better. He's the man in charge of NATO intelligence for Western Europe. He's a good man. We've worked with him on several tasks."

"What's our mission?"

"We want Rahmil alive, if possible. But, believe me, nobody will shed a tear if you punch his ticket in the heat of battle. We'd like to talk to him should the opportunity arise. And we want the mother and daughter free and the NATO information secured."

Raven let out a low sigh. The mission objective couldn't have been the other way around. CIA interests first, always. Never the victims. But Raven had his own way of dealing with the bureaucratic garbage he faced more often than he liked. Fisher knew how he felt, and gave him permission to handle the situation in his own way. Fisher didn't like spy bullshit any more than Raven did.

"What about Ward?" Raven said.

"I don't understand."

"He's gone by the book reporting the ransom demand, but will he buckle under pressure? Will he give Rahmil the list?"

"Get his family back in one piece and we won't have to answer that."

Raven didn't like non-answers to what he considered important questions, either. "Who do we see when we land?" he asked instead.

"You'll meet with Ward and Admiral Leonard, the current man in charge at the headquarters. Leonard isn't a fan of special ops, so he may be a little frosty. But he also knows he's not equipped to handle this kind of situation. Their intel people ride desks, not jets across the world. Sam?"

"Yes?"

"Be nice."

"I'll be my usual diplomatic self, Chris."

"That's what I'm afraid of."

Fisher blinked off.

Raven turned to his teammates. They sat on his left, having listened and watched Fisher's presentation. One woman, three men. Victor Matson, Carlos Vega, and Billy Anzell—all three were trim, muscular, young; expert marksmen, proficient in combat, electronic surveillance of all forms, the kind of shoot-and-loot specialists the stalker teams sought for recruitment. All three had some amount of facial hair, unlike their boss.

Mara Cole, with her fierce green eyes and long, curly dark hair, preferred a less direct approach to their assignments. She liked setting up scenarios where the enemy came to *them*, if they put themselves in the right spot and remained patient. Her method had its pluses and minuses, and a long list of successful missions, too.

14 BRIAN DRAKE

"You heard the boss," Raven said.

"But?" Victor Matson said. He grinned a little.

"I'm not interested in prisoners," Raven said. "Kill *all* of them. The idiots on the top floor will have to be upset. Our goal, our *only* goal, is freeing the wife and daughter and protecting the NATO secrets."

"You think he's going to crack?" The question came from Billy Anzell, who sat next to Victor. Billy was more than curious. He liked questions which probed for unspoken answers in an attempt to bring them to light.

"Would you?"

Billy shrugged. "I found it frustrating Fisher didn't answer."

"Oh, don't worry," Raven said, "I'll look Ward in the eye and ask him personally."

"He might not," Mara Cole pointed out.

Raven looked at her before answering. They were occasional lovers, going through an on-and-off-currently-off phase. He wished it wasn't so complicated with her, but they were too much alike for their own good. She'd tied back her hair, but the rebellious curls found a way to break free, giving her a tousled look. With her green eyes and pouty lips, the look was enough to make any of the men glance twice.

"We'll see," was all Raven said in reply. They didn't talk much during an "off" phase. He wished they got along better, but their relationship problems hadn't compromised their work. Yet.

"What about the Admiral who doesn't like special ops?" said Carlos Vega, usually the quiet one, asked.

"We've dealt with his kind before. This won't be any different."

"I suggest," Carlos continued, "we lock Ward away and

handle this ourselves. If you're nervous about him cracking—"

"You're reading my mind, Carlos."

The pilot's voice came over the cabin loudspeaker. They'd land in ten minutes.

"Double check your gear," Raven said, "and get ready to be back on solid ground. We're going to be busy."

———

AN OFFICIAL ESCORT MET THEM AT THE AIRPORT HANGAR. They traveled in a black SUV. A second vehicle carried their gear. Raven sat in the back with Mara. She took his hand and gave it a squeeze. He looked at her. She smiled. A nice confidence booster. She said a lot without saying anything. He wondered if they could switch their relationship back to "on" when they finished the job.

The drive to the NATO headquarters wasn't long, and the facility made a big impression. One large building, a massive squared-off design with two extensions on one side. Smaller buildings of similar design were spread around the complex, with more parking space in one place than Raven had ever seen. The massive steel gate opened to allow their vehicles access, and a team of security officers checked each one of them before allowing the SUVs to continue into the main plaza. At the entrance, standing at the foot of wide steps, stood a man in a full Navy dress uniform, and another in Army Class A attire. Leonard and Ward. Raven exited the SUV last, and went to them. His crew unloaded the second SUV.

"Admiral Leonard, I presume," Raven said. He stuck out

his right hand. He and the Admiral shook. He noticed the Admiral's eyes, the lines on his face.

"I am. This is Colonel Ward."

Ward's hand felt cold in Raven's grip.

"It might have been anybody, Colonel," Raven said. "Don't blame yourself."

Ward tried to reply, but Leonard jumped in.

"We can talk in my office. I have a staging room where your people can wait."

"Let's go," Raven said.

He left Victor Matson in charge of the team.

THEY RODE AN ELEVATOR TO THE TOP FLOOR AND WALKED down a chilly hallway to Leonard's office. Raven ignored the view. The windows overlooking the east side of the complex appeared so clear as to be invisible. NATO kept Windex in business.

Leonard took the chair behind his desk. Raven and Ward sat in front of the desk. Ward kept his eye on the floor. Raven watched him with concern. *He's already losing it.*

"Has there been an update?" Raven asked.

Leonard answered. "We had a second call prior to your arrival. Rahmil, again. The meet is set for tonight, eleven thirty, downtown."

"Me, alone, with the names," Ward added. "I'll be picked up in a car and taken to my family."

Raven jumped in. "They'll kill you, dump your body, take the names, and maybe let your family live. But Rahmil and his people will be long gone. You can't be serious about doing this."

"They know what I look like," Ward said. "We can't use a stand-in."

"Let's fake the names."

"And wait for them to retaliate when they find out?" Ward said.

Raven turned to the Admiral. "You need to at least send out a warning to your people, let them know they may be compromised. Start the process of exfiltration."

"It'll take time," the Admiral said. "And while we are waiting, some may lose their lives. And pulling our assets will ruin years of carefully cultivated information."

"I get it, Admiral, but unless you want to hang your spies out to dry, you don't have much choice."

Ward's face blanched. Raven noticed. "Are you sure you're up to this, Colonel?"

"What are you saying?"

"Admiral, I think the Colonel needs to step away. Let my people handle this."

The Admiral shook his head. "Based on what intel? You know nothing more than we do. Our only chance of getting near the terrorists is to let Colonel Ward meet them."

Raven pressed his lips together.

The Admiral continued. "I don't want a major shooting match in the streets of Naples. I don't want you here at all, Mr. Raven. But I see we have no choice. We need to make this happen, one way or another, and you're our best bet. But Ward plays on the team. He has a vested interest."

"Which is the problem," Raven said. He glanced at Ward again. "All right, the Admiral has a point. We don't have time to look for where they're hiding. We'll be on your six all night and if it looks kinky, we're moving in."

"Okay."

Raven suggested they go meet the rest of the team. He saw the Admiral's glare, but ignored him.

Raven didn't work for NATO.

———

A FOUR-PROP DRONE, PAINTED BLACK TO MATCH THE NIGHT sky, hovered above Garibaldi Square. Small hi-def cameras mounted on the bottom watched the streets for incoming cars. There were few at the late, or early hour, depending on how you looked at the clock, but Raven and his team wanted to see any vehicle approaching the plaza.

The large statue of Giuseppe Garibaldi at the center of the square was a landmark of Italian history; general, patriot, revolutionary. He stood proudly, holding a sword pointed at his feet, atop a stone column. He'd been part of the nine-teenth-century political and social efforts resulting in the unification of different states on the Italian Peninsula into a single Kingdom of Italy. He remained revered over 100 years later. Raven hoped his spirit was alive and well with them; they needed all the help they could get.

One block away, parked curbside on Garibaldi Street, Raven and Mara sat in a minivan with tinted windows. Raven was behind the wheel; Mara occupied the middle bench seat behind him. Using a laptop, she monitored the drone's four camera shots. A remote unit on her left operated the drone. For now, the drone hovered in place.

"How's Ward?" Raven asked. He looked at Mara's reflection in the rearview mirror as he spoke. The glare of the laptop screen made her face look gray.

She consulted one of the camera shots. "Pacing near the base of the statue."

"All right," he said.

"If the bad guys are on schedule, they should be here in another ten minutes."

None of the cars or trucks passing through stopped; none of the drivers behaved as if they were a scout crew. Raven wondered if the other side had the manpower. He also wondered if the scout crew arrived on foot after parking a few blocks away and found hiding spots in the many nooks surrounding the square.

But then, if they had, his shooters would have spotted them. Matson, Vega, and Anzell were spread around the area, checking for such activity.

From his seat in the van, he faced the opposite direction. The rear of the van pointed to the statue. He wanted the van to be another anonymous vehicle parked curbside, interior dark, nobody bothering with it. Mara served as his immediate eyes and ears; his shoot-and-loot trio were positioned closer if the plan went sideways.

Raven checked with his three shooters over a wireless com link. All three responded with an all-clear. If there was a scout crew, his gunners would have noticed. But he still tapped the steering wheel with nervous fingers.

"Knock it off," Mara said. "Why are you so jumpy?"

"He took the real names."

"He *what*? We gave him fakes!"

"I checked before we left. He accessed the real list on his office computer. I knew he wasn't going to be able to take the heat."

"Oh, boy…"

———

20 BRIAN DRAKE

COLONEL WARD WAS RISKING MORE THAN HIS CAREER AND had no illusions about the consequences.

Which made standing in the plaza in the shadow of Garibaldi much harder. If he looked at the statue, Ward knew he'd see a look of condemnation. He didn't look at the statue.

He held a leather briefcase in his hand, and it was too much for the single file folder within. But what the hell. He needed to put it in something, and the briefcase fit the bill. He'd indeed looked up the names of current NATO informants in jihadist circles, having tossed Sam Raven's make-believe list, as accurate as it may have looked. If Rahmil kept his word and let him and his family go once he received the names, they'd forever be in danger. Because Rahmil would eventually discover, and very fast, the list wasn't genuine. He might even know one or two of the names already, and compare the data with the list in the briefcase. The man couldn't be stupid enough to take things at face value—like a good lawyer, you never ask a question you don't already know the answer to. This way, at least, Rahmil had the real names to check against whatever information he currently possessed, and wouldn't come after Shannon and Faith again.

His fate, though...

He'd already made up his mind, when all was said and done, to confess. He'd do time, but in exchange for his confession he'd ask for protection for his family. At least they'd be safe while he was locked away—for however long the sentence might last. Which included the rest of his life.

Ward checked the luminous dial of his watch. An anniversary gift from Shannon. A blue-faced Invicta Pro Diver which he appreciated very much, and liked even more telling people who complimented the watch who gave it to him. He and

Shannon had a good thing going, and it was a shame how it was going to end.

But they'd be safe!

Ward thought if he kept repeating the mantra, it would come true. He could even begin to believe it himself.

He knew enough about people like the man called Rahmil that he and his family might not survive to see sunrise, no matter how they complied or what they did.

He looked at his watch again. The pick-up time had passed. Rahmil's people were five minutes late. His heart began to beat faster. Had something gone wrong? Had Raven and his CIA cowboys intervened?

Did it mean he was in the clear? Burning the list would be easy, and he could carry on without ever telling a soul…

Bright headlights appeared on the right.

The big car turned the corner, and Ward held up his free hand to block the glare of the LED headlamps. The car looked like a big Mercedes in the glow of the streetlamps, but the make and model really didn't matter, Ward decided. He needed to get into the car, make the trade, and hopefully be done with the tortuous ordeal. One last night with his family, and then he'd take the next step.

The car stopped in front of the statue. Ward looked at the tinted windows. He saw nothing inside. The door didn't open for him. He took a bold step toward the car, opened the rear door, and looked inside.

"Come in and sit down, Colonel," said the man in the back seat. He wore a nice suit, and a whiff of expensive cologne wafted out. "I am Rahmil. I don't believe in sending somebody to do what I can do myself."

Ward cleared his throat. He slid into the back seat and pulled the door shut. The car left the curb. One man drove, another sat in the passenger seat. They faced forward. Ward figured both were armed. Rahmil's suit looked carefully tailored, and fit tightly. Ward didn't think he was armed, but did it really matter? He had no weapons of his own, either.

———

"CAR COMING."

Raven copied Mara's report and raised his shooters on the com link.

"You guys watching?"

Matson replied, "Black four-door Mercedes with tinted windows."

"Mara?"

"Ward is getting in. Car's driving away. It'll pass us in three, two…"

The Mercedes cruised by the van. Raven watched it go. The driver halted at the stop sign at the end of the street, signaled for a left turn, and drove around the corner.

"You got a lock?" Raven asked Mara.

"We've locked. Drone is tracking."

"Matson, Vega, Anzell. Get back here, fast."

———

IN THE TIME IT TOOK FOR WARD TO ENTER THE MERCEDES, Mara "pinged" it with a tracking laser from the drone. The laser acted much like the laser sighting systems for missiles. As long as the beam wasn't interrupted, the drone would follow the Mercedes wherever it went, transmitting video all the way. Of course, in a city, there were plenty of dangers to the beam and the drone itself. If the drone crashed into a light pole, building, or power line, they were out of luck. But Mara set an altitude to keep the drone out of sight and above such things. She figured the drone would be safe. She also counted on the terrorists not traveling very far.

Mara watched the footage. She fed the route to Raven turn-by-turn, and with the three shooters back in the van, they followed the big Mercedes. As Raven steered, he hoped they weren't driving into an ambush. Rahmil had to know Ward wouldn't keep the problem a secret; there had to be a contingency plan in case Ward tried a rescue. He could question and speculate, but what he really needed was to get inside Rahmil's head. They knew next to nothing about him.

Well, the CIA hadn't sent Raven's team for nothing.

If any Stalker Tam had the edge on victory, it was Raven's.

But they'd messed up before, too. They couldn't win every battle, even when they did everything right. Sometimes mistakes derailed victory; sometimes, the enemy was simply better.

———

"YOU NEED TO RELAX, COLONEL."

Ward held the briefcase on his lap, hands resting on top; his hands were shaking. Visibly, too. There was no way to hide it short of jamming them into his pockets.

"You're holding my wife and child hostage, you've threatened us, what am I supposed to do?"

"I've done no such thing, Colonel."

Ward let his anger rise, but checked it with a deep breath. "You know better than that, Rahmil. The threat was implied."

"And you know all about people like me, right? Terrorist

monsters? I'm a *business* man, Colonel. I'm only here for what your list will bring on the open market. Speaking of, let me see."

Before Ward replied, Rahmil took the briefcase from his lap. He paused with his fingers on the locks. He grinned. "If I open this, will it explode?"

Ward shook his head. His face looked drawn, exhausted.

"I believe you. Plus, if it does, you die too. Then what happens to your family?"

Rahmil flicked the locks and the briefcase clasps snapped up. The snap sounded loud in the car, like a gunshot; Ward figured he was the only one who saw it as such. To the others, the sound was benign.

The "business man" laughed as he removed the printed list from the file folder. He flipped on his cell phone's flashlight, scanned the names, and snapped a picture. Ward felt his heart sink into his gut. He had all he wanted and needed nothing more. If he sent the pic in an email or text message to another contact, there'd be no putting the genie back in the bottle.

But Rahmil didn't send the picture anywhere. He put the phone away and read the names again.

"Looks real enough."

"It's genuine," Ward said.

Rahmil grinned at him. "I'm supposed to believe you, Colonel? You can mistrust me, but not the other way around?"

"It's real. I figured you either had suspects and wanted confirmation, or you had one or two names already. Either way, you'd know if it was a fake. It's not."

"How interesting," Rahmil said. He turned off the light and put the phone away. "I should have thought about telling you I knew one or two of the names. I don't have anything to compare them with. But whoever *buys* this list surely will, and they'll appreciate the assurance you've provided, Colonel."

Rahmil smiled again. He closed the case.

"I don't know about you, Colonel, but I like jazz music. Care to listen?" Rahmil gave the order. The man in the passenger seat turned on the stereo. Sofit piano and sax filled the Mercedes.

"How much farther?" Ward asked.

"Hmmm?"

"How long till we get there?"

Rahmil checked his gold Rolex. "Oh, another five or ten minutes. I told my driver not to break the speed limit. You know, just in case."

Ward shifted in his seat. His thoughts turned to Sam Raven and his CIA team. Maybe he was wrong to think of them as cowboys. Right now, they were truly the only hope he had of getting Shannon, Faith, and him, out of the lion's mouth.

———

MARA COLE KEPT THE DRONE FROM CRASHING WHILE THE laser beam dragged it behind the Mercedes. She advised Raven where to turn, and when to hold back. When she said they were getting too close, Raven pulled curbside for a moment.

"Any idea where they're going?" Raven said as he pulled onto the roadway again.

"They're approaching some warehouses," Mara said. "I'd bet one of them is home base."

"Are we getting itchy trigger fingers, boys?" Raven asked.

Matson, Vega, and Anzell responded in the affirmative.

Raven said he wanted to shoot some bad guys, too.

TWO GUNMEN TOTING SUBMACHINE GUNS SHOVED WARD ahead of them. They traveled down a short hallway to a door. The light was low, but Ward had seen enough of the gunmen to know he could take them down had circumstances favored such a move. The men had their weapons on safe, and he was familiar with what they carried, the HK MP7. He could take one down, grab a weapon, switch the safety off, and kill the other. But then he'd have to deal with the rest of the crew.

Stop! This isn't the time!

Ward had never considered himself a coward, nor would anybody he ever served with level such an accusation. He'd served with distinction throughout his career, including two combat tours. But that was before Shannon; *way* before Faith; he had a hard time watching the resolve with which he'd fueled his past performance fade into nothing.

Where's Raven?

One of the gunmen yanked him to a stop a foot or two from the door. The other used a key on the lock. The door swung inward. The colonel heard his wife cry out when she saw him. A hard shove, and Ward tumbled into the room. His impact on the concrete floor hurt. One of the gunners yelled, "One minute!" and the door slammed shut.

Ward jumped up to crush his wife in his arms, then grabbed Faith and lifted her off the ground. He held his daughter longer. He felt her tears stain his right shoulder.

"What's going on?" Shannon asked.

"I made a big mistake, hon."

"And *this* is the result?"

"Babe, I can't explain now. But there are people coming."

"What?"

The door swung open. The gunmen entered and moved toward Ward. He handed Faith to Shannon. The gunmen grabbed him.

"You said one minute!" Ward shouted.

They dragged him out and slammed the door once more.

———

RAHMIL WAITED IN ANOTHER ROOM. HE STOOD BETWEEN A chair and a camera mounted on a tripod. The gunmen carried Ward into the room and forced him onto the chair. Rahmil handed the NATO Colonel a sheet of paper.

"Read those words into the camera."

Ward read down the page. A red flush crawled up his neck.

"This is a confession," he said. He looked up into Rahmil's face. "This wasn't a part of the deal!"

"I told you I am a business man. This *confession* is my insurance policy to make sure you keep your mouth shut."

"I've done everything you asked for! *Everything!*"

"And you did well. Now, read those words into the camera and you and your family may go."

Ward looked at the script again.

They wanted him to say he'd given up the undercover spies because he was sick of "American imperialism" in the Middle East. *Usual bullshit*, he thought, but they had him over a barrel. He didn't see any way out. He had to try and stall until the CIA team –

Rahmil moved behind the camera, aimed the lens at Ward, and pressed the Record button. A red light came on at the front of the camera.

"Begin, Colonel."

"I won't say this. It's not true. You'll use it to blackmail me."

Rahmil signed. "Colonel, must I remind you—"

"You have what you want!"

"You aren't listening, Colonel. I need a little more."

"When those men on the list start turning up dead, you'll send this out."

"You have my word it's only for insurance. In case you try anything stupid. I am a man of my word."

"No."

Ward tore the sheet in half. He dropped the halves on the floor. Another cold, concrete floor like the one in the room where they held his family. He glanced at the two gunners. Their HK MP7s remained "on safe." Rahmil, he was certain, didn't carry a pistol.

Rahmil snapped an order.

"Bring the daughter."

One of the gunmen turned and went out.

Good.

Rahmil then unbuttoned his blazer, and moved his right hand to the leather sheath on his right hip. Ward's eyes widened. He carried no pistol, but he did carry a knife. Rahmil pulled out the blade. Seven-inches of tempered steel and razor sharp. He swallowed. This wasn't going to end well. Not at all.

Rahmil said, "I wish you hadn't—"

But whatever Rahmil wished, he didn't get to say.

An explosion rocked the warehouse walls. Men began yelling. Bursts of gunfire crackled.

And Colonel Adam Ward made his move.

———

RAVEN, MATSON, VEGA AND ANZELL RAN INSIDE, FEELING the residual heat of the flaming doorway as the blast from Vega's C-4 charge dissipated. Wearing night vision goggles, they looked at the open area of the warehouse. The interior lay before them in a green glow. Armed with 5.56mm Galil ACE-23 automatic rifles and Glock-17 pistols, they spread out to engage incoming targets.

Raven's eyes followed the length of the Galil from rear to front sight. The two-legged creatures ahead weren't people. They were *things*; at worst, insects to step on and remove from existence.

And the insects carried weapons as deadly as his.

Rahmil's gunmen entered the wider area of the warehouse via a passage between the storage area and a perpendicular hallway. Raven wanted to get to the hallway. He fired on the run, the Galil spitting flame. One gunner went down; his buddies scattered, only to drop like chopped trees as the 5.56mm slugs from Raven's team cut through them. Raven swung left to fire at the last man, who dived behind a stack of 2-by-4s. The enemy gunner poked the muzzle of his sub gun over the top. Raven fired. The hand holding the MP7 became a jagged, bloody stump as the rounds destroyed flesh and bone. As the gunner screamed, Raven reached him and fired another burst. The screaming stopped.

"Hold the area," Raven said, changing mags. "I'm going for the hostages."

"Copy," Matson said. He and the other two took up security positions. Raven radioed to Mara that the warehouse was secure. She advised she was watching the exits for any escapees.

———

WARD LEAPED FROM THE CHAIR AND COLLIDED WITH THE remaining gunman. Rahmil's man had been in the process of flicking off the safety of his weapon. Ward brought him to the floor before he completed the action. The MP7 wasn't attached to a sling. A sharp elbow strike dazed the gunner, and Ward rolled off of him with the MP7 in his hands. The safety switched off with only a little pressure from his thumb. He swung the sub gun at Rahmil.

Who wasn't where he'd been standing, behind the camera, any longer. He was almost at the door, running fast. *He can't escape with his phone!* Ward shifted and triggered the HK. The burst only gouged the floor and smacked into the door. One shot might have scored—Rahmil screamed—but Ward didn't see what he'd hit. Rahmil made it through the doorway.

Ward jumped to his feet. The CIA team was here; let them deal with Rahmil. He had to get to Shannon and Faith! The gunfire has ceased. He paused in the doorway. Which way had Rahmil gone? He risked a peek in each direction. No sign. Ward broke left and ran hard. He reached the door and tried to open it. Locked! He yelled for his wife to get Faith away from the door and shot the lock. The door knob separated from the door and clattered to the floor. He ran into the room. Shannon's eyes widened as she looked over his shoulder and yelled, "Behind you!"

Ward pivoted, bringing up the MP7, but held his fire when Sam Raven yanked off his night vision goggles and yelled for Ward to stand down.

"Where's Rahmil?" Raven asked.

"He took off. I had to protect my family."

"We'll find him. Stay with them. We'll take care of the rest."

"The list is on his phone!"

"What?"

"The *list.* He took a picture of the list."

"All right." Raven turned on a heel and ran out.

———

RAVEN RADIOED HIS TEAM AS HE RAN. "RAHMIL IS ON THE run. Mara, any sign?"

"I got a lone figure slipping out a side exit. Looks unarmed. He's looking for a ride and there are two cars on our side of the building. One's the Mercedes."

"That's him. Matson, you and Vega and Anzell take care of Ward. He's in a room down the hall with his family, then get them out of here in the van. Mara, get out of the van and see if that other car has keys. We'll take that one."

"Copy."

Raven reached the side exit. He pushed through the door into the night.

———

THE MERCEDES SCREECHED RUBBER AS RAHMIL DROVE OFF. Raven ran to another car, a sedan, with Mara behind the wheel. They'd left the keys inside, apparently, and lucky for Raven. Now the others could use the minivan to get away from the combat zone.

Raven dropped into the passenger seat. "Is the drone still tracking?"

"Batteries went out," she said. She gained the road and followed the red tail lights of the black Mercedes. The engine under the hood of the sedan had a lot of power, and closed the distance between the vehicle ahead quickly. Raven powered down his window and prepared to unleash the Galil ACE-23. He hoped the Mercedes wasn't armor-plated, but noted it moved too fast to have the extra weight caused by bullet-resistant panels.

Cold air rushed into the car as Mara kept the Mercedes in sight. Other buildings flashed by. Raven was grateful for the late hour—no civilians at risk. But that didn't mean there'd be no police. They were running the risk of proving the Admiral's point on why covert ops in a major city was a bad idea, unless he pulled a few strings somewhere along the way to keep the law off their backs.

The road curved, Mara staying on target, the Mercedes unable to pull away. Raven leaned out with his rifle. One burst, two bursts, flame flashing from the muzzle. He aimed at the trunk and rear tires. He had to score one way or another and keep the Mercedes from getting away.

Raven's next burst took out a rear tire and the Mercedes fishtailed, tire rubber screeching as Rahmil tried to avoid a light pole. The car almost turned a hundred-eighty degrees, the back smashing into the pole, turning the rear of the car into a crumpled mess of metal and broken glass.

But Rahmil made it out. Raven saw him tumble from the driver's seat and onto the sidewalk as Mara stopped the sedan. He left the Galil behind and charged after the terrorist. He grabbed the Glock-17 9 mm autoloader from the holster on his right hip.

"Sam!" Mara shouted. Raven ignored her. He didn't bother to tell her to stay, either.

Rahmil made it into an alley. Raven fired a shot. The slug whined off the pavement. He charged after Rahmil and fired again, two rounds this time, and Rahmil stumbled and fell behind a stack of broken pallets. Other debris littered the alley. Raven advanced slowly, the Glock in a two-hand grip. A step closer.

Rahmil lunged from cover.

The light from the street glinted off the seven-inch knife Rahmil clutched. Raven dodged back as Rahmil swung. His foot hit a piece of debris—Raven toppled, landing hard on his back. Winded, Raven rolled left, kicking out, his combat boots scoring a blow in Rahmil's abdomen. Rahmil exhaled with a cry and doubled over.

Raven jumped up and tried to level the Glock with one hand, but Rahmil slashed despite the pain of Raven's kick. The razor-edge of the blade cut into Raven's right arm. The Glock dropped from his grasp. His right hand lost its strength. Raven then felt Rahmil shoving him into the alley wall, the hard brick biting through his pack; Raven wedged a leg between them as Rahmil drew the knife back for a plunge at Raven's neck.

Raven smashed his forehead into the bridge of Rahmil's nose. *Crack!* Rahmil recoiled with a scream. Raven pushed away from the wall and dived for the fallen Glock. He could shoot plenty well with his left hand. Then Rahmil kicked the gun away; it spun across the pavement, bounced into a wall. Rahmil kicked Raven in the face. Raven tried to grab at Rahmil's legs, but missed. Raven flopped onto his back again, then sat up and threw his weight forward to grab the Glock. He grasped it, dropped back and rolled onto his belly. Rahmil was running, blending into the alley shadows further down. One shot—*crack!* The running figure did not stop.

Raven rose, gripping the Glock in his left hand. There was no catching up in his condition. He felt the flow of blood on his right arm—and the searing pain making his eyes water. He needed medical attention, and fast. As he began to turn back for Mara, he spotted something on the ground. The light from the street, same as it had glinted off Rahmil's blade, now partially shone on something else. Raven stowed his gun and picked up the item. The cell phone. Rahmil's cell phone. With a now-cracked screen. Raven grinned. Well, at least he'd recovered the phone. As long as Rahmil hadn't sent the list along, the undercover spies were safe. He moved as fast as he could to where Mara waited. She met him halfway, gasping at the blood on his fatigues. She helped him into the sedan and told him the others were heading to NATO head-quarters. Raven said they needed to get back there, too. She started driving, turning back the way they'd come. The medical staff at HQ would take care of all the poking and prodding and stitching and Raven remarked he'd be out of action for a few weeks. Mara suggested they take a vacation. Raven grinned again. She must have switched their relationship back to "on" but he didn't point it out to her. Better to make vacation plans before she changed her mind.

———

RAVEN AND MARA RETURNED TO NATO HQ AND THE HECTIC activity within. The Admiral had ordered medical support staff and other officers to remain on duty till the rescue ended —one way or another—and he was glad when everybody returned in one piece. Medics tended to Raven as well as the Ward family, though the colonel kept refusing his own check-up. He insisted he felt fine. Only when his little girl snapped, "Daddy, do what the doctor says," in the only way a child could manage, did he agree to a review of his condition. There were plenty of medics to go around. Nobody had to wait.

Raven turned over the phone to the intelligence people. He didn't mention Rahmil having taken a picture of the list. He'd found the picture, and deleted it. He also confirmed Rahmil had not sent the list to anybody. It made sense. He wouldn't want something so valuable in the hands of a contact or associate who'd try to cut him out of the deal.

It wasn't until Raven, alone in the medical unit while his attendant went for more gauze, that Ward approached.

"You know what I did, right?" the colonel said.

Raven sat on the edge of a gurney. "Yup. I erased the picture he took. It wasn't sent anywhere."

"I...appreciate it, I guess. But it will all come out. I'm finished here."

Raven shook his head. "Don't worry about it."

"What do you mean?"

"The briefcase we recovered will be empty when they look inside."

"Raven, I don't—"

"You should have followed my plan, but I understand why you didn't."

"Do you? Really?"

Raven blinked.

"I appreciate the support, I don't deserve it, but one of these days you may be in my shoes. I hope you aren't. When you are, I hope you remember how desperate I was. I'm not a bad man."

Raven took a deep breath. Ward was making him uncomfortable. "It's over, Colonel. What you do next is up to you. I suggest you spend some time with your family and help them through this."

"Rahmil got away."

"That was my fault. But don't worry. I'll see him again *very* soon."

The attendant returned; Ward excused himself. The medic finished wrapping Raven's wound.

BUT RAVEN WAS WRONG. HE DIDN'T SEE RAHMIL AT ALL. The "business man" terrorist went so far deep into hiding nobody heard from him again.

Until…

CHAPTER ONE

Ten Years Later

THE CAR FINALLY STALLED.

Leslie Rose-Brooks yelled, "No!" and steered the car off the road. She bumped the curb on her left and shut it off. The street was empty, tall lamps lighting the way ahead, but the other car coming up behind her made any chance of escape less than 100 percent.

She had no way to reach the man she was on her way to meet. Sam Raven, an old friend from the old days, hired by her boss to bring her in from the field. She'd been undercover the last few months, but somehow the enemy had found out and came for her the very night she planned to pass along the intelligence information she'd managed to collect. The zippered leather pouch on the passenger seat held her notes; she grabbed it, and left the car. There was no need to close the door so she left it open. Her left hand grasped the pistol on her hip. She held it tightly and ran.

The men chasing her had fired several shots into the

back of the car, punching holes in the gas tank. She'd made her getaway leaving a trail of petrol for them to follow. She was somewhere in downtown London; closed shops, dark buildings, darker alleyways. The headlights of the chase case shined over her as she ran for an alley. The car jerked to a stop, doors opening. She pivoted, bringing the pistol up, and fired twice. Two men were getting out of the car, neither one the driver. Her shots went wide, but sent the killers diving for cover. One returned fire and missed, but Leslie tensed when she heard the *whip-crack* of the pistol shot.

Leslie's job hadn't seemed complicated at first, but quickly turned near-impossible. Formerly of British intelligence, she'd left official government employment to join a covert intelligence network run by UK socialite Ana Gray. Rumors of a major charity organization funding terrorism currently had their attention, and Leslie's mission was to work her way into the charity and discover the links, if possible. She did. But they discovered her, too. And now she was running for her life.

Running across the sidewalk, her tennis shoes pounding hard, she only focused on the darkness within the alley as a place to disappear and ambush the men chasing her. She heard them running over the sound of her own pounding heart and heavy breathing. Almost there. *Almost.*

She was tall with long dark hair, pulled back into a ponytail. Pale white skin, she could never visit the beach without layers of sunscreen, otherwise she'd turn as red as a lobster. Dressed in jeans, blouse, and a light jacket, she only carried the bare minimum. No purse. Her ID was jammed in her back pocket. All she needed was her pistol and the leather pouch.

Another shot cracked.

She felt the impact in her lower back. No pain, but a heavy punch throwing her off balance.

Leslie pitched forward and crashed onto the concrete of the sidewalk, inches from her refuge. The leather pouch flew from her right hand. She tried to move but her body wouldn't respond. She started to scream. But another shot cut off the sound and then there was nothing.

———

RAVEN EASED THE CAR TO THE CURB AND SHUT OFF THE engine. Movement across the street caught his eye. The street lights shined on three men with guns. They had their eyes on him, one shouldering his weapon. *Move!* Raven opened the door and rolled onto the wet street—a moment before the shooting began. Muzzle flashes flared; slugs hammered into the rental car. Raven scrambled across the pavement to the back of the car. Glass shattered and metal puckered as the salvo continued, the gunners shifting their aim. Raven jumped up and ran to an alley. Bullets chased him, but the shooters ceased once he joined the alley shadows.

Raven dropped low. From under his leather jacket, he whipped out his Nighthawk Custom Talon .45 ACP autoloader and flicked down the thumb safety.

He wasn't supposed to have been caught in an ambush. He was in a dark and deserted London neighborhood at 3 a.m. to pick up an agent coming in from the cold. Leslie Rose-Brooks was her name, and she was special to Raven. He'd responded to the SOS because Leslie had saved *his* life once, and now it was time to return the favor. The ambush meant Leslie was dead, and *he* was next on the list.

Voices. A man giving orders. He wanted his men to

spread out and approach the alley from multiple directions. Raven waited in the dark. He faced at least three gunners plus the leader, whom he hadn't caught a glimpse of. Unless the leader was part of the three. He assumed four until further notice. Better not to get taken by deadly surprise once he tagged three without realizing he still had one to go.

He glanced down the length of the alley and saw two choices. He could run, or try the fire escape. Better to gain the high ground. Raven lunged for the ladder and began his climb, stifling grunts as he pulled up with his hands and dangled until he could quietly place his feet on one of the rungs. He climbed to the second landing and stopped. A dirty, sealed-shut window blocked any escape into the building. Raven braced to fire on the gunners. With luck, they couldn't see him. The light from the street lamps didn't extend into the alley.

Then the street light highlighted a gunner crossing the street at a quick pace. The man clutched a submachine gun. Raven settled his glowing sights on the man and fired once. The bark of the .45 sounded loud in the alley confines, and the hollow-point slug did as designed. The gunner stopped as if striking an invisible wall; he collapsed onto the street. The other two yelled to each other. They'd have to enter the same narrow space Raven had used to get into the alley, and Raven didn't think highly of their strategy. He wanted to know who they were and who sent them; he wanted to know if anything of value remained on the body of the woman he had been sent to collect. Or had the information she promised to deliver died with her?

The two remaining shooters found cover on either side of the alley entrance. One stuck his head too far around the right corner. Raven fired and missed. But his slug tore a piece of brick out of the wall and the gunman's startled scream was reward enough for now.

He climbed higher, stepping on and grabbing rungs fast. Almost to the roof. Never mind the noise. The metal shook and clanged against the building. Pot shots smacked the wall. Neither shooter wanted to get closer. Somebody yelled—the boss again. He was the man Raven wanted to talk to.

Onto the next landing and up one more ladder.

He reached the roof and rolled over the edge to the top. He wasn't going to wait for his assailants. He needed to get back down and attack from behind—if possible. The team leader urged his men forward and must have taken the lead. Metal clanged against the building once more. They were coming up fast.

Raven's shoes scraped on the surface of the roof as he moved. He kept a solid grip on the .45, and didn't turn his back to the fire escape. He checked over each shoulder as he moved, shifting around pipes and utility boxes until he reached the opposite edge. A peek down—no fire escape. *Dammit!* So much for a flank attack. Raven dropped behind a large A/C unit. He'd have to face them head-on. The clanging stopped.

The night kept getting better…

Raven didn't want to fire until he had a solid target. A stray round would fly until it ran out of energy, or hit somebody he didn't intend. Raven wasn't in the business of creating more victims of violence. He fought a war without end to stop such violence. So, he'd wait…

It was too late to save Leslie. But he could avenge her and find out why the men coming after *him* murdered her. The team leader rolled onto the roof as Raven had, dashed to cover, and whistled for the other two. It took time, but the pair arrived, spreading out. They stayed close to the fire escape and didn't try to search him out—yet.

"There's no way off the roof!"

Raven grinned at the team leader's taunt. There certainly was, but he had to go through *them* first.

One of the gunners moved. Raven fired once. The shot smacked the gunner down and he stayed put. The other gunner fired a string of rounds. Raven ran from the A/C unit. Bullets shredded the sheet-metal box; his return fire dropped the gunner where he stood.

Raven dropped flat. He called out, "Only the two of us now!"

He could taunt the enemy too.

The team leader had no snappy comeback.

Raven listened, but the echo of gunfire still rang loudly in his ears. He watched where the team leader had been, darting his gaze left and right to catch peripheral movement. *I need this one alive!*

No movement. No noise. Had the man gone back to the street? Not likely. He'd have made too much noise doing so.

Raven rolled left and flat-crawled back to the A/C unit he'd abandoned.

The team leader had the same idea. They made eye contact at less than twenty feet. The boss had his pistol extended, and Raven didn't hesitate. He triggered the Nighthawk and watched the hollow-point cave in the other man's face.

So much for making him talk…

Everything's gone to hell tonight!

But dead men still had a tale to tell if you knew where to look. Raven ran to the body and began checking pockets. The man had plenty of muscle and a medium build. Dark skin.

Sleeve tattoo on his right arm. No wallet, but he had a phone in a jacket pocket. Raven took it. He put away his gun and hurried down to the street. With no car—at least, no running car—he had a long walk ahead. But at least he had a place to go.

CHAPTER TWO

RAVEN SLIPPED OPEN THE IRON GATE BLOCKING OFF THE walkway to the ornate residence in a neighborhood of many such dwellings. Notting Hill was known for its posh homes, and this one was no exception.

Raven's arrival in London three days earlier wasn't without a reminder the city was no longer London of old. The Muslim population was making themselves seen and heard in a big way. Calls to prayer five times a day; full burkas everywhere. On his second day checking out Hyde Park, twelve men on prayer rugs remained quiet, but another pair nearby made a lot of noise. They'd stood behind a long table; one gave out Korans, another talked through a loudspeaker telling passersby they had better convert or their families would burn in "eternal fire."

In some ways, it amused Raven, the British getting a taste of what it was like in the nations the empire once ruled—and with an iron fist, too. They probably deserved to get their land taken from them as they had done to so many others—karma, right? And polite British subjects went along without protest, or they faced penalties—arrest and imprisonment—for speaking out. Nobody wanted to be seen as "bigoted," especially since the words they used were now as policed as their actions. Better not say the wrong thing, guv'nor, or you'll end up in Old Bailey! Better not post the wrong thing on social media, mate, or you'll never see the sun in jolly old England again! (The obvious response being, well, it's an island; it rains a lot; the rest of the time it's cloudy; how often does anybody *really* see the sun? Maybe you tyrants with your bad teeth need to try another kind of threat.)

Criticisms aside, Raven wondered about the unintended consequences of current policy. How many jihadists operatives had snuck in with the rest of the "refugees?" How had England exposed itself to a mass casualty attack in the name of welcoming immigrants to a so-called better life? How many Britons had to die before the politicians and social justice warriors performed a hundred-eighty-degree turn? Or would they instead double down and make excuses for the violence knowing British subjects had no power to truly respond?

Like many questions related to government agendas, the answer never came until it was too late to prevent the consequences.

He pulled the gate shut again. The electronic lock engaged, but Raven didn't understand the need. The edge of the gate and low wall around the house only came as high as his stomach. Easy to climb over if one desired, but then there were interior security measures to deal with, which Raven didn't have to worry about. He punched a code into the keypad beside the door. Another electronic lock clicked, and Raven entered like he owned the place. He didn't.

Lights burned throughout the lower floor. Raven crossed

the front room, with its mostly antique furniture, to a small hall and stopped in a doorway midway.

Ana Gray rotated her chair away from the twin flat screen monitors on her desk. Her smile faded.

"You're alone."

"Yes," Raven said.

Ana Gray wore her dark hair tied back, a tight white blouse fitting almost like a corset to accentuate how thin she was and what little she packed up top. Black Capris rode low over the flare of her hips. The Gray fortune left her a billionaire when the title passed, and she used the money to support her covert intelligence network. London society had no idea. Ana Gray regularly made the most eligible bachelorette lists circulating through the world's wealthiest singles, but never attempted to end the streak.

"What happened?"

Raven leaned in the doorway, folded his arms, and related the events of the night. He was sore, tired, sweaty; his clothes were dirty, and he wanted answers. When he finished, Ana's face lost color.

"Oh, no."

Raven's mission hadn't sounded complicated when Ana first approached him for help. Leslie Rose-Brooks needed an escort home after a long-term undercover assignment. She informed Ana she'd discovered what she'd been sent to find, but the enemy found out, and she had a target on her back.

Ana hoped Raven could get her home in one piece.

But now Leslie was dead, and Raven almost bought it, too.

"I found this cell phone on the team leader's body," Raven told her. He took out the phone and handed it to Ana. She said nothing more. Taking the phone, she plugged it into one of the many peripheral devices connected to her computers, and Raven stood behind her chair as she worked the keyboard and brought up data on the right-hand screen.

A check of the text message folder was her first stop. Somebody sent the team leader a picture of Leslie. The phone number rerouted half a dozen times when Ana attempted a trace. The dead man's name was Sebastian Fellows. Freelance killer for various clients. Long record. Ana cursed in frustration. He was a dead end, she explained. Had nothing to do, she said, with the people she'd sent Leslie to investigate. "Except being hired," she added. Obviously, she believed, they'd hired Fellows and his gunmen to do the dirty work while they remained in the background.

"He's still worth checking up," Raven said.

"Find out who hired him by talking to his friends? No, Raven, you have no idea who we're dealing with. They wouldn't be so sloppy as to leave a trail. It took us months to get anywhere with Leslie and Piper. They cover their tracks well."

"Who is Piper?"

"The other agent I need you to bring back. She's in Cairo. And, now, I assume, she's in as much danger as poor Leslie was."

"Are you sure she's even still alive?"

"She made her check-in this evening. Unless something happened after, she's all right."

"Did you expect me to leave tonight?" Raven asked.

"First thing tomorrow morning. I have a private jet scheduled. You better get some sleep."

"You going to tell me what this is all about?"

"When we get Piper, Raven. She'll tell us everything."

"Sounds like you're not even sure what it's all about."

"I'd only be sharing rumors. Piper and Leslie went for the hard data."

"But it looks like the rumors are true."

Ana scoffed. "Go to bed, Raven."

Raven grunted. He'd try and sleep, but wasn't hopeful of getting real rest. Ana supplied a spare bedroom upstairs for him. He went up, showered to get the night's grime off his body, and swallowed a sleeping pill to help get him to sleep. But he still had trouble dozing off. His brain continued to spin with questions. He hadn't, after all, seen a body. He wasn't *certain* Leslie Rose-Brooks was dead. If she had evaded her killers, she was still out there, hiding, while Raven was already off on his next mission. If she was still alive, he hoped she could hang on a little longer. If not, he'd get answers, find out who killed her, and show them the meaning of *payback*.

CHAPTER THREE

ANA SHOWED HIM THE NEWS HEADLINE VIA HER SMARTPHONE the next morning. Police found a woman's body along the Thames near the Waterloo Bridge. Ana didn't need the cops to tell her the body belonged to Leslie. Raven finished his breakfast with a grim set to his face. The early police report stated she hadn't died near the bridge. She'd been killed elsewhere and dumped.

The private jet took off on time. Raven sat without moving. His mind was focused on an old friend he'd never see again who didn't deserve to be murdered.

His history with Ana Gray went back several years, and he helped her out from time to time. She'd also been involved in a recent operation Raven undertook involving sensitive photographs of the US president. She'd had the pictures in her possession, with unknown intent, only to have them stolen from her safe thanks to an employee who wanted a few extra bucks on the side. A dark cloud descended on Raven as he recalled the matter. The woman who had stolen the pictures—Megan, no last name—had briefly made him think he had a chance to go through life without being alone. It was a mistake. She'd been taken from him same as the most important woman in his life other than his mother. He'd never forget either of them. Megan in particular had been a woman after his own heart. With her by his side, the predators of the world would never have a chance.

But she was gone. He was alone. And perhaps that was the way it had to be. He didn't understand why, but the ghosts of battles past, who directed his war without end, surely did. He had to trust them.

Raven had spent much of his life on the front lines, covert or otherwise. 82nd Airborne; Special Forces; CIA Ground Branch; a career serving his country in hostile environments around the globe. A multitude of enemies and brushes with death. His days as an official government man were over. He left the life behind to settle into civilian life, until tragedy struck, compelling him to take up arms again. Not for his country; not for himself. He fought to keep others from experiencing the tragedy he had. When he failed, he avenged with fire and fury. Like now. Again.

The jet touched down five hours later. The jolt of the landing jerked Raven from his trance.

Cairo. Not Raven's favorite city. But he had no favorite city any longer. The world had changed too much—and not for the good. Every place looked like everywhere else. The Western influence on even the most *non*-western of countries ruined much of what once made the world, and traveling throughout, unique and an experience to look forward to.

He made the drive from the airport into Cairo in a rental car, a small compact with a weak four-cylinder engine and so lightweight it let in a lot of road noise. But he needed quickly available transportation, which meant not relying on cabs or ride shares. He was under the gun—Ana's agent may have already met the same fate as poor Leslie—and he had to work fast. The heavy traffic on the highway allowed him to glance at a few Cairo landmarks in the distance. The Cairo Tower, in particular, scratched the clear blue sky; if he had the time, a visit to the Egyptian Museum in Tahir Square would have been nice. But there wasn't time, and he wasn't in the mood.

As nice as some parts of Cairo and Egypt were, and the country had much to recommend it, Raven still had his gripes. The edge of Giza, neighboring Cairo, stopped where the pyramids and surrounding ancient structures began. City developers had to fill every square inch with houses, shopping, etcetera—they might as well have torn down the pyramids, since dead pharaohs aren't prompt with their property taxes. The luster and legend of the land had vanished; worse, it was a mecca for the Middle Eastern music and film industries. Who cared about the old things anymore? Dead pharaohs don't make TikTok videos.

He had the address of Piper Shaw's hotel memorized; as he drove, he thought over Ana's description of the young woman.

"She's probably too young for you—or maybe she isn't since I'm apparently too old," she began, forcing a laugh at Raven's raised eyebrow. She was always trying to get him into bed, and Raven always refused—without saying why. Ana Gray *used* people to further her version of the greater good; he had no desire to fall into her web. But when she needed help, *serious* help, such as with her stray operatives, he set his prejudice aside.

"Here's her picture. See? She's not hard to look at."

Raven only grunted in affirmation. Piper Shaw would

have turned on any man who liked them a little thicker, and with short hair, too.

"She's former SIS, left to do modeling, then said the hell with it because she wanted a cheeseburger now and then, and now she works for me."

Raven saw the look. Blonde hair, blue eyes—thinner, she would have been the model type. Now, she looked ordinary. Perfect look for a spy.

Except, of course, in this case. The other side wanted her dead because they knew she discovered secrets they wanted to keep hidden.

"Bring her back alive, Sam," Ana said.

He fully intended to.

————

RAVEN TURNED OFF THE HIGHWAY AND DROVE INTO downtown Cairo. Traffic inched along. The A/C fought against the outside heat, but Raven still felt warm. A layer of sweat covered his back against the car seat.

Piper Shaw, according to Raven's instructions, was waiting at a hotel across the street from the Café Tambourine, owned by another contact of Ana's. On the opposite side of the café was the Mosque Sultan Hassan, and Piper's placement near both spots wasn't an accident.

Ana explained: "Louis Jordan is the fellow who runs the café. He's keeping an eye on Piper till you get there, and he has men to spare if you need them. The mosque is another advantage. The imam there is very anti-crime, and he has some of his followers, at all times of the day, hanging around the sidewalks making sure nobody attacks the tourists or engages in anything the imam doesn't approve of. You'll notice them—they wear white."

Raven spotted the Sultan Hassan "watchers" as soon as he turned the corner and started up the street. They were men in their twenties or forties, a decent mix, all loitering and wearing white *thobes* and head coverings as they scanned the street. Passersby didn't pay them much mind, and they kept out of the way. Raven caught one eyeing him as he drove by the hotel. He found a place to park the car farther down the block and locked the car to make his way back along the sidewalk. He felt guilty locking the car, oddly. With so many "watchers" hanging around, he figured he could leave the car unlocked, the windows down, and the engine running, and nobody would mess with the vehicle.

He took a moment to examine the street further. Traffic was heavy, cars moving slowly, their progress hampered by tourists crossing the street and street vendors hocking items to tourists with loud calls to buy what looked like cheap junk— trinkets worth far less than their retail price. But a good street hark can make a chump believe they are buying something of tremendous value which will last for many years to come… and then fall to pieces in the suitcase during the flight home. The idea made Raven smile. He knew the scenario was true, because it had happened to him.

Then he saw four people sitting in a parked car watching the hotel.

Great. The enemy was already there, waiting for a chance to strike.

He started for the hotel entrance.

Other guests kept the desk clerks busy checking them in; Raven bypassed them and found the elevators. In the car by himself, he pressed the button for Piper's floor. As the elevator ascended, he called her number on his cell.

"Yes?" Her voice was soft, tinged with uncertainty, and her natural accent.

"It's Raven. On my way up."

"What's Ana's favorite color?"

Raven hated such questions, but understood the need for them. Now and then.

"Black," he said. "Best way to blend with the shadows."

"I appreciate you not saying *gray*, Mr. Raven."

He laughed. He could hear the smile in her tone now. The elevator stopped and the doors slid open. He said, "Be ready. I'm ten steps from the door."

He tapped a code on her room door, one worked out between her and Ana in advance, and Piper answered with tote bag in hand, jacket zipped, and no questions.

"That's all you brought?" Raven asked as they started down the hall.

"Always travel light," she told him.

Raven steered her to the stairwell. He didn't want them both in the elevator at the same time. He probably should have skipped it himself, he reflected, as they began going down the steps.

"Any trouble getting here?" she asked. She looked a little better than the picture Ana had shown him. Her hair was longer and curled, and had lost a few pounds since the photo. No makeup, and comfortable clothes for travel. Jeans, sneakers, and a T-shirt showing under the jacket. He figured she had a pistol under the coat. She'd regret wearing it in the afternoon heat, same as he regretted his, but you couldn't go walking around most places on Earth with a pistol exposed.

There were many, many people who'd take exception and go running for their safe spaces.

"We might have trouble *leaving*," Raven said, and mentioned the surveillance crew he'd spotted.

They turned to go down another flight.

"They won't make a move while the Hassan people are watching the street," Piper said, "but we won't have them around once we leave the block."

Almost to the lobby…

"Got any ideas?" Raven asked. "Maybe the Jordan fellow Ana mentioned?"

"Exactly. I know a way to the café without having to go outside."

She pushed through the lobby door and turned left. They were going away from the main entrance, traveling down a passage lined with small shops and restaurants. It was a mini-mall attached to the hotel. Piper explained an underground passage dug under the street ended at the Café Tambourine. It was the reason Piper had chosen the hotel. Along with the imam's watchers, she had more security than poor Leslie ever had.

They had to slow their brisk pace because of other foot traffic, but Raven used the time to quiz her a little.

"You heard about Leslie?"

"Yes. I promise somebody is going to pay for that."

"Ana's refusing to tell me what your mission was all about. Care to—"

"Not saying a word, Mr. Raven. If Ana is keeping you in the dark, she has her reasons."

"Guess I'm just an errand boy this time."

"I'm sure she's paying you well."

Raven grunted as they continued. He *was* being well paid, but money wasn't everything.

Presently the passage took them below the street. The shops ended, and the walls became faux-rock, with ads displayed, with the concrete walkway remaining constant. Signs in several languages were mixed with the ads announcing the Café Tambourine straight ahead, and as they neared a set of wooden steps, Raven hoped this Louis Jordan person had a spare car. Or at least somebody to drive them to Ana's waiting jet. How the opposition found them he had no idea; most likely, they'd had Piper under surveillance for a while and were waiting for her to make the run for home before attacking.

"This Jordan fellow couldn't run you home himself?" Raven asked.

"He'd want too much money. And he'd send one of his men. Ana and I talked about it and decided he wasn't a good fit. She trusts you—and you're cheaper."

"This job is doing wonders," Raven said, "for my self-confidence."

Raven only wanted to avoid a fight in public. He knew the opposition wasn't so inclined. They never were. Bad guys didn't care if innocent people got hurt in their crossfire— Raven did. This underground trick of Piper's was keeping a fight from happening where one shouldn't, and Raven didn't have to find an out-of-the-way spot where they'd be free to fight. Better to avoid a battle altogether. Rule Two—no gunfights in public. He adhered religiously to Rule Two. His first rule, no roots, was his other guiding principle. And every time he thought of it, he saw the faces of those he'd failed to protect, the ones he let get close to him when he knew better. As long as humans craved other human contact, it would be the rule he struggled with the most. Rule Two was much easier to follow.

They reached the steps and went up. Stepping into the entryway of the café, they stopped. A velvet rope blocked the doorway.

The café's dining area was a wide circle, bar in the center. Uniformed wait staff hustled to take down chairs from tabletops, and prepare for opening. They were closed, and the white-haired maître d' who came over to them said as much. He was an American, overweight, with white hair and a jowly face.

"I'm here to see Louis," Piper said. "Tell him it's Piper Shaw."

A loud voice from across the room called out, "Let them through, Mitchell."

The heavy-set white-haired man removed one end of the rope from a hook, and allowed them to pass. Raven said, "Thanks," as Piper made a bee-line for the man who had spoken.

Raven examined Louis Jordan as they approached. He waited beside the bar. He was tall and lean and his arm muscles bulged under a button-down work shirt. Black hair with a streak of gray; his graying goatee covered much of his chin and upper lip.

He smiled as they neared. "What do you need?"

Piper jumped in before Raven had a chance to speak.

"There's an ambush outside waiting for us. We need a ride to the airport. Or a car if you can spare one."

"I can take you. No sweat."

Raven said, "Got a big enough back seat for us to lay down?"

"I even have a few hidden Uzis in case your friends find a way to catch up." Jordan laughed.

Raven didn't think it was funny but didn't say so. He only said avoiding a fight was his main objective.

"Come on," Jordan said. "My car's out back. We'll get you out of here without shooting off any artillery. It would be bad for my business, too."

Raven and Piper followed him out back.

CHAPTER FOUR

"I don't think you're getting out of here without a fight, Raven."

The escape had gone well—too well, considering the enemy wasn't far away. Jordan had led them to the parking lot adjoining the Tambourine, one shielded from the road by palm trees and other edge growth, and they piled into a white Mercedes. Jordan made sure to exit the café lot on the street opposite the one Raven had parked on to avoid the eyes of the crew he'd spotted spying on the café.

But another vehicle—a truck, not the car he first saw—with enemy thugs aboard picked up their trail as soon as they hit the road. It took two blocks and a couple of extra turns for Jordan to identify the bad guys.

Raven rose from the back seat, telling Piper to keep her head down. There was enough traffic to make it tough for any surveillance effort, but Raven wasn't taking anything for granted.

"They're trying to look inconspicuous," Jordan said.

"Nice try," Raven said. He reached under his jacket for the Nighthawk .45.

"Whoa, not here!" Jordan said. "Let me get away from all this traffic first."

"A man after my own heart," Raven said. "But just in case they try to open the festivities first, we need to be ready."

Piper sat up. "Where are those Uzis you mentioned?" Piper said.

"Panel under the seat," Jordan told her. "Behind your feet."

The Mercedes was an older model, maybe twenty-five years old, with a chugging diesel engine. Jordan turned off the air conditioner to get the most out of the engine. "Might get a little warm!"

Raven rolled down his window. Hot wind entered the car. Piper worked the panel behind her feet as Jordan described and pulled out a mini-Uzi with a loaded mag. She checked the chamber and set the weapon between her and Raven.

The car's interior warmed up fast, but Raven figured it was less from the outside temp and more from his rising pulse rate.

Raven twisted around, looking out each window, trying to get a sense of where they were. The buildings and street activity blended together. At least they were moving—at maybe 35 miles per hour—and not stuck.

"Where are we, Jordan?"

"The 26th of July Corridor," the café owner answered. "It's an impressive roadway and Cairo is very proud of this freeway. The truck is sticking close, by the way."

Raven looked out the back window. "I see him."

Piper Shaw seemed bored. She rested a hand on the Uzi submachine gun between them. "First time, Raven?"

"Shut up," he told her.

She laughed.

He was thinking of Rule Two. And how, sometimes, the enemy forced his hand, preventing him from keeping the innocent out of the line of fire. The only strategy in those moments was to shoot true. Don't miss. Take out the other side before they harmed others. But with so many people around, in cars or on the sidewalk, the odds were not stacking in Raven's favor. He felt for the sterling silver locket under his shirt. He never went without the locket, the motivation contained within—the ghosts of battles past who often directed his war without end. They sent him where he needed to be. Knowing they were with him calmed Raven's racing thoughts. He settled back in the seat. And held on to his gun. The fight was coming soon. He'd handle it as he had so many others.

He wasn't going to let the enemy kill Piper the way they had Leslie.

Jordan changed lanes, moving to the left, and increased speed. The Mercedes' V8 growled, cars in the middle lane flashing by. A portion of the Nile lay ahead, slicing through the city in its twists and turns, and they crossed over the bridge at speed. Several large ships were docked on either side of the canal, large container ships, Raven noticed. Piper sat with her eyes fixed ahead. She was waiting for action same as him.

Jordan moved across the road to the right lane, cutting off a car or two, ignoring the angry blasts of horns. Raven checked behind them. The old truck kept up. Maybe three car lengths back. Not getting closer, or aggressive. They were waiting for a second car. A support team. *The sedan he'd seen*. Raven took a deep breath and sat forward.

"They'll make a move when they're ready," Piper said quietly.

"We're already ready," Raven said.

Jordan turned off the freeway and began cruising through city streets. He kept the speedometer at thirty-five or forty. Everything looked arid despite the density of the buildings. The dusty desert motif was everywhere Raven looked. But there were fewer and fewer cars and Jordan continued, and fewer and fewer people about.

"Where are we going?" Raven asked.

"I don't need any more trouble from the cops than we're already going to get," Jordan said, "so I know a little playground where we can settle our differences and go on our way."

"Which way?"

"Up or down, depending on the state of your soul, my friend."

———

RAVEN THOUGHT THEY WERE CLEAR UNTIL THE OLD TRUCK turned the corner behind them and sped up to close in. Another car, the sedan, followed the truck and pulled alongside. The sedan was for sure the car he'd seen outside the hotel before he met Piper. Both truck and car converged on the Mercedes as one.

"Backup car made it," Raven announced. Jordan made a sharp left. Raven put away the Nighthawk and fiddled with the panel under his seat. He removed the other mini-Uzi. The compact version of the famed Israeli submachine gun warmed in his hands.

"Got any spare ammo for these squirt guns?" he asked

Jordan. A 30-round mag was locked into the gun, but a single magazine wasn't going to last long against two carloads of bad guys with high-powered weapons of their own.

The café owner leaned over to the glovebox without taking his eyes off the road. He opened the box and grabbed two spare magazines. Handing them back, Raven took both and passed one to Piper. Sixty rounds each. Raven's .45 pistol. Two carloads of enemy gunners. They needed more ammo and maybe a few more shooters on their side, Raven realized.

"I hope you're hiding an M-60 in the trunk, Jordan," Raven said. "We're outgunned and outnumbered."

Piper said, "Is there a difference?"

"We'll be down one more," Raven told her, "if you keep up this spoiled teenager act."

She grinned. "I'll tell you what this is all about if we survive."

"Then make every shot count, Piper. We won't have a lot of room to groove."

Jordan yelled, "Here they come!"

Raven noticed Jordan never said what extra firepower, if any, he had in the trunk.

CHAPTER FIVE

THE OLD TRUCK SMASHED INTO THE REAR BUMPER OF THE Mercedes.

The crash of metal on metal sounded loud in Raven's ears. He felt the jolting impact in his bones as the seatbelt kept him restrained. He let out a sharp grunt of discomfort nonetheless. He hoped he didn't have a case of whiplash. The blow flung the Mercedes forward, Jordan jerking the wheel but unable to keep the rubber on the road. The big car lurched to the right, jumped the curb, and skidded across the concrete sidewalk. It finally stopped in a dirt lot. Raven saw they were in a construction zone. Partial wood frames and a trailer with a company name on the side occupied the lot. There were no workers around but plenty of neighbors across the street. Raven cursed as he unlatched his seatbelt and yelled, "Everybody out!"

Raven shoved open his door and rolled onto the dirt. He stopped on his belly. The truck jumped the curb and turned into the lot. The sedan stopped in the street. Raven wished

Jordan had stopped closer to the building frames, but he had to deal with the battlefield he'd been given.

The truck kicked up a cloud of dust as the driver turned slightly, steering away from the Mercedes a little. Raven steadied the Uzi—

A wave of dirt crashed onto his left side, striking Raven's face. He spit and ran his left hand over his face. The motion cleared the mess out of his vision. The Mercedes sped off toward the building frame. Raven and Piper had only a second to gape in shock before movement at the truck forced their attention back to the enemy.

The cab doors swung open and both driver and passenger jumped out. They clutched CZ Scorpion EVO submachine guns which had a higher rate of fire than the mini-Uzis, but it meant nothing if the shooters weren't accurate. Raven figured they knew how to use the weapons as well as he would and kept his mini-Uzi on single-shot. He needed to conserve ammo. He fired three times and yelled for Piper to get to cover. The ejecting brass bounced in the dirt beside him. He fired three more, focusing on the driver, registering in his peripheral vision that the crew in the sedan weren't engaging.

At least, not yet.

But they were watching.

The driver used the truck's door as cover, but the gap between the bottom edge and the ground left his ankles exposed. The second string of 9 mm projectiles closed the distance between Raven and the driver in the blink of an eye. Two smacked into the hard steel door. The third slug punched through the driver's left foot. The driver screamed and staggered back, bumping into the body of the truck, almost stumbling to the ground. He fought to keep his balance. But as he fought, he fully exposed himself.

Raven flipped his selector switch to full-auto and squeezed the trigger. A longer burst this time, flame flashing from the muzzle, and the salvo spread across the driver's chest. When he fell to the ground, he fell to stay—he lay still and didn't move.

"Raven!"

Piper shouting from cover. He heard her firing behind him. The passenger of the truck returned fire, but not at Raven. Piper was the immediate threat. He fired at her. Raven jumped up, squeezed off a burst in the passenger's direction, and ran for the wooden frame behind him. His salvo missed, punching through the front windscreen, but the bullets drove the passenger to cover and gave Piper a chance to change locations.

Raven leaped over a low wooden beam and moved left, where a wall had been erected on one side of the wooden skeleton. The structure was square, with multiple levels; the start of an apartment building, or multi-story office park. Raven didn't care. The structures presented places to hide while the enemy tried to kill him. And he hoped he could kill *them* before they got *him*.

Planks behind him formed part of the floor. The spot he crouched in hadn't been covered yet, so his shoes sank into soft dirt. Piper was in the right corner, angling for another shot at the truck's passenger. Raven peered around the corner at the sedan, still parked curbside. The occupants weren't coming out. But one in the back seat appeared to have some sort of telescope or camera. Watching.

It made no sense.

"Where the hell is Jordan?" Raven yelled.

The truck's passenger opened fire over the top of the truck's cabin roof. He'd climbed into the back. The position exposed his head, but not enough for Raven and Piper to take a shot as the rounds hammered into the wood around them.

Bullets slapped at the wood skeleton like angry hornets dive-bombing an aircraft carrier. Wood beams splintered, shards flying, none coming near Raven as he adjusted his shooting position and –

The hammering of a heavy machine gun made him jerk. He felt the concussion of the muzzle blast despite the wall on his right. The weapon wasn't aimed at him or Piper. The firing came from around the other side of the wall. Whoever lay behind the machine gun knew where to put the rounds. The truck's front tires popped, the front end sinking, the jolt of the drop throwing the gunner off balance. Raven and Piper cut loose. Their crossfire cut down the now-exposed gunner. He toppled out of the truck and joined his dead partner on the ground.

The sedan's engine revved, and the four-door took off in a tire-screeching U-turn. Raven and Piper left cover and ran around the other side of the wall, where they stopped short. Louis Jordan hoisted the bipod-mounted M-249 from the ground. He grinned.

"Had it in the trunk," he said. "Come on."

Raven laughed despite the situation. He and Piper followed Jordan through more wooden skeletons to the chugging Mercedes. As Jordan dropped the machine gun into the trunk, Raven and Piper returned to the back seat, hurriedly strapping in. Jordan slammed the trunk twice before it stayed closed, but the back end didn't have as much damage as Raven would have thought. Dropping behind the wheel, Jordan shoved the car into gear. The rear tires kicked up a wave of dirt at the press of the accelerator. Jordan steered for the pavement.

"Those guys owe me a car wash! And a new bumper!"

Raven wondered how the café owner planned to collect but let it ride. He had more urgent matters on his mind as he stowed the dirty mini-Uzi back in its hiding place. They had to get back to London fast. He wanted to know what was going on and who the son of a bitch with the camera in the back seat of the sedan might be. The enemy already knew about Piper. Now they knew, or soon would, about Raven. No matter what motive Ana had for keeping him in the dark, Raven was now up to his neck. He needed to know who he was fighting, and why, in order to finish the battle before more lives were lost.

Piper held onto her Uzi. Raven figured, if it made her more comfortable, it was best to keep his mouth shut.

CHAPTER SIX

THE MAN IN THE BACK SEAT OF THE WHITE SEDAN REMAINED stoic as the driver raced away from the construction zone.

His hair was thick and dark but showed a little gray on either side. Despite the lines on his face, he looked younger than his fifty years, and he retained the sharp jawline of his youth. He wore a white suit, polished shoes, a gold Rolex. His name was Rahmil, and he was still in the revolution business. He held a digital camera with an extended lens on his lap.

"Are you all right?"

The question came from the man seated on his right. Rahmil turned to Borja Elim and frowned. Elim was the head of Rahmil's base of operations in Cairo, a man he trusted with the intricate secrets of the global organization.

"It's fine, Borja. I know who we are dealing with now."

"Who did you see?"

Rahmil glanced at the camera. The long telephoto lens had shown him all the detail he wanted. He'd print the photos for his men to examine, but there was no need for his own copies. He remembered Sam Raven's face. Like him, Raven was older, but also like him, the changes weren't so much as to make him unrecognizable.

"An enemy who bested me ten years ago," Rahmil said. "Somebody I should have dealt with long before now, when time is short and our plans on such fragile ground. But here we are."

"Why didn't you?"

Rahmil shrugged. "Other priorities. Or maybe I was afraid of losing again and *permanently*."

Borja Elim added nothing to the remark. Rahmil knew he wasn't invincible; to say otherwise, even in jest, denied physical reality. Rahmil was far too aware of himself to lie to his own reflection.

"But now?" Elim asked.

"Now? This time? Oh, have no doubt." Rahmil smiled. "This time, only one of us walks away."

The sedan drove on.

———

HE WASN'T IN GOOD ENOUGH SHAPE TO RUN FOR LONG.

But if he stopped running, Little Jimmy White would kill him for sure.

Garrett Ranch shed his jacket and let it fall behind him. He didn't need the drag. He pumped his arms and legs harder —he needed distance. His lungs burned, his breathing labored, sweat dripping into his eyes. He looked for a place to hide, but there was no escaping Jimmy unless he dug a hole in the ground and crawled to China.

Blonde haired, scrawny, Ranch was in no way a prime physical specimen. Mentally, he was quite sharp. He knew his math backward and forward which made him a good numbers man, and when he was hustling, his fast talking could run a mark in circles to the point they wouldn't know which end was up. He started young, as a teenager, running around London for Old Man White as he worked his way up. He had his own crew and nowadays delegated most of the work while he took it easy and stayed out of sight. He ran numbers, moved drugs, whatever legwork Old Man White needed. He answered to Lil' Jimmy, the Old Man's kid. The White Organization valued Ranch, but then he got greedy, got arrested, and thrown back into the organization as a grass. Now the White Organization, and young Jimmy in particular, wanted Ranch dead. And if he didn't get away, Lil' Jimmy would get his wish.

Ranch had abandoned his car at the intersection of Glamas Road and The Highway, and high-tailed it through the King Edward Memorial Park. Behind him, between the park and the road, a tall wall of trees shielded him, but it wouldn't hide him for long. Jimmy White was too close for the trees to throw him off.

Ranch's work boots dug into the soft ground under his feet, and as he crossed the middle of the field the cramp hit. It struck like an undercut. He veered to the right. Buildings ahead. Shadwell Pierhead and a pub. He imagined storming into the pub, out of breath, sweaty, shaking, saying something stupid like, *"Hey, mate, pour me a pint. I'm a grass running from a bloke who'd like to shoot me."* But there were other buildings around Shadwell. Places to hide. Maybe people. Lil' Jimmy wouldn't shoot with other people around. Right? Ranch tried to laugh. Of course not. Jimmy didn't care. Jimmy had his father's protection to rely on. Jimmy's father knew all the right people in all the right places. Ranch could sit in the corner of the pub and Jimmy would waltz up to the table and empty the magazine into his face, then buy a round for the house for their trouble.

A grass. An informer. A rat. All three and all in one. Ranch might have been smart, but he wasn't lucky. Any crook who let the cops nab him and turn him against his buddies not only truly screwed up but deserved whatever misfortune befell him, which had always been Ranch's philosophy…until it happened to him. But he knew Jimmy wouldn't be interested in talking things over.

He heard a bump, almost a crash, and an engine rev. He looked over his shoulder. Ranch found the energy to run again. He ran hard. The silver car had jumped the curb, and now the tires dug into the field as the car came at him like a shark smelling blood. Full speed. The car overshot Ranch, started to turn; Ranch tried to cut left, but then the car spun toward him. He felt the impact with the front end, a hammering blow. He left the ground. His vision spun— twirling sky, rising ground, *impact*. He landed on his back and his breath left him. He couldn't tell the difference between gasping for air and panic. Oddly, he noticed the overcast sky. Clouds of various shades of gray—light, dark, in between. Typical London. Why couldn't he die on a sunny day?

The car doors opened.

"Lookie, lookie," said Jimmy White. He exited from the left side, his buddy the right. Jimmy took a gun from under his jacket.

James White wasn't little. He was tall and lean and wore nice street clothes. He might have been mistaken for a Holly-wood actor. He kept his hair perfect, his face clean-shaven, and his fingernail manicured.

LONDON ASSAULT 73

"Lookie, lookie, lookie," White said. He stopped to look down at Ranch. Ranch laughed. White had a double chin with his head tilted down the way it was. He wouldn't have appreciated the information. "Grass on grass," White continued.

Ranch finally had enough breath back to talk. He wasn't conscious of the pain throughout his body. A small consolation. He had no idea how badly hurt he actually was.

"Jimmy...*James!*...you gotta hear me out—"

"It wasn't your idea? You had no choice? I've heard it before, Garrett. You're not the first and you won't be the last. But you know how it goes. We find out you're talking to the cops, you gotta go. Believe me when I tell you this will hurt me more than it hurts you."

"Wait!"

The gun cracked twice. Whatever Ranch had intended to say died with him.

CHAPTER SEVEN

"Right, job done," James White announced. "What'd you even get out of the car for, Phil?" He laughed. His number two, Philip Deen, pulled something shiny out of his own coat pocket.

"I got the shears, remember?"

"Ha! Right! Left thumb, good chap."

Philip Deen was a little shorter than James White, but they shared similar builds and taste in clothes. Deen leaned down, grabbed Ranch's left hand, and used the sharpened shears to cut off Ranch's left thumb. The bones broke with a sickening crunch, and Deen had to press hard several times, but he broke the digit from the hand—*pop*. James winced at the sound. Such dreadful work. But it had to be done.

James White hated the nickname "Little Jimmy." He preferred his proper name. His father had taught him an important lesson early in life when James proclaimed he was going to smack the next guy who called him Little Jimmy. The Old Man said, *"If you complain about the nickname, they'll use it to get under your skin. Better to leave it alone, son. It'll die out by itself."*

"Why's it gotta be the thumb?" Deen said. "Why not the pinky? Pinky'd be a hell of a lot easier, mate."

Deen put the bloody stump of thumb into a sandwich bag. Shears and bag went back into his jacket.

"I like thumbs," James said.

Deen grinned and turned back for the car and gestured for his boss to get back inside. "Because you're not the one with the bloody shears."

"Literally and figuratively," James added.

They drove back across the grass to Glamas Road. The car thump-bumped back over the curb and onto the pavement. Deen made a left and joined the flow of traffic.

"One down," Deen said, "one to go. You sure leaving his body—"

"The cops will get the message," James said.

"They'll put the pressure on, you know," Deen said.

"Like it will matter. They haven't nailed my father on anything in forty years. You think they'll get *me* for murdering a runt like Ranch? Please. Just drive. It's under control."

Deen drove.

———

ANA GRAY STOOD WITH ARMS CROSSED OUTSIDE THE PRIVATE hangar at Heathrow. The dark clouds above reflected her mood. She was glad Piper had made it out of Cairo alive, but the fact the opposition killed Leslie and almost killed Piper meant MI-6 had been right. Piper and Leslie were targets because they found proof. Worse, the fight wasn't over. There was still plenty of work to finish the battle the government had no power to fight.

She dressed for the chill, designer jeans hugging her legs and hips, leather boots, a warm coat. She'd tied back her hair to keep it from blowing with the wind. The coat looked big and made her look smaller than she actually was. She hated being thin, yet couldn't put on any mass. The only thing she hadn't tried was a full spaghetti dinner every night before bed for a month. The thought occurred to her often. Ideally, she'd plump right up. But knowing her luck, all she'd get was indigestion.

An SUV waited behind her, driver behind the wheel; she watched as her jet taxied toward the hanger. It was time to bring Raven fully into the picture as well. She'd need him to take Leslie's place. If he was willing. She'd have to up his payment for sure, but she knew him well enough to know he wouldn't turn her down. And not only because he had a history with Leslie.

Ana Gray only had bits and pieces of their full background together because neither had been able to divulge the truth. Need-to-know and all that. But they'd worked on a joint CIA / MI6 mission somewhere in the Balkans and wound up facing tough opponents. An ambush almost cost Raven his life; Leslie, spotting the gun crew ahead of time, opened fire, compromising her own position but allowing Raven to escape the line of fire and take out the gun crew. All they'd say about the rest of the mission was that they'd achieved their desired goals.

The whine of the turbine motors increased, then settled into a low drone as the jet stopped twenty-five yards away. Ana didn't leave the hangar, but she did smile a little as Piper exited first, followed by Raven. Raven covered a yawn as he came down the steps. Piper walked briskly, pulling away from Raven, who maintained a slow pace. He didn't look happy. She wondered if Piper had told him anything during the flight. What else was there to talk about?

"Are you okay, Piper?" Ana asked. She had to raise her voice over the drone of the jet engines, even at their idle level. The otherwise empty hanger created an echo effect as well. She wanted to get back home as fast as possible.

"We got the bad guys dead-bang, boss," Piper said. "And I'm all right. Raven was a good choice."

"Of course." Ana looked over Piper's shoulder at Raven. He frowned at her.

"It's time we had a talk, Ana," Raven said.

"I'll tell you everything Piper didn't know."

"Didn't know?" Piper said. She raised an eyebrow.

"Need-to-know, luv." She smiled. Ana loved the phrase. "Let's go." She turned on a heel and started for the SUV. Raven and Piper followed.

———

RAVEN'S BODY ACHED. HE WANTED TO SLEEP. DROWSINESS stalked him like a cat hunting for mice.

He and Piper had talked a little on the plane before he cut the conversation off to try and rest. Nobody talked during the ride through London, which he didn't mind. They'd talk and then he'd crash. He needed to recharge before they started after the enemy again. He wasn't afraid of an attack on Ana's place. It was fortified to withstand any assault. Unless the bad guys brought a tank, which he didn't think was in the realm of possibility, but he didn't want to assume. Maybe they had one under a tarp somewhere tuned up, armed, and ready for use.

Raven dozed and was glad Ana didn't try to wake him. But when they pulled into the garage at Ana's place in Notting Hill, he snapped awake and followed the chatting women inside. Ana ushered them into a plush living room and left to make tea. Raven knew why she had no servants in the house. One had betrayed her once and let in a burglar who stole sensitive information. Now, Ana did everything herself. Raven and Piper sat opposite each other with a glass coffee table between them. The leather sofa was soft enough to make Raven wonder if he could keep his eyes open.

The living room displayed Ana's usual taste in things expensive. The mantle above the fireplace was white marble; the carpet matched. A glass display case contained various pieces of silver serving containers; the paintings on the walls could have funded the university educations of ten less-fortunate kids. The temperature wasn't too hot, wasn't too cold, and none of the street sounds from outside penetrated the walls. There was a feeling of seclusion while in the middle of a huge city.

Ana's fortune and the rewards from her espionage activities paid for her extravagant tastes. She'd made sure to construct her house in Madrid so it faced the Madrid airport. She liked to sit on the upper balcony and watch the jetliners fly over the house, and spent winters there when London became dreary and unbearable.

Ana was somebody dedicated to something greater than herself, yet still Raven didn't see eye-to-eye with her. The surface was fine. Beneath the surface, he wasn't sure, and his combat senses told him to stay wary. She wasn't going to betray him; of that, he was certain. But she wasn't somebody he wanted to get close to, either.

His gaze settled on Piper. He wasn't sure what to think of her. He didn't like her attitude. She'd held up under fire, but Jordan had bailed them out with his M-249 so fast he didn't think it was enough of a test. If Ana wanted to keep him around to finish the job, which seemed likely now, he hoped he wouldn't be forced to work closely with her.

She watched him, too. Her blue eyes studied him, as if she was examining every inch and making the same considerations as he. The look made him shift. Her face showed no emotion, her lips a flat line. He wondered what she was thinking. Then again, it was probably better he didn't know.

Ana returned with cups and a teapot on a silver tray. The matching pot and tray shined bright. What else would a proper Englishwoman serve tea with?

Ana poured for them both.

CHAPTER EIGHT

THE DARK BREW STEAMED. RAVEN HELD THE CUP AND SAUCER on his lap.

Ana sat on a leather seat to Raven's left and Piper's right. She addressed the blonde woman first. "What did you tell him?"

"Not everything."

"Okay." To Raven: "What do you know about charities funding terrorism?"

"I know it happens a lot," Raven said. "Sometimes the charities aren't aware, sometimes they're involved. I'm sure if you look around, you'll find the US alone has several active cases checking out such things."

Ana didn't reply, so Raven continued.

"It's not new. The IRA used a charity in the US—Noraid, or Aid to Northern Ireland—to buy guns and bombs to attack the British. They tricked Irish Americans into thinking the donations went to help civilians affected by the fighting."

It wasn't the first time the bad guys used a charity to raise money; it wouldn't be the last. A few weeks back,

Raven heard through the grapevine about a discussion at a counter-terrorism conference in Bonn how NATO and its allies needed to step up their investigations of suspicious charities, because the money was flowing too freely for anybody's comfort. Canada's intelligence community worked hard auditing various organizations working within their borders to make sure their spending was on the up-and-up, but lack of staff and budget hindered their efforts. They lacked staff and money because the top brass didn't think such investigations were a priority. Like everything else related to the so-called Global War on Terror, nothing became a priority until bodies littered the streets. Then the people who needed the money received what they asked for.

"Now we have another such case," Ana said, "but they do enough genuine good work to fool everybody. Leslie and Piper were investigating a charity run by Thomas Granton. Old money billionaire. Friend of the King. He uses his charity to donate to various causes around the world, quite legitimate."

"Except?" Raven sipped his tea. It had cooled enough to drink.

"Granton made several trips in recent months to the Middle East and set off a few alarms doing so," Ana said. "MI5 noticed suspicious behavior in his emails, too. And phone calls. He's been talking to people MI5 has classified as 'jihad suspects.' Sympathizers. Money men. So far, they haven't linked any of them directly to terrorism, but I empha-size 'so far.' The links are there if they look hard enough. But they're afraid to look too hard because if Granton complains to the King—"

"King Charles will shit all over them."

"Yes," she said. "You could put it that way, sure. I'd prefer a different phrasing, however." She grinned at him.

Raven didn't smile. "They asked you to poke around?"

"Unofficially. And quietly. It would be a huge scandal if it's true."

"I see." *Politics as usual...*

"We found a few things—"

"Like what?"

Piper jumped in. "Granton converted to Islam."

"Nothing illegal about changing your religion," Raven said. "It would also explain his Mideast travels."

"But he's been siphoning money," Piper said, "from his charity to terrorists. Not any specific group, but he's funding a 'money man' who then distributes the funds. A man we know only as *Rahmil*."

Raven's face changed. He looked grim.

Ana picked up on the look. "Mean anything to you?"

"I know Rahmil, yes." Raven explained the ten-year-old Naples mission. He left out the later fate of his team. Matson, Vega, and Anzell—his deadly trio of sharpshooters—were dead, killed well after their CIA careers ended when the fallout over an old mission came back to haunt them. Mara? Still alive. She'd been living in London until recently. Raven didn't know where she was now. The memory of her, and how they'd parted for the last time, made him sad.

He said, "That was Rahmil in Cairo, wasn't it? In the white sedan?"

Piper nodded.

"He knows I'm involved now," Raven told Ana. "He'll be coming after me. And I'll be waiting for *him*. We have a score to settle."

Piper said, "My job in Cairo was to gather information

from Granton's office there. The money is supposed to go to refugee support. But I have copies of spreadsheets showing income and outgo. A portion of the outgo shows money going to other, smaller charities who are jihad fronts."

Bigger charities subcontracting to smaller charities was also nothing new, and perfectly acceptable. Often, the larger organizations lacked personnel in areas in need of help, but local organizations had their assistance infrastructure already in place. It was easier for the big outfits to help the smaller ones instead of setting up their own people.

But subcontracting came with risks. Often, any misappropriation of funds took place with the smaller charities.

"What Piper found," Ana said, "backs up my own data."

"What about Leslie?" Raven asked. "Did she—"

"We don't know," Ana said. "Whatever she found, died with her. But she was looking at Granton's end of things here in London."

"How did they find out about you two?" Raven asked Piper.

Ana answered. "I suspect there's a leak in MI5. Either my contact or somebody close to him."

"Well," Raven said, setting his cup and saucer on the coffee table, "we're going to finish the job."

"And I wish I could say the hell with MI5," Ana said, raising her voice. "I want Granton and Rahmil wiped out. Dead. Gone. But we need to get Granton to confess and surrender. This has to be done cleanly, by the book."

"Piper's evidence isn't enough?" Raven said.

"Imagine you're a defense attorney."

"I'd rather not," Raven said with a smile.

Ana's expression remained flat. "We can't have this thrown out of court because the defense raises doubt of the authenticity of Piper's data or how it was obtained. I need *hard* proof. Irrefutable."

"I'm going to need a closer look at Mr. Granton," Raven said.

"He's throwing a party in two days. One of his many fundraisers. The cream of British society will be there. I'll make sure you and Piper have invitations."

"Is it smart to put Piper back in play?"

"I'm not sitting out, Raven," Piper declared. She looked angry. "Leslie was a friend of mine, too. And my being there may spook Granton into making a mistake."

Raven admitted she was right but added: "Granton won't screw up if he can help it. We're playing with fire here."

"And bringing a can of petrol," Ana added. "Or *gas* to you, Raven. Why do Americans call a liquid *gas*?"

"It's short for *gasoline*, dear. We don't call a liquid *gas*, give me a break. We're just too lazy to say the whole word."

Piper stifled a laugh. Raven smiled at her.

Ana sighed and shook her head.

CHAPTER NINE

Owen Yates left London at high speed and pushed his little car along a two-lane road. He kept checking his rearview mirror. A box sat on the passenger seat, half open; inside, the bloody stump of a thumb and a note from James White saying Yates was next.

He was in the same situation as Ranch had been. He'd helped Ranch get his police deal. Somehow, White had found out. Now they were both marked men, Ranch was already dead, and Yates needed help. He needed guns. He needed people on his side who knew how to use guns. Which meant there was only one place to go.

Leaving London had been his last option. When the box with the thumb showed up in the post that morning, he'd tried to call his MI5 contact. No dice—the man didn't answer the phone. Yates left a message, but there'd been no call back. He had no other police contacts, which meant no police protection. He wondered if they'd bother to help him anyway. He wondered if they'd say the hell with it and leave him out to dry and the last option he was heading for anyway.

He slowed as the wire mesh fence appeared on his right; the barbed top allegedly electrified, but he knew it wasn't. The fence blocked off the road from a large vehicle scrap yard, dead hulks of cars stacked high.

He slowed for the driveway, noted the sign announcing RYAN's AUTOMOTIVE PICK-N-PULL, and turned right. He drove up the dirt driveway to a pair of portable buildings. They were surrounded at the rear and sides by more stacked hulks. He stopped near a trio of other cars and jammed on the hand brake. The pick-n-pull was a legitimate business on the outside, but beyond the main building was another shop—a chop shop, where stolen cars were broken down to parts or had their VINs and paint changed for resale, usually to overseas clientele.

By the time he exited, two blokes were stomping down the steps of one of the portables. One was blonde, thin, wore black; the other had darker hair, wore ripped jeans, and a faded Smiths T-shirt. Alec Wayne and Joe Carson. Alec owned the place—the original owner, Ryan, was long dead. Alec was his grandson.

"What's the matter, Owen," Alec said. He stopped to light a fag and blew a cloud of smoke. "You look a little pink, mate."

"You're not going to believe this," Yates said. He rushed around the front of his car to the passenger door. Why hadn't he thought to bring the box with him when he exited? Whatever. It was hard to think when his heart was racing. He didn't feel the breeze blowing, the leaves rustling, the birds; none of it registered. He opened the door, grabbed the box, and turned around, stopping short when he saw Alec standing close in front of him. He hadn't heard Alec's shoes crunching on the rock-strewn ground.

"What's wrong?"

Alex actually looked concerned. It showed on his face. Yates held up the box and explained where it came from and what was in it.

"No way," Alex said. He tucked the cigarette in the left corner of his mouth and grabbed the box to see for himself.

When he lifted the lid, his face lost some color.

"See?" Yates said. "I told you."

Alec raised his eyes to Yates. "This was Garrett?"

"Yeah."

"White did this?"

"Yeah, Alex. You think I'd make this up?"

"Because he was a grass?"

Yates swallowed hard. "He might have been a grass, but he was still our friend, Alec."

The blonde-haired man raised an eyebrow. "You a grass too, Owen?"

Yates stuttered his reply. Before he got any words out, Joe Carson, who remained near the portable, tugged a pistol from under his shirt.

"Car coming!" Carson shouted.

Alec thrust the box back at Yates, who turned to look at the incoming car. It made a slow turn into the driveway and eased toward them. Yates began to shake; he tossed the box back into his car. He turned back to Alec.

"I don't have a gun!"

"Better keep your head down," Alec said. He took out his own pistol. The faces of the pair in front of the arriving car were clear enough for him to identify. "Me and Little Jimmy are gonna have a few words, is all."

Philip Deen stopped the big car behind Yates' vehicle. He

and James White stepped out. White held his arms out lengthwise and gave Alec a weak smile.

"Lookie, lookie, Alec," James White began. "We're here to pay a visit, say hello, share glad tidings."

"What's with the thumb?"

"My thumbs are fine." The gangster made a show of looking at each of his thumbs, then back at Alec. He shrugged. "What's this with thumbs?"

"The one who took from Garrett."

"Oh! *His* thumb. Should have said so. Well, I had to make a statement, didn't I? Who's that hiding there? Hi, Owen. Lose a contact lens or something?"

"Um—" was all Yates managed. His voice shook. He stayed low.

"Ranch was a grass," James explained. "You know how to deal with traitors, Alec. Your grandfather taught my father a few things, remember? He always talked about not tolerating traitors and making an example of them."

"Garrett was a friend of mine."

"I understand. I'm sorry. It had to be done, Alec."

"What are you here for, James?"

"Owen was helping Garrett. Owen was actually the first traitor I found out about, and he helped Garrett get set up when Garrett got busted. So now I need to deal with Owen."

"Dammit, no!" Owen screeched from behind his car. "It wasn't like that!"

"Tell me how it was, Owen. Tell me how it was."

Alec raised his gun. "Nobody's getting killed on my lot, James."

"Alec. You aren't going to give me trouble too, are you?"

"You're not going to kill Owen today. We're going to let him get out of town, and he'll never bother us again."

"You're doing a bad thing pointing your gun at me, Alec."

Philip Deen made the first move. Alec was too busy looking at James. But Deen didn't see Joe Carson looking at *him*.

Deen drew his pistol; Carson fired once. His pistol *snap-cracked* and Deen let out a choked cry as the bullet hit him with a wet slap. He stumbled against the front of the car, hit the ground, stayed still.

James White dove left, in between his car and Owen's, as Alec opened fire. The windows popped and slugs *thunked* into the metal. James grabbed for his gun and, staying on the ground, tipped to his right to lay on his side. He fired at an upward angle, three shots in rapid succession, his autoloader cycling faster than the eye could observe. The trio of slugs ripped through Alec Wayne's black shirt one, two, three. The blood didn't show, and as he fell, he revealed Joe Carson swinging his gun in line with James' face. James White fired again. One shot. It was appropriate, because one shot had killed Deen, too. The slug tore through Carson's head and flung him back. He landed with a thud.

James White was red with rage. He put his feet under him and rose, breathing hard. He rounded Owen's car to the hunkering man near the front passenger tire.

"This is all your fault, Owen."

Owen Yates' face was wet with sweat and his face twisted with tears in his eyes. "I swear—"

"Shut. Up."

James fired twice, then twice more, then rapidly dumped the rest of the rounds in the magazine into Owen's body. It was unnecessary. The first shot had killed him. The rest were because he was mad.

James lowered his smoking pistol, closed the action, and

put the gun away. He brushed off his clothes, rocks and dust flying away from him, but what would have annoyed him to no end in any other circumstance made no impression on him now.

He had to go through Deen's pockets, and he leaned over the body to accomplish the unpleasant task. He found Deen's cell and wallet. Taking both wouldn't keep the cops from identifying Deen, but it would cause a short delay. Long enough for James to get his alibi squared away. Long enough.

He slid behind the wheel of the car. Deen had left the keys in the ignition. The engine started. James made a U-turn and headed back to the road, back to London, driving at a moderate speed. He tried not to get upset. His chest felt heavy as he sat alone. He hated leaving his buddy's body behind. But he had to be done. It was business.

When the first sob forced to the surface, he took a deep breath and forced himself to stop. There'd be time later. Not now. He had known Phil since they were kids, but he had to get back to London and home base. Then he could grieve in private. In his position, he couldn't be seen a vulnerable, not even to the loss of a friend.

CHAPTER TEN

JAMES WHITE WANDERED CAREFULLY INTO HIS FATHER'S office. The room was a mass of wood and leather—wood on the walls and floor, polished to a fine shine. Leather couches and seats all around. Glass display cases showed various trophies and antique artifacts. It was either a school headmaster's office or the "man cave" of a fellow who enjoyed good spirits and cigars, as testified by the corner bar and another glass enclosure which served as a humidor. Shelves of cigar boxes filled the enclosure. Jimmy cleared his throat and the old man raised his head. The big boss, Billy White, sat behind a huge mahogany flat-top looking like a prosperous, legitimate businessman. He liked to cultivate that view outside in the regular world, but most knew him as the Teflon king of the London underworld. The police had tried to put him in prison for years; their cases always fell apart, somehow. It helped to have insiders. The "good guys" had their share of grasses, too.

"You look rough," Billy White said. He put down his pen. The younger man couldn't see what his father was working on; frankly, he didn't care. "Sit down, son. You can't just stand there. You'll tip over."

Billy White left his seat while his son collapsed into the chair in front of the desk.

They were a striking contrast, but age had a lot to do with it. While James was tall and lean, Billy was tall and getting thicker in the middle with each passing year. But his arms still bulged with muscles, and his rough face showed he'd survived plenty of scrapes. Nobody wanted to challenge his position, and only fools made the attempt to topple the king. When they tried, James went out to handle them. It was a fine arrangement.

As he sat, James wondered if his father noticed he didn't have Phil with him.

Billy poured a drink at the bar, Jack Daniels and a splash, and handed the glass to his son. Jimmy held the glass but didn't drink. He didn't understand why some people went for booze after a stressful event. It never calmed him. Not at all. Booze only hyped him up. But his father was trying to help, and James wasn't going to tell the old man no. He swallowed a mouthful as his father eased back into the desk chair.

"What went wrong?"

James grinned. Straight to the point, Dad was. No need to engage in useless chit-chat.

"I lost Phil."

"Oh, no."

"Fucking Wayne's buddy shot him. One shot, pop, that's all it took and Phil was dead meat."

"One shot is often all it takes, boy."

"But Phil—"

"Friends since you were lads, I know. It's never easy. I

can still tell you all the names of mates I lost. All the old timers can. Happens to everybody. It's the business."

James drank a little more of the whiskey and water, then placed the glass on the desk unfinished.

"You never finish your whiskey, boy," his father said, grabbing the glass and tossing back what remained.

"But I got Yates, and Ranch, so the leaks are plugged, and they only told those MI5 bastards what we wanted them to say," Jimmy said.

"Good. We can continue. The ship will arrive with no incident."

"Our man at MI5 will steer the raiding party somewhere else," Jimmy added.

"I like that man. I mean, he's a piece of shit, but he's done well for us."

"I know what you mean, Dad."

"Day's still early. What are your plans?"

"I have to go see Phil's girlfriend. She needs to know before the cops show up and tell her. I was there. It's my responsibility."

"You shouldn't go alone. Bring that girl of yours. The new one. Tracy?"

"No. Tammy. Tammy Granton."

"Right. Bring her with you. Women like having their own kind around when somebody is delivering bad news. Then get some rest. Anything else you have to do can wait awhile."

James nodded and rose from the chair. He said goodbye and made his way to the door. He knew his father was watching him, but he didn't look back. Always forward, his father said. What's behind you is history and should be dropped into the rubbish bin.

But James White didn't like leaving a part of himself

behind. Until they put poor Phil in the ground, he wasn't going to feel right. And maybe not even then.

BILLY WHITE REFILLED THE EMPTY GLASS, BUT THIS TIME left out the water.

He felt sorry for his son. Losing a longtime friend wasn't as bad as losing a wife, but it was up there on the list of things he'd liked to have avoided in his life. But the experience would make James stronger in the long run. When he finally took over the organization, he'd have the mental fortitude to carry on as needed. With the ruthlessness required. He'd finally put to use everything his father had taught him and all the knowledge he'd gained on his own. *He'll be better than me*, Billy thought, and wanted nothing more for the wish to come true.

But now, back to work. Even gangsters had to do boring stuff. His days of smuggling guns and drugs with a close group of mates had ended long ago. Now he ran the empire instead of existing only as a cog in the machine.

He returned to his desk and settled in to finish.

THE TEXT MESSAGE FROM JAMES READ:

I'M COMING OVER. GET READY.

Tammy Granton had been lazing around her apartment in sweatpants and an old T-shirt and no bra prior to the text, but she hurried into the bedroom to dress properly. The sweats and T-shirt went into the hamper, replaced by stockings, a knee-length skirt, black; red blouse, and the push-up bra he liked. She left the top two buttons of the blouse undone to give her boobs a little air. It was more than she wanted to wear on a day off. She'd expected to stay home and do nothing, but the text from James changed the entire day. Not that she was complaining. Tammy hadn't expected to see him till her father's charity party in two days.

She was on the couch, sitting straight with her legs crossed, anxiously looking blankly at the TV while also checking her watch. James had that effect on her.

Tammy lived well. She worked for her father's charity part-time, and another part-time job with a flower shop. Her apartment was furnished with high-end items, and plenty of decorations marked her territory. She wasn't much for artwork, like her father was, but she liked plants and flowers, and both types were in abundance. One wall had a few family pictures, including a large one of her late mother. She'd put Mom in the center. The other pictures were hung in a circular orbit around her. Just like when she was alive. Everything revolved around Mom and her shepherdship of the clan.

When she heard the key in the lock, she stood up and went to the door. She stood a few feet away with her hands behind her back and her chest puffed out. The door opened. James entered with his head down. He looked up at her and didn't smile. He shut the door. They embraced, but he didn't react with any of the usual excitement. She made sure to press her breasts into his chest and whispered into his ear, "Zipper's on the side and I have the *tiniest* panties on," but he pushed her back and shook his head. She looked shocked.

"What's wrong?"

"Phil's dead." His voice cracked.

She gasped and put both hands to her face. If he noticed her red nail polish matched her lipstick, he gave no indication.

"Oh no! What happened?"

He stepped around her into the living room and sat on the couch. She knew he wouldn't want alcohol, so she didn't fetch any.

James explained the shooting at the junkyard.

"That's awful," she said.

"My friend is lying in the dirt and there's nothing I can do about it."

She scooted close and rubbed his back.

"And it pisses me off," he added.

"Have you told Fiona?"

Fiona Hatcher was Phil's girlfriend.

"No. I thought you might come with me."

The implied question was another out-of-character moment. James didn't ask. He made a statement, and you said yes.

She'd never seen him this crushed before.

"Of course, I'll go. You can't see her by yourself. We should leave right now." She stood up and buttoned the rest of her blouse. Taking his hand, she helped him to his feet. He kissed her.

They left.

CHAPTER ELEVEN

IT WAS A LONG DRIVE ACROSS LONDON IN HEAVY TRAFFIC. Tammy had offered to drive, but James refused. He steered the black BMW through the stop-and-go.

"Are you still up for my father's party?" she asked. The inside was quiet; she wasn't used to the lack of noise. Usually, he had the stereo on. Today, only the low drone of the engine noise, pumped through the speakers, filled the silence. The black leather interior felt like a cocoon, as usual. It was a nice car. Today, though, it didn't seem as comfortable as usual. She felt anxious, nothing was safe; a reaction to Phil's loss, yes, and hopefully a temporary sensation.

"I don't want to go right now."

"Understandable."

"Might change my mind later. We still have time."

She agreed. Then they stopped talking for a while, and the silence bothered her. She didn't know what to do. She wasn't sure he knew what to say. He and Phil had been inseparable, so much so that she and Fiona often joked they were happier together than with either of them.

"Well," she finally said, "I *have* to be there. You know Dad will expect me to help with the fundraising."

James scoffed. "Yes. Your father will need you. He'll need you to help fleece all his rich friends."

"He's not *fleecing* them, James."

"The only difference between him and me is I might end up in jail for what I do."

She let out a sigh and a mumbled "Uh-huh." It was an old argument. She didn't want to press him when he was feeling the way he was. He was reacting to Phil's loss, not trying to goad her into a fight.

"Fuck it," he said. "I'll go. It will do me good to do something normal. Phil wouldn't want me to mope around."

She reached across the center console to give his leg a squeeze.

The slow drive continued.

———

TAMMY BEGAN TO HESITATE AS THEY APPROACHED FIONA'S front door. James walked ahead of her with a confident swagger she knew was false. He was behaving the way he thought he was supposed to. But when they stopped at the door to Fiona's flat, the swagger was no more. He swallowed before knocking on the door with a rapid triple tap.

The lock snapped back and Fiona pulled the door open in an angry rush. Tammy almost stepped back. Fiona's eyes were red; face streaked with tears; she already knew. The cops had beat them.

"You son of a bitch!" Fiona shouted. Blonde, short and stocky, she flung herself at James like a battering ram, fits hamming, a guttural scream coming from her gut. James deflected as many of the blows as he could, but plenty landed. He only let out a grunt with each hit, and Tammy backed away till the wall behind her stopped further movement. By then, James had both of Fiona's wrists clutched in each hand. She kicked him instead. He pulled her to him. The impact of her body against his almost knocked him off balance, but he leaned close to her face to get her attention.

"Stop it, Fiona! Stop!"

Fiona froze, and stared into James's face. Her own expression was twisted with a mix of anger and pain. Then she started crying again, and fell against his chest, and James put his arms around her and held her close.

After a while, Tammy suggested they go inside.

———

THEY SAT AROUND THE KITCHEN TABLE. TAMMY FILLED glasses with water and set them down before taking a seat. The table was chipped around the edges, but the top looked okay. She watched James and Fiona stare at each other. It felt like they didn't know she was there.

"The cops tell you?" he began.

"They left five minutes before you showed up." Fiona spoke softly, but they had no trouble hearing her.

"I tried to get here first."

"You weren't fast enough."

"I'm sorry."

"Good lot that does."

"I was there."

Her expression remained flat. "One of your jobs?"

He nodded.

"Tell me what happened."

James explained the situation with Ranch and Yates. He told how the fight at the junkyard began. And ended.

"Did you get the man who shot Phil?"

"I did."

"Well, that's something."

Another knock at the door. The three of them froze. Fiona shook her head—she wasn't expecting anyone. James looked at Tammy and jerked his head toward the door. She left the table to answer.

A man in a suit stood in the hall. Dressed in gray, clean cut, with a perfectly knotted tie, he held up an ID. The card showed his picture with MI5 displayed in one corner.

"Fiona Hamilton?"

"No."

"I'm Declan Barlow, MI5. Where is Fiona Hamilton?" He put the ID away.

"Inside."

Tammy stepped back to let the MI5 man into the flat. She hoped he didn't ask her name, and raced to make up an alias. If MI5 knew Thomas Granton's daughter was involved with the son of Billy White…

"There you are," Barlow stated as he cut through the kitchen. He stopped a few feet from the table. Fiona stayed seated. James rose.

"What are you doing here?"

"James White, right?"

"So?"

"So, I have questions, and Fiona may have answers."

"About what?"

"Come now, James. About the death of Philip Deen. Friend of yours, right?"

"She's in no mood to talk, Mr. Barlow."

"Now, now, this is only a routine inquiry. Her boyfriend was found with a bullet in him, after all."

Fiona sucked air sharply.

"You're disturbing her, Mr. Barlow."

"James, if I may, you're next on my list, so I'm glad you're here. What do you know about the death of Philip Deen?"

"Your police pals were already here. We've only just learned ourselves."

"How convenient. Pardon me if I don't believe you weren't with Mr. Deen during the unpleasantness. You two have been glued together your whole lives."

"I wasn't there."

"You sure?"

"Positive."

"You can prove it?"

"I can," James said.

"Hmm. Ms. Hamilton? Anything to say?"

Fiona choked out the words. "Not to you."

"I'm afraid we'll have to make this official at some point. Today you should grieve the loss of your lover and friend. My condolences, of course. Quite unfortunate. Don't wander too far from London. I *will* be in touch."

"Bring a warrant," James said. "I'll bring a lawyer."

Declan Barlow started for the door. He said over his shoulder, "One of your father's best, James?"

Tammy held the door, and her tongue. But the MI5 man smiled at her as he passed.

"Good day, Miss Granton. My best to *your* father."

And he departed. Tammy shut the door with shaking hands. She turned the locks and walked back to the table.

"He's only trying to stir things up." James sat down again.

"Be careful when you leave," Fiona said. "He may follow you."

"He must have arrived with the cops, but waited to see who else showed up," James said. "Don't worry, they follow me all the time."

"But this time—"

"Worry about yourself, Fiona. It's under control."

Tammy said, "He knew my name."

"Sure, he did, luv. They knew we were together long before today."

"I guess I thought I hid it well."

"From your father, yes," James said. "Not MI5." He reached out to squeeze her hand and smiled. The gesture didn't help Tammy settle down. Not one bit.

CHAPTER TWELVE

DECLAN BARLOW EASED BACK BEHIND THE WHEEL OF HIS CAR and watched the apartment building up the street. He was too far away to identify anybody who exited—the cost of having to park a half block away. He'd seen James White and the Granton woman arrive because they'd driven past him. Neither noticed, and why should they? Barlow had never interacted with the Whites prior to today.

MI5 handled counterintelligence matters and threats to the internal security of Great Britain. Normally, needling a known gangster wasn't on the ministry's to-do list. Investigating organized crime was the responsibility of the National Crime Agency. But MI5 had knowledge Billy and James White, the father-and-son gangster duo, were branching into areas where the UK's internal security was indeed threatened. And agents like Declan Barlow were on the case. He found it odd James White hadn't mentioned the fact that he shouldn't be bothering with a homicide. White knew as well as Barlow why he was visiting the flat, which only confirmed for

Barlow that his superiors had been correct and the Whites were up to something bad for sure.

Exactly *what* they were involved with still needed investigation, but they were on the right track. Barlow wondered if the Deen homicide, along with the deaths of the others in the scrap yard, and, of course, Branch and Yates, all tied together. He knew for sure Ranch and Yates died because they'd been discovered. What frustrated MI5 was the informants were found so fast. It was like the Whites knew they'd been sold out as soon as Branch and Yates agreed to turn grass in order to protect their own necks.

And then there was Tammy Granton. Barlow *really* wanted to know how she was involved. With her father's connections, she couldn't *only* be Little Jimmy's girlfriend. Her value was in what she brought to the scheme. She wasn't good-looking enough to make James' pulse race; she needed something else. Like the keys to certain people and places overseas. Either that, or James White really liked her tits because her face wasn't much, at least in Barlow's opinion.

Enough sitting, Barlow decided. Time to go back to HQ and report. He started the car, checked for a break in traffic, and drove away. He could at least tell his boss about a close contact with the primary suspects.

———

WHEN JAMES WHITE DROVE AWAY FROM FIONA'S BUILDING, he checked the rearview mirror and announced nobody was following them.

Tanny frowned. "How can you tell with all these cars?"

"All these cars passing? That fellow honking? We're going too slow. Nobody is lagging behind," he told her.

She hadn't noticed him driving slowly, or the cars going around. She hadn't heard the other driver honk as he passed. Her mind was elsewhere.

"Step on it, will you?" she said.

James laughed and increased speed to catch up with traffic.

Tammy tried not to clench her jaw too tightly but felt herself doing so. She opened her mouth to keep from grinding her teeth.

"What's wrong?"

She scoffed. He had to have an idea. He must have wanted to hear it from her directly.

"If we have MI5 on our tail—"

"Could be bad, yes," James admitted. "Our new thing is riskier than my father's usual activity, but we have it covered."

"How?" Tammy asked.

"I have to keep *some* secrets, darling. It's better you don't know everything."

"I'm doing as much work as you, James."

"You are. There's a lot we couldn't have accomplished without you. But if the worst *does* happen, it's better you don't know everything. Understand?"

"I think so."

"This is bigger than selling drugs at Oxford."

"No shit?"

"You know what I mean." He smiled.

She didn't.

And for the first time, Tammy Granton began to doubt she'd made the right decision by getting involved with the Whites.

She'd graduated from Oxford only a few years before. To

cover her expenses during her university time, she'd sold drugs. It was an easy way to make money to buy clothes to make all the other chavs look like trash. Her dealing brought her into contact with Billy White. Nobody sold drugs in London without giving him a cut. The old man arranged for her to give her cut to his son, as he was in charge of the street dealers at the time. Soon, their business relationship became much more. Her father wouldn't have approved, so they made up a story about what James did for a living and she'd never revealed his last name. Her father thought he sold cars. Which wasn't *entirely* a lie, but it was a no-show job to pay his taxes. Everything was on the up-and-up. They'd left drugs behind for something more lucrative; much more. Human trafficking. The two rats James set out to kill had threatened the scheme, and they'd only found out about the treachery of Branch and Yates because of their insider at MI5.

James thought everything was cool with the rats neutralized. But MI5 knew her name. Tammy didn't feel confident in her anonymity any longer. If they'd gone after Branch and Yates, they might come after her, too.

But she had to trust her boyfriend. Now wasn't the time to get cold feet. She was "in it" up to her neck. No going back now.

She decided to change the subject.

"Are you feeling any better?"

"No," he said, "but I'm also not as mad as I was. It felt good to tell Fiona that Phil's killer was dead. She seemed to appreciate the information."

"Uh-huh." She didn't want to commit to more than a basic acknowledgment. The information didn't mean anything, and certainly didn't bring Phil back. He was fooling himself.

"She'll be fine," James continued. "Fiona will find another chap and the cycle will continue. Probably by the end of the week. Or maybe she'll wait till after the funeral." He laughed again.

"Come on."

"Fancy some lunch?"

She said okay. James took the next motorway on-ramp and they picked up speed. He wanted to go to an Italian place he liked a lot.

CHAPTER THIRTEEN

DECLAN BARLOW CHECKED IN ON HIS RETURN TO MI5 HQ AT Thames House. He entered under the big arch on the north bank side, forgetting his usual habit of pausing a moment to look at the water before entering. He enjoyed his job and liked coming to work in the big stone HQ building with so much history, but his drive back coupled with continued thoughts about his exchange with James White left him sure of one thing. He was mad.

He wasn't interested in employing the usual polite terms: slightly cross. Not best pleased. Miffed. The problem with the Whites was not a "kerfuffle" or a "fuss." It was a direct threat to His Majesty and Declan Barlow was pissed off.

James White knew more than he let on. Barlow had watched White and his girlfriend arrive minutes after the police departed. And he'd known the officers who delivered the news to Fiona Hamilton were going to visit White next. If he was nowhere near the crime scene, as he claimed, how had he known his pal had been shot? On one hand, it meant White had been present during the shooting. On the other, perhaps a witness survived and told him? If so, it was another person Barlow had to find to get to the bottom of what happened, and what it might mean.

Barlow stepped out of the elevator onto the fifth floor. He proceeded along the echoing hallway. Footsteps, voices, they all bounced off the walls to considerable annoyance. The building was old. Everybody understood the quirks. One could only remodel and dress up the place so much. He reached the door to his department. The knob turned easily, and he entered the bullpen with his eyes on his corner desk. He was fortunate to be next to a wall with a window. He could look out at the Thames and London's gray skies as he completed paperwork and wrote reports. Privilege came with rank and experience. Other desks lined the wall, too, and others were shoved front-to-front around the rest of the room. Some of his compatriots said hello as they walked by. Barlow nodded or waved in return. His eyes were on his computer monitor; his fingers tapped commands into the keyboard. The presence of Tammy Granton bothered him, too. He wanted to learn more about her. See if the official record had anything the tabloids failed to report.

He read down her file when the data appeared on his screen. An old picture of her accompanied the information.

No arrests. Strong suspicion of drug dealing at university —Oxford, no less—no evidence. If she was selling drugs, she was working with the Whites, which explained how she became involved with James. He read further.

Employed at a flower shop and her father's charity.

Barlow frowned.

Was the flower shop a no-show job arranged by the White? Or was she off today and able to spend the afternoon with James?

Probably a no-show gig, he decided. Arranged by the Whites to keep her taxes up to date while she dabbled in whatever she and Little Jimmy had going on. She was dirty. Somehow. The question was, did her father know?

A shadow fell over him.

"Whatcha reading, partner?"

Barlow eased back from the monitor to look at Agent Mick Taylor, his partner. They hadn't made the trip to Fiona Hamilton's flat together because Taylor had a dentist appointment.

"How're your teeth?" Barlow said.

"Still messed up." Taylor took a seat at the desk opposite Barlow's, another front-to-front arrangement like the other desks around them. "What's the deal with Tammy Granton?"

"Just checking on her."

"For what?"

"Saw her with a suspect today."

"Really? Which one? The White kid?"

"Yes."

"Think it means anything?"

"I think it means a lot," Barlow said. "How to handle it is the question."

"Her father knows King Charles."

"Really? I had *no* idea, Mick. Seriously, what would I do without you?"

"Come on, mate, no need for the attitude."

Barlow cursed and closed the file. "You should have seen him, Mick. Sitting there like he hadn't a care in the world."

"I don't get what you mean."

Barlow told Taylor about his visit to Fiona Hamilton's flat, and the semi-confrontational conversation shared with James White, Tammy Granton, and the Hamilton girl.

"Gave you a good shine-on, huh?" Taylor said.

Barlow raised an eyebrow. "That's one way of looking at it."

"What do you want to do?"

"Let's keep hitting the bottom players in the White Organization, the ones connected to those who died at the scrap yard. I want to build a story of what led up to the fight there."

"Dec, come on. They found Yates there. I can tell you what happened."

"Okay. Tell me."

"Yates went running to the scrap yard for help. Deen and Jimmy White show up, have the fight, and Jimmy gets away."

"Come to think of it," Barlow said, frowning, "his suit looked a little dirty."

"Like he'd been rolling in the dirt?"

Barlow nodded. "Maybe."

―――――

WEARING A SUIT AND TIE IN THE MIDDLE OF A STICKY HOT summer in Washington, D.C., was not Callum Hill's idea of a good time. Not that Frankfort, Kentucky, where his political career began, served up anything different in summer…or winter. Both places sucked. Hot and humid or bitch ass cold, and the price he had to pay if he wanted to serve the people. Callum Hill tolerated the discomfort because of the greater good he fought for on Capitol Hill.

The Kentucky independent took his coffee order from the young barista who said, "Thank you, senator," when he dropped a few bucks in the tip jar. He made his way through the crowd in the small coffee shop and stepped outside. Nobody harassed him. Sometimes they did—usually after he went on TV and said something people didn't like. He ruffled feathers on the left and right. Both sides deserved the ruffling. With a tired sigh, he eased into the back seat of his driver's black Lincoln and pulled the door shut. There was no need to say anything to the driver. The closing of the door meant Hill was ready to go. The driver shifted into gear and headed for the street.

Hill was thin, in his sixties, with curly gray hair. Plenty of lines on his face. A little extra skin hung below his chin, and with his pasty white skin made him appear out of shape. He wasn't in terrible shape, he jogged at least, but sitting around talking most of the time did him no good.

This morning, he had a lot on his mind. Usual agenda on the Senate floor to deal with; more importantly, he had a smaller meeting to host. The weight of the subject wasn't lightweight. The meeting was also secret. Only him and two others. Eventually, Hill would make the subject of the meeting public, but not until he had the input of the other two.

Hill managed to get up the steep capitol steps without getting tangled in a conversation with passing colleagues. They were going about their business—some of it for "the people" but others for their own benefit. The amount of corruption, the lining of their own pockets, Hill's congressional colleagues engaged in often left him enraged. Only the young congresswoman from Vermont—who'd only been elected on the last cycle—seemed to share his view. Yet, unlike him, she hadn't been locked out of any committees or found herself frozen out of other activity. And it was only because she was attractive. The old men wanted to sleep with her. Once they found she was taking part in Hill's private meeting and resulting resolution, she could very well see her committee assignments vanish. Hill had told her this. She didn't care. She was as dedicated to solving the problem they faced same as him.

He made his way through the crowded and noisy first-floor corridors to the stairs. He preferred stairs to the elevators. Reporters liked to corner members of Congress in elevators. A few news people had stopped other representatives in the halls. Jackson from Mississippi was telling a blonde woman much shorter than him about social security—same old, same old. A House member from Wisconsin talked about farm subsidies. Nothing they said would get on TV. The reporters had a smart game plan. Stick microphones in faces to make them feel important. Let them talk about their pet issues. Then, they'd be happy to come on TV or talk about more pressing matters when they came up. When the crises were invented. And every so-called crisis, Hill felt, was manufactured, ginned up by not only his colleagues but a willing media who needed butts in couches and eyes on televisions. Such events always, always, without fail, took time and effort away from real problems. The real problems were smaller problems, and Hill wanted to fix those rather than pretend to fix fake problems.

He shook his head in frustration. Time to ignore everything not important to his meeting. He had to keep the meeting top of mind. Now was not the time for distraction. He also didn't want to be late.

Second floor, left turn; he passed a few closed doors and a few open ones. The open offices held other private meetings—representatives talking to lobbyists. Scum of the earth. Hill would let lawyers live if he was allowed to kill all the lobbyists.

Hill opened his office door and went inside. He spotted

the concerned expression of his secretary, a plump middle-aged woman named Shannon. She sat at a cluttered desk to his left. To his right was a small waiting area. It looked like something from a dentist's office, complete with outdated magazines on a low coffee table.

"What's the matter?" Hill asked. But he already had an idea.

"Sloane backed out," she said.

Hill shook his head. Word was out. The campaign to stop him was in effect.

"All right." He sighed and crossed into his private office. He always left the inner and outer doors open—a sign of transparency. Shannon knew what the meeting was about. He had nothing to hide from her.

He placed his coffee on his clean and organized desk. Before he could sit, a knock on the outer doorframe sounded, and he turned.

Jacqueline Bennett, Senator from Vermont, entered. She said hello to Shannon and stepped into Hill's private office.

"I hear Sloane quit," she said.

"Did anybody hassle you?"

"Bet your ass."

Hill invited the thirty-something dark-haired woman to sit. She did and crossed her nyloned legs. She wore a knee-length cream skirt and matching blouse. Her long dark hair matched her heels.

"Who?"

"California and New Mexico. I'm not uttering those bastards' names." She folded her arms and looked mad.

"Typical." Hill sat behind his desk and leaned back a little.

"Just us," Jacqueline said.

"Yes," Hill told her. He'd known his proposal faced obstacles, but for the first time, he feared he couldn't overcome the resistance.

"Too many of our fellow representatives," Jacqueline said, "are getting a kickback for these missile sales."

Callum Hill planned to sponsor a resolution to stop missile sales to Saudi Arabia. The United States government, perhaps six times a year, sold a batch of small arms and ground-to-ground missiles to the Saudis for use in their military action against insurgent forces in Yemen. The Saudis were part of a nine-country coalition from West Asia and North Africa who aided Yemen in their civil war against the Sana'a by-Houthi insurgents, who wanted to overthrow the sitting government. The insurgents had scored major victories and appeared on the verge of winning when Yemen asked the Saudis and the coalition for help. The US and Britain agreed to supply arms to help the effort.

The fighting had, by independent accounts, led to a humanitarian disaster, the near genocide of the opposing forces and anybody suspected of being allied with them.

Hill didn't believe the United States had any business in the war.

But, as always, the Military Industrial Complex had other ideas. There was big money in bombing people. The more bombs the military dropped, the more money the government spent to replace the used ordnance. And when the stores got full, they found a reason to use a few.

"Okay," Hill said. "You're still willing. I'm willing. Let's talk about how we're going to do this."

Another knock on the outer doorway. Hill perked up. Jacqueline turned in her chair. A man with gray hair in an expensive suit, entered. He smiled at Shannon and approached.

"Cal," the man said, "this may be the only time you and I are on the same side of an issue."

Democrat Zachary Roberts. Powerful. Distinguished. Committee chair. He was a big name in the Senate. Idaho kept electing him, and his acclaim grew year by year. During his first term, Jacqueline Bennett had been crawling across her mother's kitchen floor.

"May I sit?" Roberts said.

Hill gestured to the second empty chair beside Jacqueline. Roberts sat. His expression was flat, but he spoke what he was thinking.

"I'm tired of this crap," he stated. "What they're trying to do to you is wrong. I agree with you on these missile sales, and I'd like to put my name on the resolution if you'll have me."

"Welcome," Hill said. "And thank you."

"We need to stop this genocide. Or at least not help it happen," Roberts continued. "You know what I'm worried about? These fancy missiles ending up in the hands of terrorists. Can you imagine our boys being killed with our own weapons?"

"It's possible," Jacqueline said.

"My thoughts too," Hill said.

"Now," the older man continued, "we may fail. The way I see it, we need public pressure. That means you and me and Miss Bennett are going on television. Or the radio. Hell, I'll go talk to the kids on the internet and tell them what's going on. We get the public on our side, and we stand a chance."

Hill allowed himself a small smile. Roberts had taken control of the meeting, as was his style, but it did get them straight to the point. Hill found nothing he could add. Jacqueline's silence signaled her agreement, too.

"Tell me," Roberts went on, "the status of this resolution. You got a draft?"

"Right here," Hill said. He pulled the three stapled sheets of paper from the center drawer of his desk. He slid it across the top.

"Got a pen?"

Hill handed Roberts a pen, and the older man flipped to the last page and signed his name below Hill's. Roberts passed both to Jacqueline, and she signed.

She added, "Public pressure only works if we can get them to give a damn."

"Too many like not knowing things," Roberts said.

"I'll get the press involved," she said.

"And I'll start making waves," Roberts said. "Maybe I can shake some assholes—sorry, Miss Bennett—into joining us. With my name on this, some of those 'fraidy cats may come aboard."

Hill nodded. Perhaps the obstacles weren't impossible after all.

CHAPTER FOURTEEN

THE MISSILES IN QUESTION WERE BUILT AT A FACTORY IN Huntsville, Alabama. Automated and manned assembly lines dealt with the missile tubes, warheads, and various components. Workers in hard hats and white protective coats monitored the automation. The robots worked with amazing precision, loading tubes on a conveyor, adding parts as the tubes moved down the line. Most of the workers wore ear protection, too. The machinery in the main assembly room made a heck of a racket, bouncing off the walls, vibrating the floor.

The facility built several hundred missiles a day, all of which were stockpiled in an adjoining warehouse and prepared for shipment to military installations around the US. Some were prepped for shipping overseas, per Pentagon contracts.

The factory sat in an open grassy field surrounded by a high-security fence and armed guards. The seclusion worked to keep the activity private and secured, but there were flaws.

Such as the rotating team of three men who watched the facility with video equipment. The crew belonged to Rahmil's organization, and they were waiting for the missiles to leave the factory. The facility director always made sure the rockets and other armaments left on time, in convoys of three vehicles with armed escorts. The fellow's attention to detail and commitment to his schedule only helped Rahmil's team make their hijack plans. It was the missiles destined for overseas they were interested in. The plan was to grab them in transit; a backup plan called to stealing them while at sea, because sending them to Saudi Arabia via ship was cheaper than flying, considering the amount of material they were moving.

Not even the worries of Callum Hill and his allies covered what Rahmil had in mind for the missiles they wanted to stop.

Stopping the Saudi sale wouldn't have made any difference. Rahmil didn't care which batch of missiles his people collected, only that they collected what was required for what he needed.

And he needed the missiles in London.

IT WASN'T HARD TO KEEP TRACK OF THOMAS GRANTON. THE Daily Mail reported on a press conference he was hosting to promote his upcoming fundraising party. Raven decided to attend and get a look at the man.

Raven mingled with the press in the banquet room of the London Hilton in Hyde Park. The empty podium at the front of the room, sitting on a small stage, bore the symbol of Thomas Granton's organization. A blue circle rimmed with gold and TGC for *Thomas Granton Charities* in the center. A sound crew in the back of the room made final adjustments to the sound system. They fussed over a mixing console set on a folding table. Not exactly high-end, but it must work for them, Raven decided. The press filled the first four rows. TV and radio were equally represented, and nobody noticed Raven's lack of audio or visual gear, or pad and pen. His "official" press pass, pinned to the lapel of his tweed sport coat, was fake, supplied by Ana. This would be his first up-close look at Thomas Granton, and Raven looked forward to seeing the man in the flesh. He wanted to evaluate the man's body language. See if he detected any malice or subversion in the man's words.

A tall order, yeah.

If Granton was as bad as Ana said, as the murder of Leslie and the attempted murder of him and Piper suggested, Raven figured he'd have his public persona locked down. There'd be no indication he was a bad guy. He'd play the role of sincere advocate for the less fortunate. The public face of many unseen helping hands. And nothing would prove otherwise.

But bad guys always had a *tell.*

Raven only needed to find Granton's.

———

GRANTON'S PRESS SECRETARY APPEARED FIRST, A STOCKY redhead in a skirt suit fitting poorly in the middle. The skirt must have been too tight—she bulged where Raven felt certain she didn't want to bulge. Welcoming the press and other media, she announced her boss planned to speak on the needs of several African nations, specifically a multi-national food program to attempt a solution to the region's food crisis.

LONDON ASSAULT 121

She announced Granton and the man of the hour replaced the chubby redhead at the podium.

Raven examined the man as he thanked everybody for their attendance.

He gripped either side of the podium as if he expected it to rocket away; or, perhaps he had balance issues. Or maybe he was behaving like a politician, one of the House of Commons, leaning forward toward the microphone, making sure every camera picked up a clear shot. He wore a tailored blue suit, which fit perfectly, almost disguising his own growing middle. He didn't attempt to dye his hair to hide the encroaching gray, either, and he had managed to keep a full head of hair. Not all men his age were so lucky—unless his head is where he spent money to fight off nature's assault. His face looked puffy and jowly, but he had a warm smile and deep voice. His dulcet tone filled the room as he detailed his plan to save Africa.

Raven didn't temper his growing dislike for the man. Anger boiled within; Ana's suspicions made sense now. How do you fund terrorist groups who make their homes in the North Africa region? Start a "hunger relief program." Once Granton called for "the charts," Raven figured the old man was going to lay on the snow job so thick, nobody would suspect the truth. Two assistants wheeled out a large display board with a color-coded map of North Africa. Granton droned on about the facts and figures of starving people, famine, war, poverty—he hit every buzzword and emotional description. He knew how to big it up, and Raven sat with crossed arms, taking it in, and had to admit Granton impressed him as a con man. He made Raven think he truly cared.

Perhaps the program would actually attempt what

Granton claimed to desire, and be appropriately funded. Surely, those who donated needed updates to show how much good their money provided the less fortunate. Unless his donors didn't care. Many who gave to charity only did so for the tax break. The rich and powerful also got to take pictures with Granton for an extra flex.

Granton went into the second half of his presentation by mentioning his big fundraising party the next evening. A second chart showed the date, time, and location—everything Raven already knew from Ana's briefing. Ana had already squared away the invitations for him and Piper. All they had to do was show up.

Granton talked about his plans for the money raised at the party. How they wanted to expand their network of contractors who transported food and medicine and other supplies into hard-to-reach places. Granton wanted to invest in modern water purification systems to get more villages clean water— the main goal of the program from the start. He was "proud" to announce they'd equipped seven of ten remote villages in Kenya alone with improved water resources.

Presently, he began taking questions. Granton didn't reveal any "tell" Raven found obvious. His second suspicion, that the man had his act down pat, was confirmed.

Which meant the food program wasn't all smoke and mirrors.

But what if…

No. Raven nixed the idea of asking any leading questions this early in the probe. Granton would pick up on the hostility; hell, he already may know Raven's face. If Raven spooked him now, he'd only create more obstacles. Raven remained seated, part of the crowd. No matter how often Granton scanned the faces of those seated, he didn't flinch when he saw Raven. Perhaps Rahmil hadn't communicated Raven's involvement in the counter-offensive yet.

The conference ended and Raven slipped out among the departing journalists. He had much on his mind as he hit the street.

CHAPTER FIFTEEN

Piper's instinct was to dress to kill. But she needed to be ready to run, jump, and shoot. The needs of possible combat dictated her wardrobe choice for the party.

Amalfi silk tank, white, with thin straps; green blazer, oversized; matching slacks. She needed the blazer a little larger to hide the Glock-19 she fastened behind her back. The blazer draped past her waist to cover part of her hips.

She stood in front of the bathroom mirror. No bulge showed at her back except the one she liked—her rear end. No gun print, which was most important. She might not pass with the big-money crowd. Worse case, they'd think she was one of the help. The thought gave her a chuckle as she left the bathroom to wait for Raven.

A small glass of wine before the evening began would have been nice, but she'd given up alcohol years ago. Piper poured a glass of sparkling water instead and sat on the couch. She was nervous. She didn't *want* to be nervous, but the butterflies in her belly had other ideas. She had the option of sitting out the night. Ana had made it clear Raven was willing to attend the party alone. But Piper *needed* to be there. She didn't think she owed Ana or Raven a reason. She *had* to attend.

A knock at the door. Raven. He knocked four times, paused, four more. Piper reached the door as the second set began. When she opened, she stopped short and blinked in surprise. Raven sure cleaned up well.

He'd chosen the "to kill" option with his outfit, and Piper felt the nervous butterflies in her belly switch to a different kind of flutter.

Damn, he looks good. And what's the scent?

"You all right?" he asked.

"Um…yes, of course. Come in a moment." She stood back to let Raven enter.

This isn't a date.

Stay professional.

But wow…

"You act like you've never seen a man in a suit before."

"Well, not you. And…um—"

"What?"

"You wear it well."

It was a blue stretch suit, the kind of material which fit snug but allowed movement, the kind of combat movement they might need if the night went south. Blue blazer, slacks; white cotton shirt, black tie, and black shoes. The blazer tapered at his waist but looked wider at the shoulders to probably accommodate his .45, but she didn't think there was enough extra material to hide the Nighthawk Custom hand cannon.

She didn't ask about his cologne. She liked the mystery. And the scent. And what the scent did to her insides. It beat being nervous about walking back into the lion's den.

"You don't have your gun under there, do you?" she asked.

"Not the .45. I borrowed a smaller pistol from Ana. An old Walther."

"PPK?"

Raven laughed. "No. The P-5."

"Good gun."

"I always thought so, too. Shall we go?"

As she locked the door, he said, "You look terrific as well."

"Thank you."

He offered his right arm. She took hold at the crook of his elbow. They walked down the hallway to the elevator like a couple on a real date. It had been a long time, Piper reflected, since she'd been on *any* kind of date. *Enjoy the moment.*

Even if it is an illusion.

Remember, this is for Leslie.

Resolve took hold once again. Nervousness departed. She was on a mission and had a job to do. She'd set aside real life until she finished the mission.

————

BACK TO THE LONDON HILTON IN HYDE PARK. ANA LET Raven borrow her black four-door Maserati coupe. He and Piper actually fit in well with the big-money crowd; at least, nobody glanced askew at them. Raven noticed the big money was mostly Old Money, but plenty of New in the form of the latest and greatest in UK sports and entertainment happy to pose for press pictures as they walked the red carpet. Loud music, bright lights, snapping flashbulbs. The jumble of a thousand voices filled the outer red carpet scene.

The ballroom inside was just as busy. The hotel had put them in the largest ballroom in the building, and Thomas Granton Charities knew how to use every piece of available space.

The room was divided into three sections. One, the largest, for dining; dance floor in the middle; and, last, an area for silent auction exhibits. Bidders had a shot at high-value items and travel destinations with all the money going to TGC and the well-publicized North African food program.

Raven decided the best way to examine the room and attendees was to spin around the dance floor. He asked Piper if she'd like to dance. With a big smile, she grabbed his arm and made him hustle to keep up.

Big, brassy music—courtesy of the small orchestra on the stage off to one side—filled the room with a steady rhythm of bass, sax, and other wind instruments. The musicians all wore white jacket tuxedos. Raven took Piper in his arms and they began a slow turn with the rest of the crowd on the dance floor.

"I feel very underdressed," Piper admitted, but her smile and bright eyes proved she didn't feel too badly about the situation. She might not have been wearing a ten thousand quid sparkly dress, but she looked fine to Raven.

"You look great," he told her, "considering the day I met you, we went diving in the dirt."

"Anything beats fighting for your life," she agreed.

"What do you notice around us?"

"They spent a lot of money. The three chandeliers overhead must have cost a fortune. They aren't Hilton standard-issue."

"Special purchase for the occasion?"

"Has to match the rest of the decorations."

"We should hit the silent auction later. Bid high using fake names and then welsh."

"One problem," she said.

"What?"

"If somebody outbids our outrageous fake big, a larger amount goes to the enemy."

"Good point. I have a feeling no amount is too much for this crowd."

They made another spin around the floor as the band continued.

"Guess we need to ignore the celebrities," Piper said.

"Now is not the night to fill your autograph book," Raven said.

"Any sign of the big man?"

"Not yet. He may show up later." Raven gave her a twirl, and she bumped into him on the return. They laughed a little. He said, "Did you ever see Granton in Cairo?"

"Never. But I could only get a glimpse of Rahmil now and then. Very tight security. Getting evidence of the two together was Leslie's job. Our thought was Rahmil would come to see him."

"Did he?"

"No idea. If he did, the proof died with Leslie."

Raven frowned but didn't voice the questions spinning in his mind. Why had the women operated without passing info as they found it? Their MO seemed to be to collect everything for a later bulk delivery; it made no sense. All it did was leave the effort open to potential failure if the worst occurred, which had.

Was it the way Ana preferred to work? He'd have to talk to her about improving her techniques.

The music, mingling, and dancing continued for another

half hour. Raven and Piper left the dance floor midway to find their table. Nametags at each place setting told them who they'd have as dining companions. Raven didn't recognize the names, but Piper did. British millionaires; industrial types. Older. She warned they might prove to be a stuffy lot. They'd need a good story to tell about how they'd come to attend the fundraiser. Raven only grinned. He and Ana had cooked up a whopper for the occasion.

"Care to tell?" Piper asked as they sat.

"Nope. But try not to look surprised if I unveil it."

"Great. If I do look surprised, they'll think I'm a paid escort."

"Not in that outfit." He smiled.

She kicked him under the table. Raven stifled a grunt.

They ordered drinks. The silent auction had attracted a large portion of the crowd.

"Granton may have ghost accounts to move the money," Raven said. "It would be nice to see the charity's finances. A good forensic review would find the hidden accounts."

"Poor Leslie probably found them."

Raven nodded. Without other pieces of the puzzle, they'd be forced to cover ground Leslie already tread. Start from square one. He didn't want to upset Piper by suggesting she'd found little of value in Cairo. She already knew.

Granton finally made an appearance as the band stopped for a break. He stepped on stage to welcome one and all and announced dinner would now be served. The tables filled rapidly. Two older couples joined Raven and Piper and immediately offered jovial hellos.

Dinner was the usual menu found at events around the world: meat, chicken, or fish. Waiters and waitresses bearing trays of each went to every table. Raven selected the meat while Piper opted for fish. They were rewarded with filet mignon and perfectly cooked salmon, along with potatoes and a side of vegetables. The older couples went for the fish and chicken. The men commented that even filet mignon might be "too much for the old system" or some such. Raven didn't understand, but they laughed at their private joke. It was a very good dinner, and the table chatter settled onto things other than respective businesses, current or former. Mostly, they talked about Thomas Granton and how often they'd donated to his causes in the past. The older couples were regular contributors, pleased to see first-timers such as Raven and Piper. They were very much looking forward to what Granton Charities accomplished in "poor Africa."

Raven kept up an affable grin during the conversation, asked a few rookie questions, and let the older folks run the conversation. Granton had a good many people fooled, for sure. But they must have seen something for the effort, right?

"You don't simply give him money blind, do you?" Raven asked.

"Oh, no, dear boy, certainly not," said the man on Raven's left. He was jowly and bald. "Mr. Granton sends regular updates on the progress of every one of his programs. We get to see pictures, charts, he'll even email us videos direct from the area we're helping, though I'll be damned if I know how to turn on the videos. I have to call my grandson for help." He laughed in a big guffaw. His wife shook her head. She was used to her husband's inability to handle new tech. Raven sided with the old man. There was too much to keep up with; the number of devices he had to deal with frustrated him too, sometimes.

During the dinner course, Raven caught Piper giving him a stink eye. She was waiting for somebody to ask Raven how he'd made his money. She was waiting to hear the cover story he and Ana prepared. Raven had to try not to laugh at her. He understood the suspense, but she really wasn't missing anything. It wasn't much of a story.

After dessert, tables broke up for more dancing and more walking through the silent auction tables. Raven and Piper decided to look at the items for auction. The overall crush of conversations filling the room made it so they could talk normally and not have to hide what they were saying—to a point.

"What do you think so far?" Piper asked.

"Granton runs a good party and keeps himself out of the limelight."

"He'll come back later," she said. "He wants everybody feeling good before he comes out and puts the final bite on the audience."

They made the rounds of the auction tables. Raven glazed over the items on offer. He didn't put his name down on anything. He found the entire process displeasing. Watching the rich line up to give their money away without realizing they were funding terrorist activities made him want to scream. It was the same old story. A con man comes around with a good line of patter, and a whole bunch of otherwise smart people fall head over heels for the rap and do whatever the con man suggested. This time it cost more than pounds and a little pride. In the end, what they were doing cost lives. Thousands of lives. You could make more money. You couldn't get back the lives lost to violence. Raven's war without end continued because of people like Granton and the people he conned into giving him money.

Piper wanted to dance again, so Raven obliged with another trip around the floor. As they followed the band's beat, he noticed a young couple still seated at their dining table. The man looked sour; the woman was trying to get him out of his seat.

"Are those two anyone of significance?" Raven asked. He turned so Piper could see over his shoulder.

"Didn't Ana show you Granton's daughter?"

"That's her?"

"Yeah. I can't remember her name. Tracy? No, it's Tammy."

"You sure?"

"Positive."

"And the boyfriend?"

"Him, I'm not sure of. But he looks—"

"Like what?"

"Like a punk in a suit."

"Lipstick on a pig."

"Exactly."

"That's my read, too. It makes me wonder—"

"Wonder what?"

"If Miss Tammy is involved, or only her father? What if she's the one funneling the money to this unsavory dude and his cronies, and they move the money to the final destination? Maybe Granton's accounts are clean."

"Granton showed up on MI5's radar, not the daughter."

"True. But maybe he's protecting her."

"Tammy didn't go to the Middle East. Or write those emails."

"You have to admit," Raven said, "it's possible. We'll know more if we get a good ID on Mr. Wonderful with the sour look on his face. Let's make a bar run."

She tried to argue, but Raven broke off the dance hold and grabbed her by the elbow. To the bar they went. While Piper ordered their drinks per Raven's request, he used a small camera hidden inside the pocket of his suit jacket to snap a picture of Tammy Granton and her not-so-happy boyfriend. She was still arguing with him, albeit quietly, and he was steadfastly refusing her pleas. Raven knew what a thug looked like. They always revealed themselves through the eyes. This fellow's eyes were shifty, cold, like pinpoints of light zeroing on targets. He was a man used to watching for weakness and then exploiting what he found. And Thomas Granton's little girl was hanging off his arm. Why? How did she fit in with the charity scheme?

Did she fit at all? Was Raven jumping to conclusions too early? Wouldn't be the first time, he admitted, but the times he had jumped, he'd been right. Maybe he was wrong this time, but there was only one way to find out.

"Your drink, dear," Piper said, with a hint of bitterness.

He'd asked for a gin and tonic, and that's what she handed him. He said thank you and took an appreciative sip. The mix was perfect; the gin flavor lit up in his mouth.

"Back to the table?" he said.

"Sure. My feet are tired."

They were alone when they sat. Both older couples were on the dance floor.

"Don't fixate on Granton," Raven said. "There may be more to it than only him and Rahmil."

"The daughter never showed herself as a suspect before," Piper said. "I'm not going to waste time with her when the two men responsible for killing my friend are right in front of my face."

"I agree, but we need to follow every possibility. This one is too big to let something slip through, and if the daughter's part of the operation, we need to know."

"You're chasing rabbit trails because you're afraid to go after the big fish when he's standing right in front of you."

"That's not true, Piper." He said nothing more. He wasn't going to start an argument with her. His suggestion made her upset; he didn't understand why. Well, you couldn't refuse to investigate every angle of a problem and expect to learn the truth. Raven wanted to pull the Granton cancer from the root. Only lopping off the top man in the chain wasn't going to solve anything if the daughter picked up the pieces and continued as if nothing happened. If she did, Raven would have to do the job all over again. Best to only do it once.

And if Piper had a problem, she could stay home like he'd wanted her to from the beginning.

Eventually, Granton made an appearance.

Raven decided to go shake the man's hand.

CHAPTER SIXTEEN

GRANTON APPEARED TO LOUD APPLAUSE AND ATTENDEES trying to get closer to say hello. Raven hung back. It took a while to break through the crowd, but Granton was making time for everyone, sharing a few words of thanks, answering questions. Presently he and Raven met face-to-face. The man had a firm handshake and didn't try to crush Raven's hand. Raven lowered his tone to seem less threatening and give Granton a sense of power over him.

For now.

"I don't know you," Granton said. "I'm Tom Granton."

"Steve Pullman," Raven said. It was a name with a solid background developed by Ana.

"You're American?"

"Yes," Raven said. "I know you're busy, but I have a question." He leaned close to talk over the noise. Granton didn't pull away. "I represent an anonymous donor who appreciates your work. He'd like to make a sizable contribution, say half a million US. Can we arrange something so my client can avoid attention?"

Granton smiled with a sparkle in his eye at the mention of the amount.

"Please tell your client I'd be most pleased to accommodate him." He pulled a flat silver case from inside his tux jacket. Opening the case, Granton extracted a business card. It had a single phone number printed on the face. "My private line. Please make the arrangements with me personally, and I'd be happy to meet your client should he or she like to come and see me in person."

"I'm sure we can set that up." Raven pocketed the card.

———

PIPER WATCHED THE EXCHANGE FROM THE BAR. BOTH MEN were tall enough for her to see them over the mass of heads and shoulders surrounding them.

She swallowed half her martini in one throw. Raven was just another man who looked good, she decided, until he opened his mouth. The *daughter*? Was he *serious*? He was ignoring everything she and Leslie and Ana had already dug up.

Wait. Take a deep breath. What if...

Dammit. He might have a point. She *did* know her job, after all. She was former MI6; military intelligence prior. She knew the ropes. Maybe being one of MI6's cutthroats for so long and her personal involvement, clouded her judgment.

Had she and Leslie and Ana missed an important detail along the way? Had Leslie died because she found the real connection?

It was a possibility she had to consider.

Piper turned from the crowd and looked at the table where Tammy Granton and her boyfriend remained seated. They made no effort to mix. The boyfriend leaned close and talked; Tammy stared ahead as if ignoring him. She wished she could be a fly on the wall and listen to the conversation.

Piper turned back to Raven and Granton. They continued their conversation. Another chat she wanted to hear.

———

RAVEN SAID, "HOW DO YOU HANDLE PROBLEMS?"

"Like what?"

"Snoopers. Reporters. My client wants to know about your security."

Granton scoffed. "We ignore such annoyances. There is always somebody who wants to try for a smear story or somebody who wants to debunk our efforts. I have more important things to think about. But we have very tight security. Our records are treated the same as any classified material the military has."

"Sounds fine. Well, be careful. You never know who's trying to hurt you. Or find out things you don't want exposed."

Granton's smile faded. The twinkle left his eye.

"I'm neglecting my other guests. Please give my best to your client and get in touch."

Granton heartily shook hands with Raven again, but it was a phony gesture. Raven watched him continue through the crowd and focused on a spot behind Granton's left ear. Where he wanted to put the barrel of his gun prior to blowing the man's face off.

———

PIPER ORDERED ANOTHER MARTINI. WHEN SHE TURNED HER back to the bar and her eyes to the crowd, she watched Raven break through the mass of people and come to her. He smiled.

"Did you get me one?" he asked.

"I drank it. This is my third."

"I had a nice chat with our friend." Raven waved for the bartender.

"You two looked like you were becoming best friends."

"Not quite." The bartender came over, and Raven ordered another gin and tonic.

He said nothing more while they watched the crowd. The band began again. Couples migrated to the dance floor.

The bartender handed Raven his glass. Piper watched him over the rim of her glass. She wished he'd get to the point.

He swallowed some of his drink and continued.

"I may have to correct my earlier statement," he said.

"About—"

"The daughter."

"Oh, make up your mind, Raven."

"I said a few things to see if he'd react," Raven said. He explained Granton's response to his security prompt.

"Do you think you sabotaged the anonymous donor thing?"

"I don't think so. Not with the amount I mentioned."

"You sure?"

"All will reveal itself in the next forty-eight hours," he said. "If Granton decides to try and kill me."

"But you're ready for anything."

"Of course." He smiled. "Where's the daughter? I'd like to take another look at her."

"Last I saw, she was still at the table."

LONDON ASSAULT   139

Raven started in the direction of the tables and Piper followed.

———

JAMES WHITE CURSED UNDER HIS BREATH AS THE BAND started another loud number.

"What now?" Tammy said.

He snapped his head to her. She looked mad. He was already mad and had been since the start of the evening. Too much day. Too much to process after losing Phil, then the MI5 man. Now this stupid party.

"Let's go to a club," he said. "Let's do some proper drinking."

"I can't leave till the dinner is over."

"You're only sitting here with me. You're not doing the *schmoozing* I expected."

"I did a lot at the beginning. There isn't much more to do now."

"Then forget it, let's go."

"All right, fine."

He left the chair faster than even he anticipated. He took her hand as she grabbed her purse, and they left the ballroom behind.

They'd arrived early but still couldn't find parking on the first level of the secure garage. James left his car on the second level, and the lift doors rumbled open allowing them to access the rows of vehicles and cold concrete. Lights blazed, some letting out a low buzz. James and Tammy moved beneath the lights. His BMW wasn't far away. He could have used the valet option available to attendees, but he'd wanted to keep the keys on him and be able to exit at any time. Only a fool let other people put his car where he had no way to find it in a hurry.

James reached for the key fob in his right slacks pocket. He wasn't looking behind him.

But Tammy saw somebody. She gasped and grabbed his right arm. "Behind us!"

James pivoted, shoving Tammy away, his right hand rising from his pocket to instead reach under his jacket.

"Don't, Jimmy."

The gunman emerged from two cars on the opposite side of the aisle. A young man, very thin, with both sides of his head shaved, a mop of black hair on top. His long jacket, zipped, went almost to his knees. The small revolver in his left hand might as well have been a cannon.

James glanced left. Tammy had fallen to the floor, but she was scooting backward to the driver's side fender. She said, "James!"

"Quiet."

"Both of you need to be quiet." The man stopped midway. He steadied his aim on James' chest.

"You killed two friends of mine, Jimmy."

"You'll have to remind me, mate. It's been a long week."

The young man scoffed. "Go easy on the jokes, they'll be your last."

"Why not die with a smile on my face?"

James shifted to cover Tammy. He hoped he was out of the line of fire. If he was going down, he was taking the young gunman with him so Tammy wasn't hurt. He still heard her sliding across the concrete floor.

"I only want you to know why you're dying, Jimmy. You've gotten away with too much for too long and now it's time to pay."

"We all die eventually, mate. What's your name?"

The young killer cocked the revolver and lifted the muzzle to James' head.

James White had played football in high school, and some things one never forgets. He bent and lunged. The young man shuffled back and tried to lower the muzzle. He fired. The bullet passed overhead and whined off the concrete wall behind him. The young man didn't get another shot, but he tried to kick. The long jacket interfered with his leg. His right foot was half off the floor when James White collided with his midsection.

The wanna-be killer folded over James' back, and James forced him into one of the cars behind him. The killer's backside slammed into the car's front grill; he screamed. James straightened and slammed a fist into the other man's belly, then wrenched the revolver from his hand. The wanna-be killer dropped to his knees. James stepped away and shot him twice in the back of the head. Whoever he was, the killer went limp and stayed on his belly as a pool of blood oozed beneath his shattered skull.

James examined the gun. An old Smith & Wesson Chief's Special. He slipped the gun into a pocket and returned to the BMW. Tammy, hair a mess but unharmed, rose from the front.

"That was close!"

James used the key fob to unlock the car. Tammy ran to her side and climbed in; he joined her. The engine rumbled to life at the first press of the starter button.

He backed out, turned for the exit, and stepped on the throttle. The BMW zoomed away.

CHAPTER SEVENTEEN

RAVEN LEANED OUT FROM BEHIND A LARGE SQUARE SUPPORT beam and watched the BMW leave. The driver made a left, tires chirping, and headed for the lower level.

Piper eased around the other side of the pillar. It was wide enough to hide them both.

"We gotta get out of here," she said.

"I know. But I think we know the boyfriend is dirty."

"I'll never argue with you again."

"Sure, you will. Next time, you might be right. Come on."

They want back the way they'd come at a quick pace.

"Who do you think got killed?" Piper said.

"I don't know, but I'm sure we can find out. How many homicides does London have?"

"You'd be surprised," she said.

They reached the stairwell and started up.

Raven hoped Ana was able to identify the man if the clandestine picture he'd taken turned out all right.

CALLUM HILL, SENATOR FROM VERMONT, LEFT THE CHAMBER and started down a long hallway. His colleagues followed behind them, but he was the only one who walked alone. He felt very much alone despite the crush of others around him, the usual suspects, the same faces as always.

He'd filed his resolution to stop the missile sales to Saudi Arabia. He wanted an immediate halt. It wasn't enough to stop after the US fulfilled its current contract. The sales had to stop *now.* Jacqueline Bennett and Zachary Roberts remained steadfastly on his side, but no others had joined them. And Hill saw the reason why break through a cluster of reporters ahead of him. The older woman zeroed on Hill with angry eyes.

Leanne Weinstein, Senator from California, who'd been trying to stop Hill since he began recruiting for the resolution. Her wrinkled face showed she'd been serving for far too long. To Hill, she was the poster child for term limits. But the idiots in California kept making stupid choices.

"Mr. Hill."

She sounded like a cranky junior high school principal scolding a troublemaker for the umpteenth time. He stopped. She stood before him and had to look up a little. She was an old bull who still thought the bucks feared her. The senators in her age group may have, but Hill wasn't impressed. She sat on the Senate Intelligence Committee, and was known as a defense hawk who wanted to bomb lots of brown people, but only because her husband owned stock in several arms manufacturing companies. Every time the US dropped a bomb, Mr. Weinstein received a dividend.

"What do you want, Mrs. Weinstein?"

"The Saudis are keeping bad actors contained," she said. "Why are you trying to sabotage what you're doing?"

"Straight to the point as always, Mrs. Weinstein. Does your husband need another yacht?"

"Stay on topic."

"Oh, I think I am, ma'am."

She soured. "If it weren't for the Saudis fighting in Yemen, it would be a breeding ground for anti-American activity. We'd have to do more than send missiles, believe me."

"You sure?"

"I sit on the *committee*, Mr. Hill, I know a lot more than you."

"You need to do your own reading instead of trusting your lackeys to inform you on events."

"Your little wish list isn't going to pass."

"You sure?" Hill said again.

She started to turn red.

"Am I interfering with your bribe checks or something, Leanne?"

Her face twisted in anger, but she knew there were too many eyes on them to go off like a rocket.

"You're crossing a line there's no coming back from, Mr. Hill."

"I'll be careful next time I'm mowing my lawn."

Hill went around the older women and continued on his way. He hid his anger well, but he was raging inside. The corruption was strong, indeed. Worse, he knew Leanne Weinstein actually believed the nonsense she spewed.

———

RAVEN FOUND ANA IN THE KITCHEN THE NEXT MORNING. He'd shaved, showered, and dressed—but still felt tired after the activity of the night before. Ana still wore her bathrobe and leaned against the kitchen island with a steaming mug of tea in both hands.

"I didn't hear you come in last night," she said.

"Piper and I didn't want to wake you."

"Have a good time?"

Raven gave her the update while he poured a mug of tea for himself, and ate a banana from a bowl in the center of the kitchen island. It wasn't much of a breakfast, but he didn't see Ana going for the bacon and eggs.

"Got the camera?" she asked.

Raven pulled the tiny camera from his jeans pocket and handed it to her. She left the kitchen for her office. Raven followed. Ana plugged the camera into a USB port to access the picture Raven snapped. It wasn't bad. The view captured most of James White's face, and she enlarged his face and ran the photo through her recognition software.

James White's police dossier flashed on the screen. She sat back and read as Raven stood behind her and watched.

"Mr. James White," she said. "He's the son of Billy White, who's the leader of one of London's biggest organized crime groups. He's been fortunate. Billy has his fingers in every pie and has bribed more cops and judges than you can count, so the police and MI5 have never been able to nail either one on anything."

"What's he doing with Granton's daughter?"

"Dating her, I guess. It's not in the file."

"Not yet."

"If they just started, no. If they continue dating, she'll eventually be mentioned like some of his other girlfriends on this list here." She tapped the screen. "But rest assured, she's associated with the biggest crime family in London, and it can't be good."

Raven told her about his theory on Tammy Granton funneling the money from her father's charity to the Whites, who in turn funneled it to terrorists. Ana considered the idea while sipping her tea. She didn't answer right away, and Raven didn't prompt her.

"Could be," she finally said. "How she stayed off the radar of MI5 and all that, I have no idea. Her father's the one who tripped all the alarms."

"Piper made the same point."

"Maybe she's learned a thing or two about covering her tracks. She should teach her father. You said you talked to him, by the way?"

Raven explained his interaction with Granton and the "anonymous donor" routine.

"I think I spooked him a little," Raven said, "but I want to play it out."

She turned her chair to face him. "What are you thinking?"

"You act as my representative and call the private line to arrange the meeting."

"Can do."

"And I'd like to see more details on Granton's travel history. May I read some of the emails?"

"Sure."

Raven reviewed the information at Ana's desk while she cooked a proper breakfast. He cross-referenced Granton's information with Piper's surveillance reports. During his last trip to the Middle East, Baghdad, and Cairo specifically, Granton met with a few men representing Middle Eastern charities. Nothing looked untoward on the surface. Raven checked the names of the Middle Easterners with MI5. The security agency listed a few as jihad suspects, but only suspects—there was nothing concrete to tie them with terrorism. The MI5 reports stated they didn't have enough information to move against the suspects, and recommended more study.

He checked out Tammy Granton, too, and read about her education and work history. No criminal record. No indication of how she could have come in contact with James White. The information gap was frustrating. Tammy Granton may not have had a police record, but she had to be doing *something* to meet the Whites. Or did they meet at a pub? Could it have been a wild coincidence? Tammy's work with her father's charity wasn't much. She assisted during fundraising events, but maintained separate employment. He wanted to check her out some more. Fill in the gaps.

Raven and Ana ate breakfast with no sign of Piper from her bedroom upstairs.

"We can do a deep dive on the daughter," Ana said, "but in the meantime, we'll get you ready to see Granton again. I'll front the half million to make it legit, and we can trace the transaction to see what Granton does with the money."

"Good idea," Raven said. Her scrambled eggs were perfect, fluffy, buttery, and the bacon was crisp to perfection. He went back for seconds, then returned to his room. He met Piper coming down the stairs as he went up. She looked very tired but managed to mumble good morning.

CHAPTER EIGHTEEN

THOMAS GRANTON TOOK A DEEP BREATH AND ROSE FROM HIS prayer mat. He remained on his knees a moment, contemplating the bare wall in front of him. He was facing Mecca by staring at the wall, and the knowledge, along with his daily prayer time, gave him comfort in light of the efforts to which he now dedicated his life.

He left the prayer room and went to change into a proper suit and tie. Rahmil was coming for a visit, and the man named Pullman was scheduled for later in the afternoon. It was going to be a busy day.

Granton's conversion to Islam took him by surprise. As an agnostic for most of his life, he gave very little thought to anything spiritual. Then a major earthquake shook Afghanistan and Pakistan and left scores dead and injured. The need for help, food and supplies, was more than Granton Charities could handle alone, but Granton led the way by personally working on scene with relief efforts. Witnessing the faith of those affected by the earthquake, he wanted to explore more about what made them so devout. Within three months, he left his agnosticism behind and joined the faithful. From there, he saw the dark side of the West's prejudice against Islam and pledged as much as he could to support jihad efforts. Peaceful outreach accomplished little.

But he had to be careful because working with people like Rahmil made him a target should the authorities get wind of the connection.

Tammy knew about his new faith, but she didn't know the rest of the story. He worked hard to keep her shielded from the other side; any consequence he faced shouldn't fall on her, too. Of course, if the worst happened, she'd feel blow-back, no doubt. And while she might live under a cloud for a period of time, her life wouldn't be ruined.

He completed the Windsor knot and admired his appearance in the wall-length mirror. Donning his suit jacket, he proceeded down a spiral staircase to make sure he had tea ready for Rahmil's arrival. The wide circular entryway at the bottom of the steps was almost all marble, with various expensive decorations abundant. A giant painting of the original builders of the Granton estate, his great, great grandparents, hung on a wall facing the thick oak double doors. He was alone on his estate. The house and grounds staff had the day off. He wanted no stray eyes on him when Rahmil showed up.

He was waiting on the porch steps when Rahmil drove his car up the access road to the circular driveway. Marble columns supported an overhang stretching from one corner to the other; the Granton family home looked like a castle, a stone and marble monstrosity known throughout the UK as the center of charity for those in need. It was Thomas Granton's personal crusade. He was in charge of the family legacy, the money, and while he and his people worked to multiply the already impressive coffers, he wanted to do something good with what he'd been given. He hadn't earned the money. He'd become caretaker of the Granton name, and he had a responsibility to do more than his predecessors had.

He was the tenth generation to occupy the home. If Tammy didn't settle down and have a family of her own, she'd be the last of the line, and he didn't want to contemplate the possibility. She'd figure out what she wanted soon enough. Only a matter of time.

With Tammy's mother having died so young, there'd been no chance for more children, and Granton remained too attached to his late wife to find another companion. And if Tammy felt pressured because of his choices, she never said. Sometimes he wondered.

Rahmil sat alone in the rental car, and he parked in front of the steps and turned off the car. Exiting, he approached Granton with a wide smile. He took the steps two at a time and joined Granton on the porch.

"You look well, my friend," Granton said. The two men shook hands warmly. Granton stood taller than Rahmil. Both wore the best Saville Row had to offer.

"It was a long flight," Rahmil said, "but it's good to see you too."

"Follow me. I have refreshments ready."

They settled in the large library, the walls lined with full bookcases; plush leather chairs, a large globe, and a corner desk filled the rest of the space. Granton and Rahmil sat in a corner, chairs facing each other, both with tea and saucers.

"Before we get to the results of your fundraiser," Rahmil said, "I should let you know about the guns."

"The ones to Boko Haram?"

LONDON ASSAULT 151

"We delivered four shipments and spread them to Chad, Niger, and north Cameroon. The brothers are pleased."

"Good."

"And the two women?"

Granton's face turned grim.

"We got one," he said, "but the other—"

"She was rescued from Cairo by another operative." Rahmil produced a cell phone from inside his jacket and began scrolling through pictures. He stopped and passed Granton the phone.

"That man is a freelancer named Sam Raven," Rahmil said.

Granton's face tightened.

"What's the matter, Thomas?"

"This man spoke to me last night. He said his name was Pullman and he represented a so-called anonymous donor. This *donor* wanted to pledge half a million US." Granton handed back the phone.

"You believed him?"

"Believed him? He's coming *here* soon. To talk more."

Rahmil smiled.

"I don't think this is anything to smile about," Granton said. His tea sat forgotten on a side table.

"Keep the meeting."

"Are you...serious?"

"I am. Sam Raven and I clashed once. In Naples." Rahmil related the story of the Ward family, the list of NATO spies, the raid by the CIA team. "He cost me several *million* dollars that night. This time, we'll finish what we started ten years ago."

"But if Raven and the Shaw woman—they *know*, Rahmil! We're in danger. *I'm* in danger!"

"They know nothing. Suspicion fuels them, Thomas. We took the first woman's collection of information; we thwarted Shaw from finding anything concrete. Once we remove Ravan and Shaw and their employer from existence, we go back to status quo."

"But—"

"Why do you think elements of MI6 called Ana Gray? Your VIP status and friendship with King Charles provides you plenty of protection. We don't have to bribe a single official. Remove Gray, Raven, and Shaw, and we only frustrate those who called on them. Frustrate them into *silence,* Thomas. They won't try again. You have to trust me."

"All right." Granton reached for his tea and took a drink. It had gone cold. He held onto the mug anyway.

"Now, about your party."

Granton stuttered as he launched into his update, but he hit the most important point right away.

"We raised four million pounds."

"Excellent! And the next one…"

"Next week. An embassy function. We're going to tap into more government grants if we can."

"You will. Because *that's* the party I'm looking forward to."

"Trying to blackmail—"

Rahmil stopped Granton with a look. "It's a solid plan. The best part is, you leave me to the details and enjoy yourself."

"Invitations are almost ready to go."

"Good. Cheer up, Thomas. It's covered. You're protected."

"I don't feel protected. I feel like a fool. Raven was within *inches* of me, Rahmil. He looked *through* me."

"He's trying to scare you into doing something stupid."

"Such as?" Another sip of cold tea.

"Trying to kill him."

Granton laughed nervously. "Your department, not mine."

"He's expecting the opposite," Rahmil said. "Stay the course. Be yourself. *Confuse* him. The *he* will make a mistake and walk right into our hands."

"If you say so, I'll believe you."

"Have I been wrong yet?" Rahmil asked.

"No."

"When is he due to arrive?"

Granton checked his Rolex. "Two hours."

"Then I should go. You need time to settle down. I recommend more prayer and reflection. Read your Koran. It has tremendous calming effects on a busy mind."

Granton agreed.

CHAPTER NINETEEN

RAVEN FOLLOWED THE CURVING ACCESS ROAD TO THE Granton house. The big mansion loomed ahead like a stone goliath, but the environment wasn't right. There was a missing piece…and it dawned on Raven as he slowed for the porch. No groundskeepers. No guards. He grinned as he stopped the Maserati. He couldn't wait to see the surveillance photos Piper was taking from the edge of the property. She'd inserted prior to his visit; she probably had a good shot of his backside as he left the car.

The car locks chirped automatically as he hit the steps. Before his left index finger pressed the door busser, the dead-bolt lock snapped. It snapped back with a solid *thunk*. The thick oak door swung open on oiled hinges—no squeaking noise.

Thomas Granton smiled big.

"Mr. Pullman. So happy to see you, old chap. Welcome. Come in, please."

Raven followed Granton inside. The older man shut the

heavy door. Raven's eyes went up to the big painting of the estate's founders.

"My great, great grandparents," Granton said. "They built this place."

"I would have loved to have met them," Raven said. "They'd be very proud of you."

"I hope so."

Granton explained his staff had the day off, but he'd prepared drinks and "some eats, as you Americans say" on the back balcony. Up the spiral staircase to the second floor, through an opulently furnished room to a set of glass sliding doors.

The "back balcony" overlooked the rear field, a wide open, flat area of grass with trees ringing the edge of the property in the distance.

Growing clouds in the sky threatened to ruin the moment if it started to rain.

"Please, sit. Help yourself."

Granton had set out sparkling orange juice, soft rolls, and cold cuts with assorted condiments. They filled most of the space on a glass tabletop with padded metal chairs surrounding it. Raven hadn't the heart to tell the Brit nobody said "eats" in the US when referring to food and had not since before Raven was born.

"Nice view," Raven said, easing into a chair. He poured a glass and made a turkey sandwich.

Granton remained standing a moment. He surveyed the property with proud eyes. "Family estate. Ten generations. My daughter will take it over someday. Hopefully with a family of her own."

"She taking the long way?"

"The long way? I don't understand."

"Enjoying her youth. Not settling down straight away."

Granton forced a laugh. "I suppose that's what she's doing." He pulled out a chair and sat.

Raven hoped the food wasn't poisoned. He noticed Granton wasn't eating. He only had a glass of the sparkling orange juice. But what the hell. He took a few bites of the sandwich.

"Don't think I'm rude—"

"Not at all," Raven said. "We made this appointment to talk business, not the ups and downs of raising daughters."

"How many do you have?"

Raven smiled, but a trace of sadness filled his eyes. "One."

Raven set down the sandwich and reached into his jacket. Anything to break eye contact. He pulled out an envelope and set it on the table in front of Granton.

"Cashier's check for five hundred thousand US dollars," Raven said. "Courtesy of my client."

Granton put his glass on the table and opened the envelope. He peeked inside, pressed his lips together, and nodded. "I don't know if I can communicate how much I appreciate this. Please give your client my warmest regards."

"I will tell him."

"We need a name for the receipt. Doesn't he want the tax write-off?"

"My client only wants to do something good."

Granton glanced at the check. "I suppose I could look up who runs the company listed on this check—"

"Mr. Granton. My client only wants to help."

The Brit smiled. "Understood. It's my nature to express my appreciation. This is a *very* generous gift."

"I know it will be put to good use, Mr. Granton."
This time, Raven smiled.

CHAPTER TWENTY

Back in Ana Gray's Maserati, Raven followed the circular drive around to where it met the access road and retraced the way he'd come. Through the gate, a left turn, about fifteen yards up the road. He pulled over sharply and unlocked the doors. Piper Shaw came stomping out of the brush and trees clutching a digital camera with a long lens.

She hurried into the passenger seat and Raven stepped on the accelerator before she shut her door. The Maserati's engine hummed.

"What did you get?" he asked, steering through the curving road.

"Proof. All we need."

"Meaning?"

"Rahmil was there. He left two hours before you showed up."

"Okay."

"That's all?"

"Where's your car?"

"Bottom of the hill and off the road. Slow down."

Raven slowed. The road straightened. He spotted Piper's car hidden off to the side, surrounded by trees in a small cutout.

"Really, Raven, I tell you we hit the jackpot and you give me nothing?"

Raven pulled over. "I want to see your pictures for myself. But good work. Truly."

She shook her head, left the Maserati, and climbed into her car. She pulled ahead of Raven, and he followed behind.

They had confirmation. Good. Raven wasn't unimpressed; he was cold about the discovery. But they had proof of Granton and Rahmil together. Now they only needed a little more to smash them and their terror-funding conspiracy for good.

There was something else on his mind, too.

"We made this appointment to talk business, not the ups and downs of raising daughters."

"How many do you have?"

"One."

One.

He touched the locket under his shirt and tried to fight off painful memories. He couldn't. Raven wondered if his little girl might have taken "the long way" as well. Because of men like Granton and Rahmil, he'd never know.

Raven put his hand back on the steering wheel, staying on Piper's tail as they continued along the road.

War without end.

It was the only solace he had. The only way to make sure other fathers didn't suffer the same fate as he. But nobody could fight forever. Someday, Raven knew, he'd meet an opponent who was faster on the draw than him.

War without end.

160   BRIAN DRAKE

Until the end.

————

ANA GRAY, IN FRONT OF HER COMPUTER MONITORS ONCE again, examined the pictures taken by Piper.

There were several. They showed Granton and Rahmil emerging onto the porch, hugging goodbye, and then Rahmil going down the steps to his car. The photo showing him going around the rear bumper was the big one. Rahmil turned his head as if looking in Piper's direction. She caught a full-frontal snap of his face. Ana zeroed on Rahmil's face and made it larger.

"There he is," Ana said.

Piper couldn't hide her excitement. "It's all we need, right?"

"What do you mean, Piper?" Ana said. She sat with her back to both Raven and the young woman. They stood behind her.

Piper looked to Raven for support. "Now we kill 'em all."

Raven shook his head.

Piper blanched.

"It's not enough," Ana said.

"*What?*"

Raven folded his arms and remained quiet.

"We have confirmation of an alliance between the two men, yes," Ana said. "Suspicions confirmed and all that. I wish we knew how they met, but we can surmise it happened through one of the jihad suspects Granton met in the Middle East."

Piper raised her voice. "What more do we need?"

"The paper trail," said Raven.

"Are you two kidding? We knock off these two, the scheme falls apart."

"No, Piper," Ana said.

"Explain!"

Ana turned her chair to face Piper. The former MI6 operative's neck was flushed red with anger. Ana wasn't happy, either.

"Excuse me, young lady?"

Piper said, "*Please* explain."

Ana counted on the fingers of her left hand.

"One, who else is involved? Who takes over if they're both killed? You know Rahmil has stuffed Granton Charities with his own people.

"Two, who are their connections? We aren't only dealing with two men, but the network they're plugged into. Who gets the money and how?

"Three, if we *knock off* His Majesty's pal without first accomplishing points one and two, we'll be charged with murder. The MI6 people who contacted me need to present *facts* to their superiors. We need to do this by the book."

"But what about Leslie?" Piper said.

Raven took over. "We'll get them, Piper. You only need to be patient."

"She was your friend, too, Raven!"

"That's why we need to stay cold."

"You're saying I'm too emotional?"

"Too *involved* is more accurate."

Hands on her hips, Piper clenched her jaw but said nothing more. Ana turned her chair to face the screens once more.

"At least we've confirmed what we set out to do before we lost Leslie," Ana said. "Granton has terrorist connections.

Some of the money he raises *goes* to those connections. Now we need to know how they work together."

Raven said, "I'm still not convinced the daughter isn't involved. How could she not be? Especially with James White in the picture."

"We need to get a fix on Rahmil and keep an eye on him," Ana said. "He'll be your responsibility, Piper. Raven, you follow up on the daughter and the boyfriend."

"Just the boyfriend," Raven said. "He may prove more interesting."

"Do you have anything to add, Piper?"

"No, ma'am."

"Good," Ana said.

Piper left the room in a huff. They heard her thumping up the stairs.

Raven watched her go.

"She'll calm down," Ana said.

"You sure?"

"You aren't?"

"No," Raven said. "If she doesn't get control of this, she's going to go off the rails and do something stupid. Something we'll *all* pay for."

"There's another problem you haven't mentioned."

"What?"

"Rahmil saw Granton before you arrived. He had to have mentioned you by now. Granton knows you're a fake. He's probably torn up the cashier's check, too. We won't be able to trace the money."

"I'm sure it happened exactly as you describe," Raven said.

"You aren't bothered?"

"No," Raven told her.

CHAPTER TWENTY-ONE

IT WAS A DAY SHE HAD TO WORK HER REGULAR JOB.

Tammy Granton had a job at a flower shop near her home. It was technically a no-show job arranged by James, and she was only required to appear a couple of times a week. She didn't do much while there. The owner allowed her to do some sorting, set product on the shelves, but nothing else. She put in her four or five hours, depending on not only her mood but the owner's, and then her obligation was settled.

She put on jeans and a T-shirt after drying off from a shower, decided to heck with her makeup, and grabbed her purse from the kitchen counter. A knock on the door made her pause. She waited. The knock came again but in a pattern this time. Two taps, pause, two taps, pause, one tap.

Oh, no.

Only one person used the particular tap code, and him showing up at her door wasn't good news.

She opened the door and tried to smile. She had to force the corners of her mouth to go up.

A slight man stood before her, dressed in an ill-fitting suit because his frame was so small. But he was well-groomed with a short beard beginning to show spots of gray.

"Mick."

"Hi, Tammy. May I come in? We have some things to talk about."

She stepped back and allowed him to enter. Putting the kettle on for tea, she grabbed two mugs and a box of English Breakfast and joined him at the kitchen table.

Mick Taylor spoke while the water boiled.

"You were with James White when my partner showed up asking about his dead friend."

"Sure."

"It's in his report."

"Okay." She felt a chill up her neck.

Mick Taylor was an MI5 agent and partner of stalwart specialist Declan Barlow. He was also Tammy's contact at the agency. A grass. She'd been paying him since her drug dealing days to let her know if she wound up on the radar.

She said, "What did he recommend? Or is it simply one line in a report?"

"No, he recommended surveillance. He's not going to get it because we're short on men. Can't afford to cover suspects we don't have hard evidence on. But there will be eyes on you periodically."

The kettle screamed as steam blasted from the spout.

Tammy poured the tea and brought Mick Taylor his mug.

"What about James?"

"He'll be watched now and then, too, but you know the Whites. They have their own arrangement. The surveillance team will go out to work, but they may have a hard time keeping him in sight."

"I see."

LONDON ASSAULT   165

"I'll do my best, but—"

"My father's a friend of the King. They won't touch me without evidence. Barlow is…overzealous."

"He is indeed, but he's also persistent. He'll figure out a way."

"I need to call James."

Mick Taylor swallowed a mouthful of tea and set the mug down. "Thanks for the brew." He stood. "I'll be in touch if anything happens. Don't get up."

She waited for the door to shut before leaving the table and turning the lock. Grabbing her cell phone from her purse, she dialed James. He answered on the fourth ring.

"What is it, luv?"

"My MI5 man just showed up."

"Tell me more."

She explained the visit and Mick Taylor's statements. James listened without comment. She ended with, "What do you want me to do?"

"Nothing. Go work your hours. We'll take it slow for a while after we're done unloading the boat. That's all they're really interested in. Phil's death is only a red herring. He's going to use it to try and find a connection."

"All right."

"Do your hours. It will be fine."

She took his word and ended the call. Traffic was heavy all the way to the flower shop, and she parked in the rear. She entered through the front entrance since the owner kept the back door locked from inside. The bell above the door dinged. The front of the store contained a long counter and several refrigerators keeping multicolored flowers cold. Other flower displays not in the cold cases filled in the gaps. The place smelled far too sweet for Tammy's tastes but found she couldn't detect the odors after a half hour of working. She found the owner behind the counter talking on the phone.

The owner's name was Brenda, and she was overweight and always wore a Muumuu and stretch pants with her dark curly hair short. She spoke to a customer in her usual cheerful manner, but it was an act. As soon as she hung up, she'd break out the Cockney accent, sour attitude, and swear words.

Tammy waited. There was nothing for her to do until Brenda told her. She always found the big woman's phone conversations amusing. This one was no different.

"I'm very sorry for your loss, but we'll have the flowers delivered to the funeral home in time for the service. Will there be anything else, sir? All right. Let's get your payment then. Will you be using a credit card?"

Presently she hung up, the transaction finished and filed the order form in a folder beside the register.

"Bloody banker's dead mum," she said, not looking at Tammy. "I'd die too if I was the type of person to stand on the necks of us little people. I can't get me a line of credit but motherfucker wants me to step and fetch it when he calls." When she finally did look at Tammy, her smile was gone. "He wants two dozen red roses. Go back and get 'em and don't fuck around back there."

Tammy said she wouldn't mess with the product. The way to the back was through a door near the counter, and Tammy went through to complete her task.

Tammy always made sure to do her best. Her family name was riding on the gig, after all. Brenda knew very well who she was, who her father was, and who her father counted as friends. But Tammy also knew Brenda didn't like her, which was fine. James secured the job because Brenda paid the

Whites protection money to make sure "nothing bad" happened to her "fine establishment."

Tammy didn't care for such rackets, but it was how James made some of his money. Not a lot, but some. He had his thugs go from shop to shop collecting the money every week. She didn't have to like it, but at least it meant James always had cash for their dates.

———

CALLUM HILL SAT ON THE STEPS OF THE LINCOLN MEMORIAL, gazing across the reflection pool at the Washington Monument in the distance. The reflection pool never held his interest. The constant battle against algae growing in the pool made it an eyesore, and under the evening lights, the algae looked like small islands within the water. The National Parks Service cleaned and drained the pool every year, but the algae always came back—like a government program, it never went away.

The sun was going down; it was cold; tourists were thinning out to let the overnight lights brighten the space. Hill struggled to decide what Lincoln or Washington might do in his situation.

He checked his watch. Zachary Roberts, one of his only two allies on the resolution to stop missile sales to Saudi Arabia, was five minutes late. Hill sat on the cold marble steps in a black suit. He'd looked out of place among the tourists. Luckily, nobody recognized him. Now with them gone, he looked like a desperate and lonely man hoping for wisdom from leaders long gone.

Would they even be able to comprehend the world Callum Hill lived in?

Another figure broke through the lights and shadows around him.

"Cal?"

"Hi, Zachary."

The older Democrat lumbered up the steps. Some joints popped as he sat beside Hill.

"Damn, Cal. I'm too old to sit like this."

"It was your idea to meet here."

Zachary Roberts laughed. "Sure was. We got too many eyes on us at the office."

"Jacqueline's on TV tonight."

"Little good it will do."

Hill sighed. "I know."

The trio had been making the rounds of television, radio, YouTubers, and anywhere else they found willing participants to spread the word about their resolution. None of the appearances generated much interest. Americans weren't calling their representatives to tell them to support Hill's plan.

"Americans can be their own worst enemy, Cal."

"They won't bother until those missiles actually blow up something they care about."

"Meanwhile," Zachary Roberts said, "Weinstein and her cohorts aren't letting up the pressure. I can't get a meeting with anybody. It's as if she's scared them into not talking to me at all."

"She's made a lot of promises to keep them from voting with us. Stuff I can't compete with."

"Your voice, Cal."

"What about it?"

"All I hear is defeat."

"I'm open to suggestions, Senator."

"Well, shit, that's the thing. I don't got none. But I'll be hanged if I don't see this through to the end."

"I appreciate you staying with me."

"All the way. No matter how it turns out."

The two men let the conversation fade. They stared into the night.

CHAPTER TWENTY-TWO

DECLAN BARLOW OF MI5 WASN'T IN A GOOD MOOD.

He sat at a long table in a conference room as the group assigned to the Billy and James White investigations went over the latest. In this case, the *latest* involved the deaths of Philip Deen and the two informants, Ranch and Yates. The loss of the informants hurt a lot, and it had taken a few days to ID the bodies and a little more time to realize what the losses signified.

To Barlow, it was simple. James White and his buddy Deen had gone house cleaning. In the process, Deen died. Now they needed to tie young James to the murders, but how?

As his squad leader droned on while standing in front of a whiteboard with pictures of the victims taped to it, Barlow let out an audible grunt.

"Something bothering you, Declan? Bad lunch maybe?" The squad leader was a middle-aged veteran of MI5, expanding in the middle, who needed to buy bigger shirts.

"I was only wondering," Barlow said, "how many dead

LONDON ASSAULT 171

informants we need before somebody noticed this department has a leak."

Silence. Not even any cleared throats. Barlow looked at the other men seated at the table, but they avoided his gaze. He turned back to Squad Leader Fitch.

"What do you think, Chief?"

"Now, Declan, we can't assume—"

"Ranch and Yates aren't the only informants to get killed. They are only the most recent. And every time we recruit another, they get killed within a matter of days or a few weeks. We have a serious problem, and I'm tired of being the only one to voice it out loud."

"But in the case of Yates and Ranch," Squad Leader Fitch argued, "we have specific information that they gave us before they died. We know where the boat is docking, when, and how many trafficked people are aboard. Once we step on the deck, we'll finally have enough to put the Whites away for good."

"Sure," Barlow said.

"You aren't convinced."

"Nope."

"Care to wager if you're wrong?"

"Twenty quid," Barlow said. "And I hope you can afford it, Chief."

The meeting broke up after more details on "the boat" and what Yates and Ranch provided. Barlow returned to his desk by the window, his colleagues continuing to ignore him as they resumed their previous tasks.

Except Mick Taylor.

Taylor took his seat opposite Barlow, where his desk had been set against the front of Barlow's. He smiled at his friend.

Barlow said, "Something on your mind, happy ass?"

"You should have bet more."

"Fitch can't afford more. How many ex-wives is he up to?"

"Well, I've had the same thoughts as you. One of our pals is bent. How do we know we got good data? What if we were given a false lead and the boat is docked elsewhere?"

"Good question, Mick."

———

MICK TAYLOR, SITTING ACROSS FROM BARLOW, WATCHED HIS partner turn to look out the window. Taylor's smile faded. Barlow was in no mood for levity.

Taylor kept his anxiousness internalized. He had to tread carefully. Barlow wasn't wrong. There was a leak. And if he started poking around looking for the agent responsible, he was bound to trip over Taylor's connection to James White and Tammy Granton.

Taylor busied himself with the paperwork on his desk. Barlow wasn't talking further. His smoldering gaze was focused out on the Thames.

Taylor hadn't *wanted* to go bad, but gambling debts forced his hand. He'd run up the debt at an illegal gambling den run by the Whites, and when they approached him with a way to wipe the slate clean, he agreed. Now they threw him a few quid now and again and he was smart with the money. He socked it away. No more gambling. If any of it came to light, he'd be drummed out of MI5 and spend the rest of his life in a cell—maybe. More than likely the Whites would snuff him before the cell door closed, just because they could.

He didn't mind when rats got killed. Who cared? One or

two or three fewer criminals on the street. As long as the Whites killed their own…

Taylor didn't want to contemplate what he'd do if the Whites ever murdered one of his colleagues. They were smart enough, so far, not to. But if they were ever backed into a corner…

The thought upset Taylor's stomach and made his bowels grumble. He excused himself.

Barlow didn't appear to notice.

———

RAHMIL LIKED TO LIVE GOOD WHILE "ON THE ROAD," AS HE called his travel activity. He had a suite at the Corinthia for the duration of his stay. While praying, he heard his cell phone vibrate. When he finished, he listened to the message, and returned the call. The call came from Washington, D.C.. From an operative named Ilyas.

The other man answered on the first ring.

"Rahmil?"

"Talk to me, brother." Rahmil sat on the edge of the bed. He wore casual clothes instead of one of his suits, and had remained in his suite the whole day.

"Senator Hill's resolution is coming up for a vote soon."

"How will it turn out?"

Ilyas worked in D.C. as Rahmil's agent, passing along whatever pieces of info he thought might be useful.

"Looks like it will fail, unless the people Hill is trying to get on his side change their minds at the last second. There's a lot of pressure for them to vote no."

"Keep me informed."

"But, Rahmil! What if it passes?"

"Not our problem right now. I'm not going to worry about what I can't control. If the worst happens, we'll find another way. But let me know what happens with the vote as soon as you know."

Ilyas agreed, and Rahmil ended the call. He set the phone on the nightstand and thought about opening the curtains. But he decided not to. He knew he was being paranoid, but there *could* be a rifleman on the roof across the street waiting for an opportunity to shoot.

What Rahmil wanted now was a nap. He stretched out on the bed. Busy days ahead. He wanted to be sharp and ready for action.

He dozed off with a smile.

The Americans were always trying to stop people like him. Most often, they did more talking than taking action, nothing they did prevented anything, and the world would soon see the consequences.

CHAPTER TWENTY-THREE

JAMES WHITE DIDN'T WAKE UP TILL FOUR IN THE AFTERNOON. It was going to be a long night, and he needed to be able to keep up. He showered, shaved, and pulled on street clothes with a designer leather jacket. The little S&W .38 he took off the man who tried to kill him in the Hilton parking garage sat heavily inside the jacket. He liked having a gun he could use and toss, and he wasn't expecting trouble tonight—bringing his usual piece of hardware wasn't necessary.

When he left his flat and drove the BMW away, he made a few turns to make sure nobody followed him. But it was tough to keep an eye on traffic ahead while trying to memorize which cars were behind him, too. He didn't *think* anybody was following him. He'd have a better idea when the streets weren't so crowded.

RAVEN GRINNED. JAMES WHITE MIGHT BE A LOT OF THINGS, but a specialist in counter-surveillance when dealing with an expert wasn't one of them. He tracked White's BMW from in front, keeping an eye on the rearview, hoping White the Younger used his turn signals. Raven had been watching the flat for far too long, getting bored with the effort. White getting started this late in the day suggested he had plans for an all-nighter.

He tracked James White to a pub and followed him inside after a short wait. Raven spotted his quarry having lunch with three other men his age. He told them "no alcohol" and they consumed soft drinks or water with their food instead. White wanted his men sober. Yup—they had activity planned, for sure. But what?

Raven finished his pint, used the restroom, and went back to his car. James White and his crew were still eating and making a racket with loud conversation. They talked football, movies, and women.

You expect them to talk business out loud? Raven asked himself. He settled behind the wheel of the Maserati and waited some more. After an hour, the crew piled into the BMW with James once again at the wheel. This time, Raven followed in the traditional manner, keeping back several car lengths and using larger SUVs for cover. A tracking device on the back bumper would have been nice, but Ana had no such equipment in her inventory. What she had provided Raven rode in the trunk of the Italian coupe. Weapons and ammo and a few grenades. Raven's .45 hung snug under his left arm.

They traveled through busy London, following the Thames at one point, eventually turning onto the A2 motorway heading south.

Where were they going? He remained far back, keeping the BMW in range as they sped along the tarmac. But not too fast. Speed cameras captured every inch of roadway. James White made sure to obey the speed limit.

They kept driving. After another hour of travel, Raven figured out their destination based on the road signs. Dover. What was in Dover besides a major port? Raven didn't know much else about the place. Hell, they could be doing anything there. He began to doubt he'd learn much; after all, Tammy Granton wasn't tagging along on this trip. Was he wasting time?

He decided to follow through after all the time invested already. Too many hours to quit. And there might be something interesting in Dover after all. The scenery off the road was nice, and gave Raven an alternative to watching cars. A lot of open and green country, and many farms.

They finally reached Dover. More traffic forced a slowdown and gave Raven a few anxious moments when they made a left and he was stuck behind a lorry. But he caught up, and the BMW headed for the port.

The Port of Dover did a little bit of everything related to sea travel and commerce since the closure of the Port of London. Ferry service, a cruise terminal, and plenty of shipping outlets. Tall cranes hovered over docked container ships. No cruise liners Raven could see. When the BMW passed through the fence gate of a warehouse, he continued driving. A sign advertised the company who owned the warehouse, with "Shipping and Receiving" below the name.

Raven drove by two more warehouses and parked around the corner of the second. He called Ana.

"What do you have?" she asked.

"I'm in Dover." He gave her the day's rundown. "Can you look up the warehouse?"

"What's the name?"

"Crawford and Son."

"Hang on."

He heard her typing in the background. It took less than a minute to find what he wanted.

"They're a legit company. Shipping and receiving, import and export, all that. If there's a deeper connection to the White syndicate, I'll need to look harder."

"The fact James drove in like he owned the place is connection enough."

"Unless he makes them pay protection, and he's there to collect."

"No," Raven said. "He'd send a local for an errand that small. This is bigger."

"What are your plans?"

"Watch and see what happens, for now. Sun's going down. I expect we'll see fireworks by the time this port closes for the night."

———

THE GIANT CARGO SHIP S.S. BONAVENTURA ENTERED THE English Channel and headed for the straight of Dover. The ship had come from Portugal with a full load; large square cargo containers stacked high filled every inch of the long forward deck all the way to the bow. The lit superstructure at the rear, bridge on the very top, towered over the stacks. More containers occupied a smaller area behind the superstructure.

The containers held genuine material destined for sale throughout the UK, but a secondary cargo was the primary reason for the voyage, worth far more than the products in the metal containers.

LONDON ASSAULT 179

Beneath the deck, in part of the hold sectioned off via a movable steel wall, a cluster of forty women ranging from 17 to 24 were jammed together and watched by a rotating staff of armed gunmen. The gunmen liked to leer despite the women being filthy and miserable and near starved. The client demanded no drugs to keep them docile; food was withheld instead. Keep them weak and hungry and dependent.

A man named Luka Bescos strolled through the compartment checking on the human cargo. Fearful wide eyes looked back at him. He wasn't an imposing figure. Thin, on the short side; but lean and strong. The HK submachine gun he held casually was probably what they were really afraid of. Bescos told the guard on duty to get the women ready to "off-board" with specific orders not to leave any strike marks should they need to smack a bitch. The client did not want damaged goods.

Bescos left the lower hold, climbing a set of metal steps to the top deck. He had a few more rounds to make before reporting to the captain. He always felt fine in the holds and narrow spaces below, but the stairwells gave him a case of claustrophobia. He hurried but knew better than to take the metal steps two at a time. If he tripped and fell against the unfinished, sharp edges, he'd be in for a bad night. He didn't know why the stairwells bothered him so much. One of the crew speculated it was because he was blocked on either side with no exit obvious until he reached the deck. It made sense. Passages had visible endpoints no matter where he was. The holds and other cabins, same.

Besco zipped his hooded sweatshirt as he cleared a manhole to the deck. The stacked cargo containers scratched the sky—they were huge, he was small, an ant among giants.

He followed the walkway to the port side, where he found other armed men on watch. Wetness hung in the air from the Channel. The chill seeped through skin. The crew of the Bonaventura wasn't concerned with other ships noticing the gunmen. Sea piracy was a real threat.

Bescos's instructions to the men on the port side were short. They'd be needed below within an hour to help "herd the cattle" and he repeated the order to those on the starboard side and bow. The cargo containers behind the superstructure filled so much space there was no room for guards back there. Instead, a pair of gunners watched the stern from the second level below the bridge.

Another set of steps up the center of the superstructure. It was nice to be out of the wind and salt water spray; now with evening arriving, the deck was going to get slick and dangerous fast.

CHAPTER TWENTY-FOUR

CAPTAIN JULIUS HARO watched through the panoramic window of the bridge. They were well into the English Channel now, almost to the Strait of Dover. Other ships weren't far from them, either traveling in the same direction or the opposite way. His radio man kept in contact with the ships, the radar operator communicating to the helmsman when to adjust their course. They were maybe ninety minutes from Dover.

The bulkhead to Haro's right squeaked open. Luka Bescos entered; his HK was slung across his back now. Haro reflected the younger man was never without the weapon, even when he visited the head.

"The cargo will be ready to move when ordered, Captain."

"You told them not to hurt the women?" Haro's deep voice matched his weathered demeanor. He was barely fifty, but years of hard living had taken a toll. He had the wrinkles of someone much older, and the white hair to match. He looked like a rock deformed by ten thousand years of erosion.

182   BRIAN DRAKE

"I told them not to leave a mark if they had to get rough."

"Very good, Luka." Haro faced forward again. Some radio chatter over the speakers filled the silence.

Bescos stepped closer to the captain.

"You look troubled, sir."

"I am, Luka. I've made many of these runs, without problems, for several years. Which means I've reached a state of comfort. Routine. Know what happens when you reach such a state, Luka?"

"Trouble."

"Trouble always follows comfort. And I'm afraid there's no way to avoid it. The trouble must happen. Then we follow a new state of awareness until the pattern repeats."

"As long as you survive."

"Survival is critical, yes. Keep your gun ready."

———

RAVEN FOUND A STACK OF PALLETS TO HIDE BEHIND. THE gaps in the wood allowed him to watch the Crawford warehouse. More cars had arrived, including an SUV with the UK customs logo emblazoned on the sides. They were expecting a boat to arrive. He wondered where White was hiding. He didn't think the gangster would openly meet customs agents and bring about the suspicion sure to follow.

He'd taken the weapons provided by Ana from the trunk of the Maserati. They were in a tote bag beside him. The main piece of hardware was a SIG-Sauer MPX-K chambered in nine-millimeter and equipped with a red dot optic. The pistol-length 4.5-inch barrel and 35-round mag made it formidable but not ideal. Raven would have much preferred an M-4 or similar 5.56mm carbine, but Ana's inventory (or

LONDON ASSAULT   183

lack thereof) struck again. Which meant he was happy to have more than only the Nighthawk Custom .45.

What he *didn't* have was a jacket thick enough to block out the chill coming off the straight. But he'd warm up once the action started.

———

THE S.S. BONAVENTURA FINALLY DOCKED WITH THE HELP OF harbor tug boats and settled at a jetty extending from the warehouse. It wasn't a quiet affair. The big ship produced a loud rumbling engine noise. Men yelled to each other. A horn sounded as the ship entered the harbor and again when it finally docked. Then floodlights lit up the back of the warehouse like daytime. The wide area between the now-open rear doors and the jetty filled with work trucks, men on foot, and two powerful cranes to unload the mass of containers. Raven remained behind the pallets and hesitated. He didn't see any gunmen. He saw a lot of dock workers. The customs agents drove out to the jetty.

He wanted to retreat. This wasn't what he'd suspected.

But the ghosts of battles past whispered *stay.* He remained concealed and watched. Using a pair of pocket binoculars, he tried to see more without getting closer. The floodlights helped with the view, while casting enough shadows over his position to leave him undetected.

The two customs agents walked up a long gangplank to meet the captain of the ship, who then escorted the two men out of sight. Raven didn't think the two agents were enough to check the containers. More likely, they'd inspect the paperwork and order the containers sealed until a larger crew performed a thorough check the next day.

Two hours ticked by. Raven shivered. He ignored the cold, but it kept reminding him it was there. With the binoculars, he scanned the dock workers. They stood around talking, waiting. No sign of James White. He wasn't disguised as one of the dock workers. No sign of his three friends, either.

A third hour. No change. Raven felt like he was freezing to the ground where he sat.

Then the ship's captain and the customs agents emerged. One of the agents held a file folder now. Raven didn't care what was in the folder. He only wanted something to happen to justify the day's effort. He was getting sore, and the cold and boredom made everything worse.

The customs men shook hands with the captain, and then somebody from the warehouse. Raven tried to get a look at the face of the man from the warehouse. When the man turned to talk the agents to their SUV, he received his wish. It was one of James White's pals from the restaurant. But still no sign of James himself.

The SUV drove off. The dock workers and others around the jetty continued loitering until ten minutes after the customs agents departed. Then White's buddy yelled a few commands, and the dock workers began a fast migration off the property. Within ten minutes, they were gone, and a long bus rumbled out the back of the warehouse to the jetty.

Raven watched closely. Very soon he understood what was taking place. The ship was unloading cargo, but nothing official. None of the containers. Gunmen finally appeared along the outer walkway, a pair in front, and a pair behind a long haggard line of barely dressed, barefoot females. Various ages and sizes. They looked frightened. Some cried as they staggered along. The gunmen herded them down the gangplank, shouting threats. Raven sighed heavily. He'd found

LONDON ASSAULT 185

what James White was up to. Fool customs with standard cargo, then bring out what they wanted to hide. The gunmen shouted at the women again as they steered the females onto the bus. And then James White finally made an appearance. He walked from the warehouse to the bus, and examined the women as they boarded.

Human trafficking. A cancer the world over, and more prevalent than anybody wanted to admit. Raven had encountered such smuggling many times, and most of those incidents involved the United States, UK, and other Western nations. Where nobody believed such horror took place. James White and his father probably planned to force the women into prostitution. Well, not if Sam Raven had anything to say about it.

The gunmen piled into an SUV. A pair went onto the bus. Somebody drove the BMW out to James White. He climbed into the passenger side. His other buddies joined him. The bus engine fired to life with a black puff of smoke out the rear exhaust.

Raven moved fast. He grabbed the tote bag and hurried back to the Maserati. He had to stop the bus without harming the innocent women aboard.

The BMW departed first. Then the bus. The SUV with the four gunmen aboard followed the bus. Still leaving the lights off, Raven slowly followed. The Maserati's engine burbled quietly.

CHAPTER TWENTY-FIVE

HE HAD ONLY SECONDS TO MAKE A MOVE. UNZIPPING THE tote one-handed, he extracted the semi-auto SIG MPX-K, glad he had a full mag in place and one round in the chamber.

The vehicles formed an odd caravan as they moved through the port, staying at the limit. Other buildings and warehouses were lit, but nobody was around at the late hour. Security guards manned the front gate. Raven would have to wait until they were beyond the port and on the road to the motorway before he made a move, but he'd have even less time. If he didn't stop them before the motorway, he'd lose his chance to save the women.

Raven let the car idle forward, only applying a little pressure to the throttle to keep it moving. He stayed well back. The bus made the three vehicles easy to follow. The slowness of the bus might come in handy, Raven decided.

They passed through the exit with only a cursory glance from the bored security guards. Vehicles leaving must not have been a concern. Presently they reached the road. The BMW, bus, and SUV turned right. Raven gave them some distance, then turned on his lights to pass through the exit gate himself. Making the right turn, he switched off the lights again and pressed the accelerator to speed up.

Raven hit the automatic window switch. The window beside him whispered down and let in the cool night air.

"I'm going to wreck your car, Ana," Raven said out loud.

But he didn't care.

The engine growled as he gained on the SUV.

———

My kingdom for full-auto, Raven thought. He extended the SIG MPX-K out the window and worked the light trigger. Nine-millimeter casings flew into the car as the weapon popped again and again, and the effect on the SUV was immediate. Spiderweb cracks covered the back window as the bullets hit; a second rapid salvo punched holes in the weakened glass. Then he was firing into the vehicle and forcing the gunners inside to defend themselves.

Raven backed off as the SUV began to swerve back and forth across the two-lane road. Raven lowered the muzzle and tried to hit a back tire. He fired several times but kept missing. The rounds only smacked into the pavement. The SIG ran dry. He was reloading with both hands off the wheel when one of the gunners appeared in the frame of the rear window. The gunner raised his sub gun to shoulder level.

Raven swerved into the right lane. The gunner missed with his first burst, then corrected his aim. A string of rounds ripped into the Maserati's fender. How they missed the tire, Raven couldn't guess, but the slugs must have hit a suspension piece because the front end began to shudder. Raven closed the SIG's bolt and fired back, spraying and praying as he steered the car back to the left lane.

The bus driver and the crew in the BMW knew what was happening. The bus sped up with a growl of engine noise and more black exhaust smoke. Raven coughed as the smelly cloud came his way. The sub gunner aimed for the Maserati's windscreen. Raven hit the gas. The coupe lurched into the SUV's back bumper. The sub gunner lost his balance and fell out of sight. Raven moved right, then swung left. His left fender crashed into the SUV's back wheel, but all he managed was to damage the Maserati further instead of forcing the SUV into a spin. The alloy wheels ground against the SUV's tire, sparks and smoke flying; nothing worth the effort. But he had a clear shot at the tire, so he took it. Raven worked the SIG's trigger and sent two slugs into the rubber. The tire exploded and pieces pelted his face. Raven backed off as the SUV's rear sank, the wheel grinding into the pavement with a shower of sparks. Raven fired more rounds into the body of the big vehicle, the trigger finger of his left hand getting sore, his arm beginning to feel fatigued from hanging out the window. But finally, the driver lost control.

The SUV veered to the right, cutting across the road, striking a ditch off the shoulder. The left side pitched up as the vehicle began to roll, and then Raven was speeding alongside the bus to get the BMW. The Maserati still shuddered at the front end, but he ignored it. As long as the car held together, he wasn't going to worry about the damage. Ana could afford it.

The BMW sped up. Raven fired twice at the car but missed. The driver cut in front of him and slammed the brakes. As the tail lights flared red, Raven stomped his own brake pedal. It wasn't enough to stop the impact. Raven kept his body loose as his front bumper plowed into the BMW's rear.

The jolting crunch shook the car and Raven, too. His body strained violently against the seat belt. The airbag in the steering column exploded, scorching his face with a blast of heat and obscuring his vision. He pressed the brakes further to the floor as the bag deflated, but it was too late for the car. It swung off the road into the ditch, the second impact harder than the first as it slammed to a stop with the nose in the ground.

The BMW screeched to a stop. The bus kept going.

Raven unbuckled and scrambled out. The crew exiting the BMW opened fire with handguns. Single shots smacked into the Maserati, tearing into the metal, popping glass. Raven rolled out with the SIG in hand. On his back in the dirt, Raven returned fire. The White crew ran behind their car for cover.

The bus drove out of sight, heading for the motorway.

Raven had to work fast. The Maserati was done for, but if he captured the BMW, he might still stop the bus before it got away.

Raven rolled to his feet and ran to the back of the Maserati. He heard White shouting orders. Raven checked the SIG. He only had a few rounds left in the mag and then his pistol. There was more in the tote bag, including the grenades. Raven moved to the passenger side to open the door. The edge jammed into the dirt after opening less than an inch—no way for him to get his hand inside.

Three of White's men left the BMW and ran toward him. They were eager fighters. Raven wondered what kind of training they had. The average city gangster wasn't that brave. Or maybe they figured one guy was easy to take care of.

Time to teach a life-altering lesson.

Raven smashed the passenger window with the SIG and reached inside for the tote bag. He found a grenade inside, pulled the pin, and pitched it over the hood of the Maserati.

Gunfire from the White crew smacked the car and punched the dirt near him. White himself wasn't firing—why?

The grenade detonated with a sharp boom followed by loud screams as the shrapnel propelled by a high-explosive charge slashed through flesh. Their bodies hit the pavement with loud smacks. Raven didn't feel sorry.

Lights. Bright lights. Coming up behind him.

Raven turned his head. More vehicles appeared down the road from near the port exit, bright headlights growing larger.

Did White have backup?

Raven turned his attention to the BMW again. The chill he felt had nothing to do with the cold.

Only James White remained alive as his men lay either dead or wounded in the road.

One way or another, he was going to punch the gangster's ticket. Then he'd have to find a way to deal with the new arrivals. But they had to catch him first.

CHAPTER TWENTY-SIX

James White, crouched at the front of his car, cursed his decision to only bring the little S&W .38 revolver. Five shots in the cylinder couldn't compete with whatever the enemy had.

There wasn't supposed to be a problem tonight! He'd given the two traitors, Ranch and Yates, false information to pass to MI5, which Mick Taylor confirmed they'd received. MI5 was supposed to be somewhere else, twiddling their thumbs; who was the attacker in the Maserati? He leaned left to see if he could catch another look. He watched an object sail over the hood of the coupe and bounce on the road. His men were running toward it. James hadn't needed to be a combat veteran to know what was happening.

"Get back!" he shouted at his mates, but the grenade's explosion drowned out his yell. The explosion was a sharp pop, a geyser of pavement torn up and tossed high, and a plume of smoke. No flames or big kaboom like in the movies. But grenades were deadly no matter how they detonated, and the screams from his mates as they collapsed in bloody heaps pierced his ears. The screaming stopped as the bodies settled into place, stretched out on the sides, backs; none of them moving.

James White began to breathe fast. His heart raced. More friends dead. Mates he'd known all his life. He stared at their unmoving forms and clenched his jaw.

He grabbed the .38 S&W and ran toward the wrecked Maserati. "You motherfucker!" he shouted. He fired once. The shot missed and the man behind the coupe raised his own pistol. White fired again. Another miss. Three rounds left. He ran hard.

THE FIRST SHOT FROM THE .38 WHINED OVERHEAD. THE second came nowhere near Raven. He scooted out of White's sight, drew the .45, and thumbed down the safety. When White came into view, Raven lifted his pistol to eye level and fired once. *Smack*. Dead center. White's upper body bent as he ran, then his feet stopped moving and momentum carried him to the ground. His breath left him as he landed face first, inches from Raven. He didn't scream, but the shock on his face was plain and obvious. Raven wanted him alive and hadn't aimed for vital areas. If the young gangster got treatment, he'd live. If not…

But White's fate wasn't top priority. The other cars speeding toward the scene were getting closer. Raven jumped over White's now-curled body and ran to the BMW. The engine still chugged. He dived behind the wheel and left a patch of rubber behind. Raven aimed the car in the direction the bus had gone and hoped he wasn't too late. He didn't want to lose the bus on the motorway.

He caught up quickly with the slower bus. Less than a mile to go. The women aboard looked out through the back window. He saw their faces in the glow of the headlights. Some looked scared. Others showed resignation.

Then an idea flashed through Raven's mind.

The bus driver would recognize the BMW...

Raven stepped on the gas and sped by the bus, cut in front with a decent gap between them, and tapped the brakes twice. Then he pressed the pedal down. The BMW slowed, and the bus slowed with it; when both came to a halt, Raven hopped out. Only then did the bus driver see the deception. He yelled to somebody inside. The driver was still yelling when Raven shot him through the glass. The older pane, not laminated as well as the newer SUV, offered no protection. The .45 slug punched a clean hole through the glass to turn the driver's face into a mask of red flesh turned inside out.

Inside, the women screamed.

A second gunman escaped the bus out the rear door. Raven heard it slam and the man's feet scrape the pavement. Raven ran to meet him. He swung the .45 as the gunner appeared around the corner. The steel gun smashed into the man's head; he crashed against the bus and fell to the ground and Raven shot him twice.

The oncoming cars were almost to him. But now another sound joined the fray. *Sirens.*

Not all of the incoming cars had flashing cheery lights on their roofs, but a few did. Cops. Maybe even MI5 or Special Branch. Raven ran back to the BMW. The women aboard the bus cried out to him, but with police near, they'd get more help than Raven had any hope of providing. He took off in the BMW and left the battle behind.

He made it to the A2, called Ana and gave her an update. She needed to reach out to her MI5 contacts right away and advise of his participation, and to check the ship. She hung up after a curt "okay" and Raven allowed himself a relaxing sigh.

He hadn't been wrong after all.

———

"STOP!"

The order came from MI5 agent Declan Barlow as his driver reached the bus. The agents in the other cars, as well as the uniformed special weapons officers assigned to them, checked out the wrecked cars and the bodies strewn in the roadway.

Barlow, Taylor, and the rest of their crew had also been at the Port of Dover, but at another warehouse far from Crawford & Son. They were at the location their dead informants had told them about. Barlow now realized they'd been fed false information as if the two informants discovered and passed them a false lead, which was how the Whites knew they were traitors.

When they heard the crackles of gunfire on the road and the emergency calls from port security, Barlow ordered the crew to leave their stakeout and intercept. It was then he knew they'd been fooled, but who was shooting?

He and Mick Taylor saw the women in the bus and ran to let them out. One by one, the frightened women stepped out, but none of them spoke English. Barlow heard them utter a mix of dialects he didn't understand. The women knew he and his men were there to help, and Barlow radioed for emergency medical services. The MI5 agents sat the women along the side of the road, and the women comforted each other. Barlow found himself at a loss as to what to do. Then one of his men yelled:

"Declan! This one's alive! It's James White!"

Barlow and Taylor ran to two officers tending to the wounded James White. Barlow couldn't hide his grin.

"You responsible for this lot, James?"

The gangster, on his back, face twisted in pain and bleeding from his wound, only groaned in reply.

Barlow was so focused on White he didn't see Mick Taylor ease away to go somewhere else.

CHAPTER TWENTY-SEVEN

In Washington, D.C., Callum Hill remained seated in the brown leather chair, arms folded, looking sour. His colleagues stood around in clusters, talking about various things, filtering out of the Senate chambers now that the end of the day had arrived. His resolution to stop the missile sales had been the last item voted on, and it went down to near-unanimous defeat. Only three votes in favor—Hill, Roberts, and Bennett. The Three Musketeers, as they'd been teasingly referred to.

The missile sales would continue until…when? Probably for the foreseeable future. Which meant the chance of theft by bad actors remained a possibility. His idiot colleagues, pressured to vote no or not, couldn't see what he saw.

Because he knew what was going to happen. Eventually.

Zachary Roberts came over and sat beside him. Jacqueline Bennett sat on the other side.

"We tried," Hill said.

"Look at it this way," Senator Roberts replied, "it's on

record. The concerns are out there. Broadcasters keep everything—so does the internet. When a bunch of yahoos grab those missiles, or the Saudis decide to make a few extra bucks on the side, we'll bring out those quotes and smear these assholes so bad they'll have no choice but to vote to halt the sales."

"Zachary?"

"Yeah, Cal?"

"You talk too damn much."

Jacqueline Bennett laughed first, followed by a hearty guffaw from Zachary. Callum Hill liked seeing the other Senators who remained look their way. The Defeated Musketeers. They weren't supposed to be laughing after a humiliating defeat. But they were.

Screw you, bastards.

"I think we need ourselves a few drinks," Zachary Roberts said. "Let's go take the edge off."

Hill and Jacqueline agreed. Zachary let Hill take the lead as they left the Senate chamber.

———

IN HUNTSVILLE, ALABAMA, WHAT CALLUM HILL FEARED WAS coming to pass.

Crews at the weapons factory loaded crates full of rockets into the back of an armored semi-truck trailer. The crates would be driven south to Mobile and the shipyards on Pinto Island, not far from the memorial to the USS Alabama battleship.

The attack happened on I65.

Rahmil's strike team, still watching the weapons plant as

the semi departed, followed in a beefed-up box truck. The team leader, Wafiq Sabri, occupied the seat next to the driver. They only needed one crate of missiles, and Sabri's plan was solid. He communicated via handheld radio with a helicopter pilot flying nearby.

The semi had two escort trucks full of armed personnel to protect the shipment. The weapons factory contracted with a PMC to provide the armed security. The chopper would take care of them with a few machine gun blasts. Sabri wanted to keep his ground crew out of the line of fire as much as possible.

Sabri wanted the helicopter pilot to fly alongside the roadway, blast the escort trucks, and then force the semi to stop. From there, he and his ground crew would raid the semi and leave behind a present for the Americans to enjoy.

After the pilot acknowledged the order, the attack began.

A steady stream of traffic rolled along I65, but it was mid-morning traffic, nothing heavy like the afternoon commute. The lightness worked to Sabri's advantage, and the gunners aboard the chopper.

He watched the chopper fly above the roadway through his window. The pilot began to descend, keeping pace with the flow of traffic, moving closer to the edge of the road. The side door of the helicopter remained closed, but Sabri knew what waited behind. A gunner at a machine gun, who was, by now, preparing to open fire.

Only a few more seconds…

———

LOGAN HART RODE SHOTGUN IN ONE OF THE TRUCKS escorting the armored semi-truck. He knew what the cargo load consisted of; it wasn't classified. What he didn't know was the enemy chopper was sneaking up on his vehicle to cut short his twenty-eight years of life.

Hart held a customized M-4 automatic rifle between his knees, a throwback to his Marine career and deployments to the Middle East. He still looked like a Marine, too. Crew cut, well-muscled yet lean, he scanned the road and checked the side mirror for any trouble. He wasn't looking for an airborne attack.

His driver, Devin Salazar, wore a pistol on his hip. Salazar's M-4 was attached to a rack between the pair. The other team in the second truck had a similar loadout. They'd been making the "missile runs" to Mobile for a few years; it was boring duty but steady work. When they weren't in the trucks, they kept the weapons plant secure.

Neither man spoke as the time went on. It wasn't because they weren't friendly, but they were too busy concentrating. They were concentrating so hard they missed the obvious. It wasn't until Salazar caught movement out his right periphery that he shouted an alert to Hart.

"What's the chopper doing?"

Hart looked to his right. On instinct, his hands grabbed the M-4, and he flicked off the safety switch. Salazar spoke into his headset radio to alert the other truck. The helicopter in question flew low beside the roadway, following traffic.

"Pilot's screwing around," Hart said.

"Logan, I got a bad feeling—"

The helicopter looked familiar, if only by shape. It was a Bell 412, the civilian version of the military's Huey chopper. The side door facing Hart and Salazar slid back, revealing a man in black who clutched a belt-fed machine gun unmistakable to anybody with Hart's deployment experience. Salazar didn't get to finish explaining his bad feeling. The machine gun started to rip; the last thing Hart saw was the flash.

––––––

"GET READY!" SABRI SHOUTED THROUGH A PORTAL BEHIND him. His ground crew waited in the back of the box truck.

Flame flashed from the machine gun aboard the Bell 412. The salvo of heavy-caliber rounds shredded the cabin of the first truck, twisting the metal, punching holes through glass. The bulk of the truck flew off the road, tumbling across the shoulder to a sudden halt against a fence. The chopper flew closer to the freeway and opened up on the second truck. The hammering of the machine gun was audible now, albeit muted. A similar result, lots of holes, lots of glass flying; the second truck veered left into the next lane, colliding with another car and flipping over. The collision set off a chain reaction of other crashes, one car into another, the crunch of metal and screech of tires loud even through the closed windows, as the driver of the box truck steered into the right lane to avoid being hit by a wayward car.

Wafiq Sabri couldn't hide his smile. The plan was going perfectly.

The chopper flew ahead of the semi-truck and stopped a few feet away from the front end. The machine gunner aimed a burst at the front wheels. The rig sank as the tires detonated and left bare metal grinding into the pavement. Traffic ahead of the semi continued on; traffic behind screeched to a stop. Sabri heard more collisions behind him, but the roadway ahead was clearing out.

"Go!" he yelled.

The truck cabin shook as the back door folded down and his men ran out.

CHAPTER TWENTY-EIGHT

The four-man ground team ran to the semi, each of them carrying automatic rifles. One toted a pair of bolt cutters.

Two PMC operators dropped from the semi cabin, but they never had a chance to raise their weapons. Rapid blasts from the automatic rifles held by Sabri's crew cut them down. Their bodies fell to the hot pavement and stopped moving. They didn't go for the driver. There wasn't time.

The team member with the bolt cutters went to work on the padlock and zip ties holding the rear of the trailer closed. He strained with effort as he squeezed the cutters against the thick loop of the lock; finally, the bolt cutters ate through, there was a loud snap as the metal broke, and the padlock fell to the ground. The zip ties were easy. The crew opened the rear doors and revealed the crates within.

A forklift rumbled out the back of the box truck, a fifth man steering onto the street to the astonishment of motorists stuck behind. The mass of car wreckage couldn't be missed, but the forklift driver didn't dwell on the smashed metal and wisps of black smoke drifting from some of the vehicles. He drove the forklift around the box truck to the back of the semi. The crates were too heavy to lift by hand. He aimed the forks at the nearest crate to the tailgate. Sliding the forks through the gaps in the pallet the crates rested on, he easily lifted the crate and rotated the forklift to go back to the box truck. The four men with rifles followed, and soon all were back aboard and somebody activated the hydraulic gear that pulled the back ramp into the closed position.

Sabri radioed for the pilot to cover them as they pulled away. He grabbed from a tote bag at his feet a pack of C-4 with a timer. Setting the clock for one minute, he waited until his driver was passing the semi before throwing the C-4 out his window. He aimed for the still-open trailer, and the bomb sailed through the opening. He told his driver to step on it. The truck sped away, though not as fast as earlier with a full load in the back. But they were far enough away when the C-4 detonated and heard the thunder of the explosion as the remaining missiles blew up, creating a giant fireball on the freeway. Car accidents? Nuts. Now there were mass casualties for emergency responders to deal with, and when they arrived with lights flashing and sirens wailing, nobody was quite sure where to start.

———

SHE KEPT THE DRAPES CLOSED AND THE LIGHTS AT A minimum. No television, no radio, no sound if she could help it.

Tammy Granton didn't want anybody to think she was home.

Word of the incident in Dover spread through the White

syndicate quickly. Jimmy's father had called her personally to see if she had any news; she had to tell the distraught father she was still in London, had no idea what happened, had no idea where Jimmy was. The news reports claimed he'd been taken to the hospital and put under police guard. There were plans to arrest him as soon as he was out of surgery. They wanted to arrest him in his hospital bed, for heaven's sake! Not even let him recover first. He'd be trapped with no way out. Not like she could pull some Great Escape routine, not at all, but she at least wanted a chance to see him before they took him away. Now, he'd be locked behind a security screen so thick she wouldn't see him again until the inevitable trial.

Then again, she'd probably end up in a cell of her own and seeing Jimmy again wouldn't matter. She was in the trafficking operation up to her neck. As soon as the government learned of her connection, they'd be knocking on the door. They might go soft because of her father and his friendship with King Charles, but in the end, it only meant they'd probably go soft. She'd still be expected to cooperate.

She stayed curled up on the couch, covered in a blanket, because she wasn't using the heat, either. She wanted nothing to suggest she was home. If she could think of somewhere to go, she'd run. But she wasn't unknown in certain circles. When the police broadcasted her picture on the television and elsewhere, she'd have nowhere to run—except off a cliff. And the thought did occur to her. She wasn't sure why she didn't act on it. Maybe she had a big enough ego to think she might survive the unpleasantness.

She'd placed her cell phone on the coffee table but hadn't touched it all day. She wasn't sure what time of day it was, either. Tammy wanted to live in a protective cocoon and never show her face again. Then the display lit up, and the phone began to vibrate on and off, rotating slightly each time the vibration occurred. It rotated to the point where she caught a glimpse of the name on the caller ID. With a gasp, she grabbed the phone.

Mick Taylor was calling.

"Mick!" she shouted.

"Where are you?" He sounded rushed.

"I'm at home."

"Get out of there, Tammy! They're coming. Barlow and other agents. They want you for questioning."

"Where should I go?" Now she spoke in a rush, near panic.

"Anywhere! Just get out of there now!"

Tammy hung up and clutched the phone in her right hand as she swung her legs off the couch and ran into her bedroom. She cursed herself for not moving sooner. Now she knew MI5 was on the way, and she'd created a self-fulfilling prophecy. There was nowhere to run when the cops were steps behind you and closing fast.

She pulled a suitcase from the closet and tossed it on the unmade bed. Throwing it open, she turned to the closet and

—

A fist hammered on the door.

She froze in place. More pounding on the door.

"Open the door, Miss Granton!"

The voice was faint, but it was Declan Barlow for sure.

When Taylor said they were coming, he hadn't said how close.

On shaky legs, Tammy unlatched the door and opened it. Barlow stared at her through the gap. If she was trying to the innocent and surprised look, she wasn't pulling it off. She felt cold; her skin must have been pale. The sight of Barlowe backed up by three other big bruisers surely didn't help matters.

"Do you want to come in?" she managed.

"I suggest you let us in, yes, Miss Granton," Barlow said. He looked cruel, angry. Ready to tear her limb from limb. "And get ready to call your attorney."

CHAPTER TWENTY-NINE

"I'M COMING OVER."

"*No*. Don't you *dare*. My *entire* staff is here at the house."

"We need to talk, Thomas," Rahmil said. "I will be there in thirty minutes."

"Why won't you—" Granton stopped talking when he realized Rahmil was no longer on the line. He tossed the cell phone onto a nearby couch and wanted to break something. But every time he eyed an item to throw across the room, he thought of how much it cost. *No. Center yourself. Calm yourself. You know better than this.*

He remained still in the quiet room, hoping his words hadn't been overheard by anybody passing by. Stepping onto the back balcony, he surveyed the grass and trees, noted the lawn care crew hard at work. The time wasn't right for a Rahmil visit. None of his precautions were in place. If any of his staff was a spy…

Now's a wonderful time to think of that, idiot. What stopped you before?

He inhaled crisp, cool air and tried to right his mind. No,

it wasn't a good time. And no, none of his staff was spying on him. Had they been, the security services would have had him tied up in a bow long ago. He could steer Rahmil away from any prying eyes once he arrived. There were plenty of areas around the estate to have a private conversation. They could walk along the eastern edge of the property, for example.

He didn't need the added stress of Rahmi's visit. He felt enough internal pressure after learning of Tammy's arrest.

The *Daily Mail* really played it up—*Charity Mogul's Daughter Arrested in Human Trafficking Conspiracy*.

His butler had a busy morning fending off calls from journalists. His security personnel were keeping snooping reporters away. What could he tell them? *No comment* wasn't the best choice of words, but what more did he have? He'd had no idea what Tammy was into; no idea she was dating a known gangster named James White; no idea she did anything other than live by herself and work at a flower shop and spend too much time at bars and nightclubs and not enough time planning for her future.

Did he really know his daughter at all?

Had he gone so far into his own world he forgot to take care of the only child he had?

Too much stress, yeah. And now Rahmil wanted to swing by for a chat.

To talk about what? Granton hoped he hadn't somehow become a liability—was Rahmil coming to kill him? Would he do so on Granton's own property in front of witnesses?

Maybe it was for the best his staff was home, after all.

And there was still the upcoming embassy function, his attempt to woo governments to contribute to his charity, to consider. Perhaps Rahmil wanted to discuss the event and ask

Granton to cancel in light of the unwanted attention from the media.

He thought it was funny, in a sad way, the media who fawned over him and his charity's successes during the good times suddenly turned on him when matters out of his control occurred. But he couldn't very well tell them he had no idea what his daughter was doing; they wouldn't believe him. It would only fuel the fires of gossip and put at risk everything else he'd built over his lifetime.

All because he had no idea what his daughter was doing with her life.

He'd made a mistake along the way, and now he was going to pay for it.

With a sigh, he returned to the house and found his prayer mat and went into the room in which he sought Allah's favor. He had some time before Rahmil showed up, which meant he had time to seek guidance and remind himself of powers greater than him.

———

GRANTON STEPPED OUT ONTO THE PORCH AS RAHMIL PARKED his car in front of the steps.

Neither of them smiled as Rahmil climbed the steps.

"Brother," Rahmil said, coming forward to embrace Granton. The move surprised the British gentleman, and he hugged back. He hoped Rahmil didn't see the surprise on his face.

But he did, and he said, "Don't be afraid. Allah will protect us. Did you have any idea?"

"None, Rahmil, I swear."

"Where can we talk?"

"Follow me."

They started walking along a stone path set in the grass to the eastern side of the property where trees lined a stone wall marking the edge of the estate.

"We're far enough so nobody can hear us," Granton said, "and nobody will be able to identify you."

"You're afraid of a spy?"

"No," Granton said. "But if MI5 ever questions my people—"

"Of course. I know it's a risk, but we had to talk in person. I know what happened with your daughter is a shock. More of a shock than you can describe."

"I appreciate your understanding. And I want to cancel the embassy event."

"We can't."

"Rahmil, the publicity will scare people away. They see the words *human trafficking* and my name in the same sentence—"

"Did you know?"

"I told you, I did *not*."

"Have you sent your daughter a lawyer?"

"I called my solicitor this morning, yes. She has good counsel."

"And you've been avoiding the press?"

"Absolutely. My guards only had instructions to let you through. Reporters have been snooping around the neighborhood trying to get close to me."

"You have to make a statement," Rahmil said. "Don't go through your attorney or a spokesperson from the charity. Do it yourself. You must go on record and not being aware of your daughter's activities, but as a loving father, you want her to have the best defense and to get to the truth of the matter."

LONDON ASSAULT   211

Granton frowned. "What good will it do? The press isn't interested in facts. They want gossip and speculation."

"It will build goodwill for you. Everybody can identify with a father who has a child gone off the reservation."

"And if it doesn't help? If the embassy cancels?"

"If the embassy cancels, it's out of your control. You need to be proactive with them, too, and have a different conversation."

"You only want your shot at Wallace."

"If we don't get Wallace under our control," Rahmil said, "the rest of my plan falls apart. I've taken too many risks to keep it in motion as it is, Thomas. We need to see it through."

"You have to understand, Rahmil—I'm not in a proper frame of mind right now."

"Which is why you should leave everything to me, brother. Do what I tell you, and we will achieve the victory we've worked very hard for."

Granton only nodded. He couldn't find the words to reply.

CHAPTER THIRTY

It wasn't easy getting close to the Granton estate this time.

The breaking news sent reporters to the house like ants over spilled honey. Armed guards turned them away from the main gate. Piper Shaw didn't spot a roving patrol, so she parked her car further down the hill than her last visit and went for a hike. The soft ground didn't help her move fast. Her shoes kept sinking. But she climbed the hill overlooking the western portion of the property and found a cluster of trees in which to hide. Her camera with the zoom lens did the rest.

The same rental car she'd seen before was parked in front of the house once again. *Rahmil's car.* Was he visiting for another conference? And how long would he stay this time since Granton wasn't receiving other visitors?

Rahmil hadn't left his hotel since his previous visit, and keeping an eye on him proved difficult. Raven was having all the fun with the gun battle in Dover, stumbling onto a crime Thomas

LONDON ASSAULT 213

Granton wasn't involved with. She felt vindicated—Raven had been wrong about the daughter, but there wasn't time to gloat. Whatever Tammy had been into must have thrown her father for a loop, and now he and Rahmil were having an emergency meeting. She hoped Tammy's scheme didn't scare off whatever the two men had planned. If Rahmil split the country now, if they began covering their tracks, it put the whole mission in jeopardy.

She watched the pair stroll back to the house from the east side, and they stopped at Rahmil's car. A handshake. Smiles. They'd agreed to something—to continue? Rahmil climbed into his car and drove away. Granton watched him go, then went back into his house.

How much more evidence did Ana need? Rahmil wasn't talking to Tammy, he was talking to her father.

Piper hurried down the hill to her car and drove faster than she should have to catch up with Rahmil's rental. She followed him back to the city. Rahmil didn't return to the Corinthia Hotel. He instead ventured further downtown to an electronics shop. She knew the place—run by Middle Easterners, they sold phones, radios, televisions, computers, anything an electronic hobbyist required. Was it actually a front for Rahmil's organization? She parked up the street and went back on foot, using the sidewalk crowd for cover. Piper found an alley across the street from which to watch. The alley wasn't smelly but still littered with debris. The shops on either side were benign. A dress shop with young women going in and out chattering about this and that, and martial arts studio. Through the wall, Piper heard the grunts of training and shouts of instruction.

Piper figured breaking into Rahmil's hotel room wasn't going to reveal much. No way would he keep anything sensitive where he slept. Perhaps further evidence waited within the shop?

Life went on around her, citizens unaware of the intrigue playing out around them. Cars and buses and bicyclists filled the street. Tourists snapped pictures and consulted maps with faces full of confusion or wonder. They didn't need to know what was happening. Piper only wanted to keep them from being hurt. And the longer Ana and Raven wasted time when the proper course of action was obvious, the greater the chances of failing to keep the public out of harm's way.

It was frustrating to say the least.

She snapped a picture of the storefront with her phone. She'd found another piece of the puzzle, and the shop deserved a much closer inspection when the time was right.

———

DECLAN BARLOW, ALONE, LEFT HIS CAR ON THE STREET AND entered a restaurant called *Vic's*. It was a private club for members only, empty at the early hour of the afternoon, and he found chairs stacked atop tables upon entering. Only one table had anybody seated around it. Billy White and two cronies.

Billy White was easy to spot, his face as familiar to Barlow as his own father's. His rough face and muscled arms stood out from the smaller stature of his companions. But their eyes fixed on him with hostility, all conversation halted for the moment.

"We're closed," White said.

"Then the door should be locked," Barlow responded. He showed his identification. "Agent Barlow, MI5. I want to talk to you, Billy."

"Come back with a warrant."

"For a conversation? Be a gentleman, Billy."

Barlow left the entryway and approached the table. The cronies shifted, one rising from his chair. Billy told the man to settle down and take his seat. Barlow halted a few feet away.

"Am I interrupting, Billy?"

"You're playing with fire, Agent Barlow."

"Maybe I am, but it's your restaurant that will burn if I drop the match."

White scowled. "What do you want?"

"I came here to gloat."

"Get it over with," the syndicate boss snapped.

"We got your kid. You're next."

"I had nothing to do with my son's activity. I'm only a humble restaurant owner trying to make a living in a very tough world."

"How cute," Barlow said. "What will you say when your kid rolls over?"

"My son will take responsibility for his action."

"Will he?"

"You people won't even let me see him."

"Correct," Barlow said. "The hospital is sealed tighter than a drum. You know what that's like, right? You've stuffed plenty of your murder victims into drums and dropped them into the ocean, right?"

Movement behind him, near the bar. Barlow sensed another man's presence but made no move. White gestured at the new arrival to step back, but Barlow knew the man was still there.

Perhaps his visit was a mistake.

Best to wrap up and get going. He couldn't take on White's entire crew single-handed.

Unlike the son of bitch in Dover who took out James White's entire unit. He still wasn't sure who the man was, but he planned to find out.

"You're on notice, Billy. I suggest you lawyer up."

"Oh, don't you worry, Agent Barlow. You're about to find out how powerful I truly am."

Barlow grinned. "Do your best."

He turned his back and went out.

CHAPTER THIRTY-ONE

THE SIGN ABOVE THE ELECTRONIC SHOP ENTRANCE READ BARNABY'S, but Mr. John Barnaby hadn't owned the shop in ten years. Upon his retirement, he sold the shop to a pair of brothers—Faraj and Sakeen al-Zakaria. They decided to keep the name because Barnaby had established himself as the premier non-brand-specific electronics store in North London, and they wanted to keep the established customer base. It also helped cover their true business behind the scenes, running cover for and supporting jihadist activity in the UK.

The al-Zakaria brothers were part of Rahmil's global network, and his visit to the shop was a planned portion of his UK visit.

Their meeting didn't take place up front. The displays of laptops and phones and other goods on offer remained under the watch of an employee, not related to the brothers but of the same mindset and belief system. Nobody who worked behind the counter depended on the shop income for their livelihood. The bulk of their earnings came from men like Rahmil, who paid them to keep an updated list of possible targets—people and places—for when the time was right to attack those targets.

Like now.

Rahmil sat in the back room with Faraj and Sakeen. They drank tea. The room was cramped with a desk, small refrigerator, and boxes of product yet to be shelved.

"Was the missile theft successful?" Rahmil asked.

"Wafiq succeeded, yes," said Faraj, who did most of the talking. He was the older of the two. Both wore casual clothes, had thick heads of hair, and were clean-shaven. They looked like college students, almost too young to be considered for subversive activity, but were in their mid-30s. Their blending with the environment around them was aided by their innocent faces. They did not have the hard faces of warriors ready to strike, or the shifty eyes of men trying to avoid detection from Scotland Yard or MI5. Both ran the shop honestly and paid their taxes; nothing untoward happened within sight of customers or passersby.

"Did you not see the news from America?" Sakeen asked.

"Been busy," Rahmil said. "Who has time to read a newspaper?"

It wasn't a true statement. Rahmil had indeed seen a newspaper in the lobby of his hotel. The front page was full of pictures and details about the gun battle at the Port of Dover. The event added another wrinkle to his mission in London, because he knew more than the authorities who were responsible for the shootout and rescue of the trafficked women.

"The Americans are trying to downplay what happened for the public," Faraj continued, "but it's hard when so many captured the incident on their cell phones. The ones not killed when the semi-trailer exploded, that is. The video is making the rounds of social media; the public is aware something other than what the government says actually happened, but there isn't much they can do except speculate.

"The government itself," Faraj said further, "is on full alert. They want to know where the missiles are going, who took them, the usual. But Wafiq says they are already out of the country and on their way to us."

"Plane or boat?"

"Boat, of course," Faraj said. "We have established smuggling routes to get the missiles into London, but it only works if they come by boat."

"Very good. You have the reconnaissance information?"

Sakeen picked up a spiral binder from the cluttered desk and handed it to Rahmil, who opened it to the first picture.

"Is this the M5 motorway?" Rahmil asked.

"It is. From the edge of the road, out of traffic," Sakeen said. "We can park the launch vehicle there, and we'll be within range of GCHQ. The missiles will take two minutes to reach the target."

Rahmil nodded. The next set of pictures showed the GCHQ headquarters, the "donut" building at the center of the facility. The Government Communications Headquarters was one of the main instruments of intelligence in the United Kingdom, responsible for signals intelligence (SIG-INT) and other strategic data for the government and armed forces. GCHQ maintained a large database of jihadist activity and those involved, and Rahmil wanted to strike at the section of the donut building where those records were maintained and cultivated—the eastern side of the donut. Faraj and Sakeen had more photographs within the spiral notebook, ones taken on scene and close-ups downloaded from the internet.

Rahmil closed the binder.

"Is the team prepared?"

"We have the vehicle," Faraj said, "and the launch platform. All we need are the missiles."

"And they should arrive—"

"Within seventy-two hours."

Rahmil handed back the binder. He told the brothers to carry on and drank some tea. They spoke about logistical matters next, what other equipment the missile team might require. Rahmil wanted them to have everything they needed for such an important mission. He wanted to set back the UK's anti-terror efforts as far as he could, delivering a direct blow to the heart of their information-gathering center. He wanted to show the Brits none of them were safe from his reach, or the reach of any other dedicated holy warrior.

The mission posed great risks. If the truck broke down, if a policeman discovered them before launch—many risks, but nothing they couldn't handle as long as they remained cold and detached and addressed potential problems before they became reality.

The problems they couldn't plan for would have to take care of themselves if they occurred.

Same as always.

Rahmil wrapped the meeting and exited the shop, walking to where he'd parked his car. He drove off, unaware of the woman following him at a discreet distance.

———

LONDON ASSAULT 221

Piper noted Rahmil remained at the electronics shop for almost a half hour. He left without buying anything.

She and Raven for sure needed to go back and see what secrets lay within. The shop itself had a big reputation in London; they wouldn't leave anything sensitive out in the open.

She stayed on Rahmil's tail all the way back to his hotel.

CHAPTER THIRTY-TWO

RAHMIL LET HIS MIND WANDER AS HE EASED THROUGH traffic. The problem with the congestion was picking out somebody following him, but he was confident in his anti-surveillance maneuvers. He'd make a few extra turns before reaching the hotel, when traffic opened up, to make sure. Even if he was stopped, he had nothing illegal on him. He was simply a businessman from Cairo making connections in London.

Raven. It was Sam Raven who was responsible for Dover, but Rahmil had no hand in that operation. The news reports stated the White syndicate was connected, with the son of the syndicate boss wounded and in the hospital and under arrest. How did the incident explain Raven's peek into Thomas Granton's life? Or was it a side trip, an unexpected piece of action, because Raven wondered if the daughter was involved in her father's work? The more Rahmil thought it over, the more he realized he was correct. Raven had stepped onto a rabbit trail, and it didn't lead to Thomas Granton. But he was sure the American would retrace his steps and find another lead very quickly.

Rahmil had to do something fast to throw Raven off, keep him occupied. Maybe even find a way to get rid of him in the process. And Rahmil wanted to do so without exposing himself or his plan against GCHQ.

His idea might require giving away a few secrets. But only what he wanted Sam Raven to know. With a slight grin, Rahmil continued through traffic.

Every problem had a solution.

———

RAVEN WAITED FOR THE CONVERSATION TO BEGIN BEFORE venturing downstairs. He heard Ana's voice clearing, joined by a male voice he didn't recognize. Once they started talking, he went down to join them.

He found Ana Gray and Declan Barlow, her MI5 contact, in the living room. Barlow paced while Ana sat. The tea she'd set out on the coffee table remained untouched.

Barlow paused mid-sentence when Raven entered the room. He looked at Raven and didn't smile.

"Is this him?"

"That's him," Ana said. "Sam, this is Declan Barlow of MI5. Agent Barlow, Mr. Sam Raven."

"Mr. Barlow," Raven said.

"Mr. Raven."

The two shook hands warily. Barlow remained stoic and gave Raven the idea he was unhappy.

Raven said, "What happened to the women on the bus?"

"They're getting help," Barlow said. "All of them were in

bad shape, starving, dehydrated. Told us they'd been kept in a hold, jammed in like sardines. Not pleasant at all."

Raven helped himself to a cup of tea and sat on the couch opposite Ana. Barlow remained on his feet.

"I suppose," the MI5 man said, "I owe you a thank you."

"I'm glad you showed up," Raven told him.

"We had bad information. Our sources told us to watch a different dock. But we were close enough to hear the gunfight."

"You were saying, Declan?" Ana prompted.

"Right," the MI5 man said. "James White remains in the hospital, and Tammy Granton is also in our custody. We've established no connection between the Whites and Rahmil. If they are in league, it is not immediately obvious. That's our official line. My opinion? There never was a connection. Tammy and her boyfriend were working on their own for Billy White."

Raven nodded. It wasn't a hard conclusion to reach.

Barlow continued. "The attention *must* remain on Thomas Granton, as much as I dislike what the inevitable solution seems to be."

"What about the leak?" Ana said.

"We have a lead," Barlow told her. "Or, more accurately, I myself have a lead. I've personally been doing the follow-up. I'm certain we have a rat. But I'd like him to nibble on the cheese a little longer."

The three paused as the front door opened and closed. Presently, Piper Shaw entered the room. She stopped short when she saw the guest standing over the seated Raven and Ana.

"What did you find out, Piper?" Ana said.

"I have a new place for us to check out," Piper said and

explained about Barnaby's Electronics while Raven poured her a cup of tea. She took a seat near Raven.

"And Rahmil is still at the Corinthia?" Raven asked.

"He's there."

"I want to see this electronics shop," Raven said.

"It's not on our radar," Barlow admitted. "I'd like a closer look, too. But I'll do it on my own. It's best I'm not seen with you. No offense, of course."

"None taken," Raven said.

"We're not used to your tactics, Mr. Raven."

"But you know my reputation."

"I do. I also know this isn't your first time in London. But please, keep the carnage to a minimum after this, okay?"

"I'll do my best."

The MI5 man didn't look assured.

————

Barlow drove his car away from Ana Gray's fancy house and remained in a sour mood. Raven and his unorthodox methods didn't contribute to his mindset; it was the mole hunt. He knew the identity of the leak, and he didn't know how to handle the information.

In the hectic aftermath of the action in Dover, he'd taken advantage of the task force's distraction and did a deep dive on the members of his team. He'd found his needle in the MI5 haystack very quickly. Mick Taylor. His partner. His friend of many years. Taylor had phoned Tammy Granton prior to her arrest. It only meant one thing. Now he had to gather more evidence before taking what he found to his superiors. Which did not include Squad Leader Fitch.

Barlow wanted a motive. He wanted a *why*. He wanted to know what made Taylor do what he did.

It wasn't a task he looked forward to.

Piper wasn't happy either.

Ana told her to get back on Rahmil's tail, and without a reason to argue, she agreed. She parked her car down the street from the Corinthia Hotel. She'd found his car in the garage; he was in his suite for the night.

Piper was tired of watching and waiting. So far, the only action they'd seen was Raven blasting away at bad guys not related to bringing Leslie's murderers to justice. She knew it was no different than what she had to deal with at MI6, and it was one of the reasons she'd left. The spy business was the same no matter where one practiced their craft. She was a good soldier who followed orders, so until Ana and Raven got their shit together—and then she stopped thinking because Rahmil's car pulled out of the garage. She started her own and trailed after him. It wasn't a long drive. Rahmil stopped at a restaurant called Vic's. Piper knew who owned the place—Billy White.

Now what? she wondered.

This was an unexpected development. And she had no way of getting inside to listen to what Rahmil had in mind.

CHAPTER THIRTY-THREE

Rahmil wore his best suit. He wanted to make a good impression.

He approached the hostess behind the front counter. She was a bright-eyed blonde with a cherry attitude and she asked if he wanted a table for one.

"I'm here to see Billy White," Rahmil said.

"I'm sorry, who?"

"Billy White. The owner."

She didn't respond, but Rahmil saw her reach under the counter. Was she pressing a call button?

"I don't know if he's here tonight," she said.

"He's here," Rahmil said. "Please tell him I know who shot his son."

"His—*what*?"

"Tell him."

Another man came over. He was bigger than Rahmil, broad-shouldered and big-chested, and he looked like a brick wall. "What's the problem?" he said to the blonde.

"He wants to see Mr. White."

The man addressed Rahmil.

"Why do you want to see Mr. White?"

"Tell him I know who shot his son."

The big man flinched. He glanced around, making sure other customers didn't hear. The restaurant was packed, every table full, the buzz of conversation filling the room. Diners were too busy eating to see the drama playing out in the entryway.

"Wait here," the big man said. He turned and went toward the bar, his long arms at his side. His arms looked like thick branches attached to a giant oak.

Rahmil smiled at the blonde. "I'm sorry if I disturbed you."

She gave him a weak smile. "Nobody ever comes in and asks for Mr. White. He works in the back and we're not allowed to see him."

"Well," Rahmil said, "he's not an easy man to reach." Rahmil excused himself and found and sat on the padded bench near the door. The hostess looked nervous as she waited for another new arrival to take her mind off his arrival.

Presently a party of four arrived. She turned her smile loose on them, grabbed menus, and led them to a table. Rahmil figured she was glad for the escape.

The big man returned. His face remained impassive. Rahmil stood to meet him.

"Follow me, please," the man said.

Rahmil followed in the big man's wake as they weaved through tables, past the bar, and down a short hallway to a closed door. The big man knocked twice. A voice yelled for him to enter. The big man opened the door and Rahmil followed him through.

Billy White sat behind a desk, his aged face examining

Rahmil as the big man stood to one side. The man gestured for Rahmil to raise his arms and gave Rahmil a thorough pat down. He turned to his boss. "He's clean."

"Who are you and what do you mean you know who shot my son?" Billy White said.

"My name is Rahmil."

"What's in this for you?"

"The man who shot your son is named Sam Raven. He's an American, a former intelligence officer doing a job, I believe, for MI5. The focus of his job is Thomas Granton, and he discovered your son's activity by following Granton's daughter, Tammy."

"And?"

"Raven's interference at the Port of Dover wasn't intentional. It just happened. But he's the one who shot your son and brought the current unpleasantness to your door."

"Unpleasantness. That's a cute way of putting it."

"All the same, he's your man."

"And what do you want out of this?"

"We want the same thing. Sam Raven didn't find what he was looking for with the woman and your son, and now he's trying to find another thread linking Thomas Granton to *my* activity."

"And your activity is what? You gonna blow something up for Allah?"

"Not quite. Not at all, actually."

"Good. I may not be an honest man, but I'm not going to let somebody like you hurt my country."

"Mr. Granton and I don't want any unpleasantness same as you. If we don't get rid of Sam Raven, he's going to do significant damage to us both."

"I still don't get why you're telling me this without asking for something in return."

"I can't spare the men to deal with Raven," Rahmil said. "And I think you'd like to do the honors yourself."

"Ah ha. So that's your angle."

"Am I wrong, Mr. White?"

"No, you're not wrong. You got a picture of this Raven fellow?"

Rahmil indeed had a printed photograph of Sam Raven. He advised both men he had to reach inside his jacket. The big man tensed. White told him to settle down. Rahmil withdrew the picture and handed it to the big man. The big man handed the picture to Billy White.

The old man examined the photograph with cold eyes. He placed it on his desk.

"All right. I know what he looks like. Where do I find him?"

"I don't know where he is, but I do have a suggestion."

"What?"

"Have your men follow me, and he will come to them."

———

"I HAVE ANOTHER LEAD WHO MIGHT COME IN HANDY eventually," Ana Gray said.

Raven sat beside her in front of the double computer monitors in her office.

"Who?" he asked.

Ana's hands worked the keyboard. "The man who recruited Granton into Rahmil's organization."

A picture appeared on one of the monitors, an older man with gray hair and a narrow face. "This is Borja Elim. He's

LONDON ASSAULT 231

Rahmil's key man in Cairo. He was one of the men Granton met with on one of his Middle East trips. I don't know how MI5 missed him among the other suspects, but here he is."

"He'll come in handy later," Raven said. "For now, I think we should focus on the electronic shop Piper mentioned."

"You want to drive by and take a look?"

"Sure. Maybe I'll buy a trinket or two."

Raven didn't buy anything, but his perusal through the shop gave him an idea of what to expect when he went back with Piper.

———

THE AIR INSIDE THE WAREHOUSE WAS STALE, BUT THEY wouldn't be there long.

By Rahmil's watch, they'd only been waiting a little over an hour, having arrived well before the appointed time.

The missiles were in the UK and on their way to him. The mission to attack GCHQ was getting close. Almost all of the pieces were in place. But Rahmil needed to make a few changes if he was going to pull Raven into the crosshairs.

Rahmil yawned. The late hours and stress of the Granton situation were beginning to take a toll. But he knew success wasn't far away. There was Granton's embassy party coming up, and Rahmil's plan to trap Defense Minister Gordon Wallace into aiding the cause. Without Wallace, the attack on GCHQ couldn't happen. The attack also required the missiles stolen from the United States. Rahmil tolerated the stale air in the warehouse because he'd see the missiles for the first time within minutes.

In the meantime, he paced the empty floor, kicking lazily

at pieces of stray debris. His contacts from Barnaby's Electronic Shop, the brothers Faraj and Sakeen, sat on an empty wooden crate. The young men bent their necks into their phone screens. Rahmil shook his head. Typical young people. Forget that, he decided, typical time wasting in general. Rahmil had noticed plenty of older people gazing into their phones as if they were crystal balls, too, during idle times. And not-so-idle times.

When they heard the chug of a worn diesel motor outside the side door, Faraj and Sakeen put away their phones and jumped into action. They ran to the side door. It slid open on wheels at the bottom edge and a track at the top. Faraj unlocked the door while his brother pushed it open. The rumble of the metal door overpowered the sound of the van. Rahmil stepped out of the glare of the headlights with a raised arm in front of his face. The van eased into the warehouse, and with squeaking brakes, stopped in the middle of the empty floor. The brothers pushed the side door closed and Faraj slammed the lock home. Rahmil reached the van first. He and the driver nodded at each other, but neither knew the other's name.

Rahmil stepped aside when Faraj reached for the door handle. The hinges squeaked like the brakes.

"Any problems?" Faraj asked.

"None." The driver hopped out. He was shorter than Faraj and wore dirty overalls. "Everything went fine." The driver turned to Rahmil. "Missiles ready for inspection."

"Let's see them," Rahmil said.

The three men went to the rear. Sakeen drove a forklift to them from a corner, the motor of the forklift whining as Sakeen angled for the van. The driver and Faraj opened the rear doors. Rahmil decided the brothers needed to upgrade their equipment—the van, the forklift, the warehouse—all of it needed attention.

A lone crate sat in the back. Sakeen ran the forks of the lift under the support pallet, lifted the crate off the van floor, and reversed the forklift a few feet from the rear bumper. He set the crate down. The driver grabbed two crowbars from his van. He passed one to Faraj, and the pair went to work popping the crate apart. Rahmil stood back. This was their show. He let them take care of the work. He was willing to let Faraj and Sakeen stare at their cell phones till they went blind if they remained as efficient as he saw them right now.

The crate cracked and popped as Faraj and the driver levered the crowbars against the planks. When the top and sides were removed, Rahmil frowned at the sixteen missiles within their long rectangular containers. A lot of straw was mixed in with the containers. Faraj and Sakeen brought the containers out and set them on the floor. It took both of them, holding the container at each end, to move the missiles from the crate. The containers looked about ten feet long to accommodate the nine-foot projectile sealed within.

The driver used a broom from his van to clean up the straw that spread onto the floor. Faraj opened the top container. He raised the lid to reveal the missile snug in a padded foam bed. The finned tube was painted white; the tip, the explosive warhead, wearing a shade of dark red.

"Launch vehicle?" Rahmil asked.

Faraj gestured to the van.

"Are you serious?"

"It's mechanically sound," Faraj said. "Don't let the dilapidated state fool you."

The driver nodded. "We'll rig the launch platform in the

back, cut a hole in the roof, and shoot from there. The jet blast from the rockets will set the van on fire."

Rahmil remained skeptical.

"What if we tried another way?" he said.

"What do you mean?" Faraj asked.

"Instead of firing from the roadway, let's use a boat. We can go up the Severn and hit GCHQ from there. Slightly further away, easier escape."

"We can do anything," Faraj said. But his face betrayed a hint of doubt.

Rahmil didn't blame him. He'd supervise to make sure the young men indeed didn't have any trouble.

"I will help," Rahmil said. "We need to start getting ready immediately."

"Tell us what we need to do," Faraj said.

CHAPTER THIRTY-FOUR

PIPER SHAW ASSURED RAVEN HER HACKING SKILLS WERE UP to par.

They'd find out soon enough.

They sat in another of Ana's cars, this one a Mercedes sedan, and Piper used her laptop to find the wireless signal connecting Barnaby's alarm to the local police. The signal allowed her to access the router; getting to the router allowed her to turn off the alarm.

"We're clear," she said.

"You sure?"

"Proprietary MI6 equipment," she proclaimed. "Used it a dozen times." She closed the laptop lid.

"Then let's go." Raven opened the door and stepped onto the street.

Piper hadn't explained anything about what her software was going to do, and only told him she was going to turn off the alarm system remotely. Raven trusted her not to lead them into a situation from which they'd have to shoot their way out. As long as there wasn't a backup alarm or a camera system monitoring the shop…

Piper exited the Mercedes with a tote slung over her right shoulder. She left the laptop on the floor of the car. She hadn't explained what was in the tote, either, and it didn't look like firearms.

They'd parked across the street from the electronics shop and crossed. No traffic at the late hour. Street lights hummed. A few other cars lined the street, all of them dark and cold. Raven hurried to the front of the store, stepping into the alcove of the front door. Now it was his turn to do some work. With a set of lock picks, he opened the door, and they slipped inside. He closed the door, turned the locks, and lost himself in the darkness within.

Piper took out a pan flash and shined it around. The store displays were orderly, nothing out of place. Their job was to make sure everything was still in place when they left. But they had no interest in the display area. Raven and Piper wanted to see what the shop owners had in the back.

Learning who currently owned Barnaby's and their background proved easy. Ana gathered the information with a few keystrokes. Faraj and Sakeen al-Zakaria had a clean record as far as the London police were concerned, but Ana dug deeper. She found they were the offspring of Yosef al-Zakaria, a very dead terrorist leader killed by MI6 five years ago. His sons may have kept their hands clean, but if they were entertaining the likes of Rahmil, they only did so to become London sleeper agents. It added up to Rahmil planning a strike against London. Raven wondered how Granton's money funded the plan, if Rahmil was indeed setting up a mass casualty event.

Piper stepped past Raven using the pen flash, and guided them around the back of the counter to a narrow hallway.

Bathroom, store room—office. The door was locked. Raven used the picks again and unlocked the door. They went through the doorway to a cluttered room with a desk. Apparently, the store room wasn't big enough, as boxes of various gadgets were stacked on the walls. The computer atop the desk remained on, the screen blank. Piper dropped into the squeaky chair in front of the desk and flipped on the monitor. The screen brightened to show a password prompt. With the tote bag on her lap, she unzipped it and rooted through the gear within. She pulled out a USB thumb drive and found the port alongside the monitor.

"What's this?" Raven said.

"More stuff from MI6," she said.

"Did you steal it or something?"

"More like I never gave it back, and they never asked."

"How efficient."

"Some things about the British are a myth, Raven."

He grinned.

A red light on the thumb drive blinked rapidly.

"What's happening?" Raven asked.

"The USB drive has a program on it that can break passwords and copy files. We'll have what they have and they'll never know we were here."

"Good." Raven examined the office further. Boxes, clutter, all around. A tight space to work in. He wondered if the brothers found ways to not spend time in the so-called office. "I have a feeling we could leave a mess behind and they wouldn't notice," he added.

"This better be worthwhile," she said. "If Rahmil is only using this place simply as a point of contact—"

"Let's think about that if this gizmo of yours leaves us at a dead end."

238   BRIAN DRAKE

The red light turned solid. Piper turned off the monitor again, yanked out the thumb drive, and dropped it back into the tote bag. She pulled the zipper closed.

Raven and Piper started for the exit, Raven locking the office door behind them.

"What else is in the bag?" he asked.

"Surprises," she said.

Outside, a need for such "surprises" waited for them.

———

THE STREET LOOKED CLEAR. RAVEN TOLD PIPER TO HANG back while he ventured onto the sidewalk. The night remained quiet and cold. No threats present. He gestured for her to come out and passed her the key fob to the Mercedes.

"Get the motor going."

Her shoes tapped a rhythm on the pavement as she crossed. Raven bent before the lock and used the picks to re-lock the shop door. His task complete, Raven picketed the pick set and followed after Piper.

Bright headlamps flashed from Raven's left, bathing him in their glare. A gun cracked.

Raven was already diving for the blacktop when the shot sounded, the whistle above his head signaling how close his war without end almost came to a permanent halt.

He yelled for Piper to get out of there as he took out his .45 auto pistol. The shooter in the car rolled out the passenger side, but the glare of the headlights made him impossible to see. More shots nicked the blacktop as Raven ran back toward Barnaby's. Reaching the cover of a bus stop, he used the bench to hide and finally saw the assassin making a break in his direction.

LONDON ASSAULT   239

Piper fired from the Mercedes, catching the assassin in the neck. The killer collapsed and tumbled end over end and finally bumped into the curb. Raven raised his aim to the car. The driver revved the engine and tried to get away, but Raven opened fire first. The Nighthawk Talon spit flame; Raven traced a line of shots across the windshield. The car lurched toward him, out of control. Raven rolled into the street as the car plowed into the bus stop. The impact uprooted the bench from the sidewalk, hurtling it forward into the front glass window of the shop next door to Barnaby's. The crash rang loud in Raven's ears, almost louder than the gunfire. The car followed the bench through the shattered pane, with a wave of glass spilling onto the sidewalk, but the narrow brick window frame closed on either side of the car like a vice grip and stopped the car from going all the way through. It stuck half in and half out, engine still running. Raven dashed to the Mercedes. Piper sped away before he shut the passenger door.

"I told you to leave," he said. She made a sharp left and pressed on the accelerator. The Mercedes picked up speed.

"And abandon you?"

"What you took from the computer is too important to lose."

"You're alive, right? Is that a *thank you* I heard?"

Raven grunted. He buckled his seat belt. "Thanks. Good shooting."

"The killer was *not* Middle Eastern."

"I noticed in the very brief second I saw his face."

"Remember I saw Rahmil visit Billy White's restaurant?"

"I do. You think—"

"He told White you shot his kid," she said, "and now White's goons are after you."

"While Rahmil carries out his mission."

"We're running out of time, Raven."

"Get us back to Ana's and find what's on the thumb drive. I'll take the car."

"To do what?"

"I'm removing Billy White from the picture. For keeps."

Piper drove on.

CHAPTER THIRTY-FIVE

RAVEN SCALED THE WALL AROUND BILLY WHITE'S HOME AND cared nothing about setting off the alarm. It was the best way to get the fight going without delay.

The electronic sensors rigged across the top undoubtedly sent an alert to the crew in the big house, and he knew White's gunmen weren't prepared for a direct assault. All he had was his pistol, but the gunners would provide whatever else he needed via their weapons. As a grizzled and cranky firearms instructor in Oregon once told him, "*What makes you think you're going to fight with your gun?*"

He was conducting a hasty and perhaps even sloppy attack, but he had experience on his side.

Raven ran across open grass. A large gazebo lay ahead. He ran faster to reach it, slipping under the thatched roof. He took cover behind a low wall and watched the house.

At least four stories, a wrap-around porch with a rail, a one-story side structure extending from the side of the house he faced. It was the one-story attachment where lights snapped on within. Presently, a door opened, and three men hustled out. One was talking. All three carried weapons—Raven thought they bore the silhouettes of shotguns, not full-auto SMGs.

"Split up," one said. "Check the east wall. Stay in radio contact."

The three men clutched their weapons and moved out. One jogged in Raven's direction. One headed for the wall. The third started for the back of the house.

Three on the outside. How many inside the house?

Raven took out his gun and waited. A semi-circle bar sat in the middle of the gazebo. Staying low, Raven moved behind it. All the shelves were empty. It wasn't the season for entertaining. But it was the season for shooting syndicate gunners who stepped into the gazebo looking for Sam Raven. He grinned. It was a joke only he'd find amusing.

The gunman approached at a brisk pace.

———

BILLY WHITE MESSED UP THE COMBINATION TO HIS WALL SAFE twice. His hands shook. He had a hard time hitting the buttons on the touchpad in the correct order. A third try—finally! With the correct number entered, the safe beeped. He turned the handle. Reaching inside, he pulled out a Colt .357 revolver. He hated having guns around. Possession of firearms carried a heavy penalty, heavy time in the slammer, and it was much easier to prove White kept a cache of hand-guns at his property than prove he was as mixed up in UK crime as MI5 claimed. He opened the cylinder and checked to make sure all six chambers had a cartridge inside, then snapped it closed and jammed the gun in his waistband. The door to his man cave opened. White turned. His chief house guard, Danny Wilcox, entered. Wilcox carried a short-barreled submachine gun.

"What are we facing?" White said.

"No idea."

"What do you mean 'no idea,' Danny?"

White's first thought was MI5. Special Branch. A special weapons unit. He'd promised Declan Barlow he'd show MI5 his real power, and White hadn't wanted his words to remain an empty boast. How to make the statement true had occupied his mind since Barlow's visit to the restaurant. Now his estate perimeter had been breached. Time was up. They were coming for him.

Unless…

What if…

What if it was Sam Raven outside?

Yes! Has to be!

"It's Raven!" White shouted. "The team I sent to Barnaby's hasn't come back."

"We need to get you out of here *now,*" Danny Wilcox said.

Gunfire crackled outside. Three rapid blasts. White jumped with each detonation.

"Let's go," he said and followed Wilcox out of the room.

———

RAVEN TENSED AS THE GUNMAN STEPPED INTO THE GAZEBO. The wood boards beneath the gunner's feet creaked. Raven froze. The last thing he needed to do was make a similar sound, and so far, he'd been fortunate. A hurried walk suggested the gunman was coming around the bar. Raven saw his left leg first. He fired the Nighthawk. The gunman screamed and collapsed; the impact of his body was heavy enough to shake the gazebo. Raven rose to fire two more rounds. One into the gunner's chest, the third to his head.

Raven jammed the hot pistol back under his left arm and grabbed the man's shotgun. It was a semi-auto Benelli. Raven removed the spare shell carrier on the gunner's belt and checked the cartridges. A mix of rifled steel slug and buckshot. He put the carrier on his own belt and left the gazebo. *Who's next?*

Raven ran for the house. No other gunmen ran out to meet him, but neither did anybody inside open fire from windows. He was aware of the man who'd gone around the back of the house; the other, who'd gone to look at the wall, was off to his left, somewhere in the darkness. Shotguns weren't good for long-range accuracy, though Raven corrected himself— with the rifled slugs, they'd be quite accurate indeed. And those all-steel projectiles didn't mess around when they tore into soft flesh. They utterly destroyed what they came in contact with.

A shotgun blast echoed across the estate from Raven's left. He dropped prone on the grass. The pellets or the slug didn't come near him. The gunner coming back from checking the wall had no idea who his target was, and Raven couldn't see him, either. The glow of lights from the side building didn't extend far enough.

But the light did go far enough to show Raven a little. The gunner who'd gone around the back of the house returned and shouted, "I got 'em!"

Raven rolled onto his side, bringing up the Benelli. He fired a blast. The gunner may have "got him," but Raven saw no sign of the man, and the shot he fired in response to

LONDON ASSAULT   245

Raven's missed it as well. Raven bolted for the side building, staying low under the window. He worked his way to the corner, spun around; there he was! The gunner was coming his way, staring down the length of his shotgun barrel. Raven blew his face off. Pivoted as the shotgun cycled, he looked for the third man—still nothing. A blast shattered the corner of the wall, bits of wood digging into Raven's neck and the back of his head. He ran for the back of the house, finding concealment in the shadows once again. He stole back a glance. Still no visible contact with the last gunner. Raven didn't have time to play cat-and-mouse with him. He had to get into the house and finish Billy White before the crime boss escaped.

Crossing the back patio, Raven shot out the sliding glass doors barring access. The shotgun blast created a hole big enough for him to go through, but he had to watch the jagged pieces still holding to the metal doorframe. He slipped through, fallen pieces crunching under his shoes as he entered. Raven grabbed spare ammo from the carrier on his belt and jammed fresh rounds into the Benelli's mag tube.

One gunner still out there…

But inside, it was quiet.

Until he heard footsteps pounding down steps.

Raven ran toward the sound, skirting furniture, running down a hall. Across the entryway, two men ran through a door. One looked back and fired a burst of 9mm rounds from a compact submachine gun. They chewed into the wall behind him. Raven fired back, the double-0 buckshot shredding the middle of the door. He ran to the wall beside the door, waited, and stuck his foot out to push open what remained. The door swung inward. Raven ducked low and went through—nobody fired at him. Because the two men were getting into a car.

Then somebody fired—Billy White, with a shiny revolver. He rolled down the passenger side window and extended his arm. The Magnum kicked and flame flashed from the muzzle, but Raven was already on the smooth concrete floor of the garage, Benelli extended. He pulled the trigger. The hate he saw in Billy White's intense glare over the top of the revolver vanished in a flash of red. Some of Billy splattered on the driver, who screamed, the car reversing back into another vehicle with a loud crash. Raven jumped up, fired rapidly through the windshield, turning the driver into hamburger meat same as his boss.

Still one more…

Raven slipped outside through another door and heard heavy breathing. The last gunner was circling the perimeter. Raven waited. When the gunner finally stepped around the corner, Raven slammed the stock of the Benelli into his face. The gunner's choked-off cry was the only sound he made, other than his body going *thump* on the grass. Raven swung at the side of his head. The jolt of the impact rattled his arms to the shoulders, but the blow put the man out for the count. Raven wanted somebody to tell the cops *one man* had done the job. One.

And he wasn't worried about the local cops showing up. They'd not dare enter the property until they could guarantee "safety" all around. British cops didn't take the same risks American cops did. But maybe they were the smart ones.

Raven dropped the shotgun and jogged for the wall. He could have taken one of Billy's cars, but Ana probably wanted her Mercedes back. And without any damage, unlike the Maserati that Raven wrecked in Dover.

Now he and Piper and Ana were free of distractions, and Rahmil no longer had proxy killers at his side. If he wanted Raven's head now, he'd have to divert some men to the task. Doing so would put his operation—whatever it was—in jeopardy, because with Raven on the loose, Rahmil was sure to make a mistake. And Raven planned to be there when he did.

CHAPTER THIRTY-SIX

DECLAN BARLOW WAITED IN THE OUTER OFFICE OF HIS supervisor, Lewis Doyle. Burly, balding, and gruff, Doyle was the man who'd run Barlow's department for the last two decades; Barlow had worked for him for fifteen of those twenty years. Barlow wasn't there on a happy errand. He held a file folder in his hand with all the data he'd accumulated on Mick Taylor. All the proof showing Taylor was a mole working for the White syndicate.

Not that it mattered any longer. Billy White was dead, his kid still in the hospital; maybe they could tell Taylor to be cool and quit making contact with whatever remained of the gang. Maybe there was no need to arrest him.

Barlow knew he was blowing smoke. No way they could let Taylor off, no matter what the change in situation may have been.

The outer office was a sparse as the inner office. Doyle didn't believe in an overabundance of decoration. Too much stuff, he often said, only gathers dust. He did allow his secretary to have a plant on her desk.

The secretary, a grandmother who'd served not only Doyle but his predecessor, finally showed Barlow into the main office after Doyle buzzed her on the intercom. Barlow cleared his throat as he entered, because in all the years he'd worked for the man, he'd never found Doyle at his desk. Doyle, as usual, head bent, stood at his window looking out at the river. He turned his head enough to tell Barlow to sit. Barlow took a seat in front of the desk. Doyle did not leave the window.

"What's so important, Barlow?" Doyle said. "You should be talking to your squad leader, not me."

"Agent Fitch and I aren't seeing eye-to-eye on this matter, sir."

"What matter? The leak?" Doyle turned from the window and fixed hot eyes on Barlow. "Did you find the leak? Or are you still sounding an alarm with no evidence?"

Barlow held up the file folder.

Doyle's face paled. "Oh, my goodness, you weren't wrong, were you?" His tone lost its edge, and he moved from the window to his desk. "Let me see, let me see."

Doyle took the file folder from Barlow's offered hand, and Barlow sat without talking as Doyle flipped through the sheets within.

"What is this?" the boss asked.

"Phone logs, mostly. Calls made from here, in our department, and from his home. Phone numbers associated with Tammy Granton and James White—I have pages breaking down where the calls were taken based on what cell tower was nearby. Not only are the numbers associated, but so are the locations, known White fronts, things like that. Taylor spoke with the Granton woman minutes before we arrested her, sir. I'm sure if we asked, she'd tell us he was telling her to run."

"Did you ask her, Agent Barlow?"

Barlow smiled. "I may have seen her this morning, sir."

"Agent Barlow?"

"Yes, sir, I saw her this morning."

"She admitted Taylor was tipping her off?"

"She thinks we already have him in custody."

"You think you're slick, don't you?"

"No, sir, just crafty."

Doyle grunted and returned to the file pages. "This other list—"

"Calls from his flat to, again, numbers associated with the Whites."

"I see, I see," Doyle said. "All right." He closed the file. Folding his hands and resting his forearms on the desktop, he leaned forward to look Barlow in the eye. "What do we do about it?"

"No sense humiliating the man, sir. I think we owe it to him to take him aside and let him know he's under arrest."

"No sense humiliating him? Are you serious?"

Barlow took a deep breath. "We don't need untoward gossip, sir, at least not right away. If we make a big show, nobody will get anything done the rest of the day."

Doyle nodded. "Okay. Pick two other men, and we'll get Fitch involved too. We'll bring Taylor to my private conference room and confront him there. Is he here yet?"

"He's not arrived yet, sir."

"Has he run off?"

"No. He thinks he's in the clear because Fitch doesn't believe there's a leak. He'll show up on time, sir."

Doyle nodded. "All right. Let me know when he does. Do *nothing* until I get there."

Barlow left the file with Doyle and started to leave the chair.

"Wait. Sit down."

Barlow sat.

"What do you know about the mess at Billy White's estate?"

"Somebody went out there and made a mess, sir."

"Dammit, Barlow."

"Pardon. I don't know anything more than you, sir. I wasn't part of the response team. But it sounds like we have collected enough evidence in the house itself to shut down what remains of the White Organization and put everybody involved behind bars, starting with James himself."

"Does he know his father is dead?"

"Not unless he's seen the news. Which I'm sure he has."

"Let's take care of Taylor and maybe go see James."

"Yes, sir."

This time, Barlow made it to the door without being called back.

————

"Wake up. Wake up, Raven."

Raven wasn't in the mood to wake up. But Ana kept shaking him, saying his name. He decided it was urgent and opened his eyes.

"What?"

"We found something. Get cleaned up and come downstairs."

Raven groaned, but Ana departed so fast he didn't have a

chance to argue. The ambush and attack on White's estate the previous night left him worn out. The entire effort in London was taking a toll. He needed a break. But if the enemy wasn't going to take a break, neither could he. Raven forced himself out of bed and wandered into the bathroom, where he stripped off his pajama bottoms and stepped into the shower.

Ana had tea waiting for him when he came downstairs, a hot mug of her usual English Breakfast blend, and a pair of sweet rolls. He found her, as usual, in front of her computer monitors.

"Can we function enough to listen?" she asked.

"I'm awake, Ana." He took a bite of one roll. He'd have preferred a hot breakfast but figured whatever Ana found took priority over slapping bacon in a pan.

"Piper's thumb drive," Ana said, "is a jackpot."

Raven pulled over a stray chair and sat next to her. "Impress me," he said.

———

"THESE ARE PICTURES OF THE BRITISH SECRETARY OF STATE for Defense," Ana said. "His name is Gordon Wallace. You can see they've been following him on a regular basis, tracking his activity, who he visits, all that. Full-blown surveillance."

Raven examined the picture. Wallace looked to be in good shape, with a close-cropped haircut. He walked with a military bearing; he may have been a desk man now, but he hadn't always spent his days pushing paper.

"And he didn't notice a thing."

"Neither did his bodyguards, did you notice? There's going to be some tough conversations coming if we don't stop them from grabbing him."

Raven said, "You think they *want* to grab him?"

"They want to make him talk. Reveal things."

"Like what?"

"The defenses of Buckingham Palace."

"What makes you think Rahmil has an interest in Buckingham Palace?"

Ana clicked her mouse and changed from pictures of Gordon Wallace to photos of Buckingham Palace. The pictures included all angles, albeit from a distance, including an overhead shot that either came from a satellite or a drone —probably a drone, unless Rahmil, even as a lone operator, had access to resources Raven only dreamed about.

"Then there's this," Ana continued. Another click.

A digital map of Buckingham Palace, taken from the internet, with red dots pinpointed around the palace perimeter. Most of the dots ran along the north side of Piccadilly, a stone's throw from the palace property itself.

"You think they want information out of Wallace," Raven said, "so he can tell them about Buckingham's defenses?"

"Anit-missile defenses, actually. Automatic cannons on the roof. Similar to what the White House has."

"What makes you think—wait, don't tell me."

"The CIA is going bughouse over a weapons theft that happened two days ago," Ana began, clearing the screen. She pulled up alerts from the CIA to all sections around the world. It was a basic "be on the lookout" notice and went into detail on the missile theft in Alabama and the FBI's failure to, so far, locate suspects or determine where the thieves took the missiles.

"You think Rahmil is responsible?" Raven said.

"It's a lot of work," she said, "but a perfect score.

Untraceable weapons bound for somewhere else. In this case, Saudi Arabia. A Senator tried to pass a resolution to stop these missile sales, but it failed."

"He should try again," Raven said. He set the tea mug on Ana's desk and ignored the second sweet roll. "I know how Rahmil works. He's used kidnapping tactics to get information out of people before, so we can assume Gordon Wallace is his target. He's going to, somehow, fire rockets into Buckingham Palace. But that's what I don't understand."

"What do you mean?"

"I've never known Rahmil to engage in an attack. Spend money, gather resources, sure; a full-on operation of his own?" Raven shook his head. "Maybe I missed something, and admittedly, I haven't been tracking him for ten years full time, but something about this…if he's doing it, it's for somebody else, or another reason. He's not going to do anything that doesn't benefit him somehow. Especially financially."

Ana waited.

"Does Thomas Granton have any events going on where Wallace may attend?" Raven asked.

"Yes. Embassy function tonight. Granton is going to try to charm governments into contributing. Emphasis on *try*. With his daughter locked up, I'm not sure Granton is going to be as useful to Rahmil as he's been in the past."

"Okay." Raven yawned.

"Do you want to go to the event?"

"No," he said. "I'm burned, remember? Granton knows my face. But I would like to know where I can find Mr. Wallace."

CHAPTER THIRTY-SEVEN

SECURITY WAS TIGHT AT THE DENMARK EMBASSY IN LONDON, but not so tight a flow of cars and party guests couldn't get through. Guests dressed to kill packed the main ballroom on the embassy's ground floor, with banners strung about promoting Thomas Granton Charities. Soft music from a small band almost overpowered the buzz of constant conversation, flowing libations, and dancing.

Thomas Granton was present physically but not mentally. He made the rounds and spoke to potential donors, both government and non-government, yet his thoughts were easily carried away. His daughter, Tammy, remained in MI5 custody for continued questioning; no bail hearing yet. No formal charges. The longer it took, the more he thought she might get away without charges. Perhaps they'd realize she was innocent of whatever her boyfriend had been doing. His lawyer, who'd seen her and been present during questioning, told him the potential charges were indeed serious, and he should prepare for the worst. Granton wasn't sure what *the worst* meant. He wasn't sure how to prepare for what he couldn't contemplate himself. He'd need to trust his attorney for sure.

But nobody refused to talk to him, which surprised Granton. He expected to be shunned, ignored; as he made his rounds, he found many eager to contribute to his programs. It was as if nobody knew about the drama surrounding Tammy. Their attitudes did not take his mind off matters. He knew he wouldn't relax until Tammy was out of custody and safe at home, preferably at his estate.

Granton for sure made a point to avoid Defense Minister Gordon Wallace, the tall, trim, affable man whom Rahmil had targeted for the night. He wasn't aware of what Rahmil wanted to do. He only knew to stay away lest he be connected somehow when the news broke. He had enough trouble already.

Rahmil wasn't at the embassy. He didn't want to risk facial recognition cameras picking him out of the crowd. And he wasn't one for disguises, either. He remained close but counted on proxies to take care of business with the defense minister. Granton had no idea who among the crowd was working for Rahmil; he didn't care to try and find out, either. He wanted only for his personal nightmare to end. It would take time.

He had a speech to make soon. Luckily, he'd written his remarks on note cards. Granton didn't want to wing it this time. He feared losing his train of thought. Rambling like an idiot wouldn't win him any new donors.

———

Defense Minister Gordon Wallace, a Royal Navy man, wore his dress uniform complete with ribbons and citations on the lapel.

Despite his fifty-two years, he remained one of the most eligible bachelors in London government and never had a problem attracting female company. Hair dye kept his hair dark and hid the gray; his workout regimen kept him trim; his six-foot height didn't hurt, either.

With his rum-and-Coke in hand, he made the rounds of various dignitaries and other assorted government people closely related to his position. He chatted with representatives from Germany and Italy, caught up with friends from the Dominican Embassy, chatted with a Colombian general who wanted to talk about efforts to block the flow of hard narcotics into the UK. It was while talking with the Colombian general that an attractive woman in a blue sequined dress caught his attention. He broke eye contact with the general to watch her walk by. He didn't see the general drop a tablet into the rum-and-Coke, which quickly dissolved in a rapid spread of bubbles. Wallace turned his attention back to the general, continued the conversation, and moved on. During the chat, he continued to sip his drink.

With his stomach feeling funny, he set the drink on a table and left the ballroom to find the men's room.

He didn't make it.

———

Wallace woke up on a military-issue cot in a cold basement with stone walls. Only a dangling lightbulb lit the room. He looked around the small space, and his eyes stopped on the man sitting in a metal folding chair beside the bed.

"Where…am I?"

"Usually, my guests want to first know who I am," Rahmil said.

Wallace looked at the man. He wore a Saville Row suit, Rolex, silk tie.

"Who are *you*?" he said.

"My name is Rahmil. And if you want to get out of here alive, you'll do exactly as I say."

Wallace tried to move his arms. They were raised above his head. He couldn't. His wrists were shackled to the bed frame. A glance at his ankles showed they were shackled to the lower portion of the frame, too.

He groaned.

"Head hurt?"

Wallace nodded. "Head. Stomach. What happened?"

"You need to keep your eyes off the ladies and on your drink, Minister."

Wallace let his head fall back. At least they'd provided a pillow, albeit a smelly one.

"What do you want?" he asked.

"Not much," Rahmil said. He picked up a digital camera from the floor, turned on the rear display, and held it for Wallace to see. He cycled through several pictures. Any color Wallace still had in his face faded.

"The press will be told she is a teenage runaway," Rahmil said. He set the camera down. "You were woozy but surprisingly accommodating, Mr. Minister. We didn't have to work very hard."

"You're sick."

"No. Pragmatic. You asked what I want. I'll tell you. I want access to the defense system at Buckingham Palace."

"There isn't one!"

"Nonsense, Minister. We both know there are automatic guns which will activate the second the radar sees a missile fired at the palace. The American White House has a similar system. I know you work hard to keep it a secret, but it isn't. I want access to the system. The codes to turn it off. I want it all, or those pictures go out. People are still at the party wondering where you went. I have people there asking, raising questions. Your absence has been noted. If and when we send these pictures to the press, everyone will know why you wandered off."

"I think I'm going to be sick."

"Not on my cot, please." Rahmil smiled. "And it would be a shame to ruin such a nice uniform."

"It will never work," the minister said. "An attack on the palace will never work. The palace has security even I'm not aware of. It's the best in the world. You'll never get close enough to fire *anything,* let alone a *missile.*"

"Who says I want to get close, Minister?"

Wallace frowned.

"You will hand over the codes within twenty-four hours, or the pictures go to the press. Do you understand?"

"Yes."

CHAPTER THIRTY-EIGHT

A STILL-WOOZY GORDON WALLACE REENTERED HIS HOME. His was shaking all over. He turned on the lights in his home, went to the kitchen, and swallowed a glass of water. He leaned over the sink with his elbows on the counter. He had no idea what kind of drug they'd slipped into his drink at the embassy, but he felt like a truck had hit him, backed up, and rolled over his body again.

A footstep scraped on the kitchen floor.

Wallace rose, facing the opening on his left. Another man stood there.

"Don't be afraid, Minister," said Sam Raven.

———

"ANOTHER MYSTERY MAN IS THE LAST THING I NEED tonight," Wallace said.

"My name is Sam Raven. Do you know who I am?"

"I recognize it. You don't look like your file photo, though."

LONDON ASSAULT   261

"It's an old one, probably," Raven said. "From better days."

"I could use some better days," Wallace said.

"We need to talk about what happened tonight."

"How do *you* know what happened tonight?"

"Because Rahmil and I are old enemies, and I'm here to stop what he's doing."

"He wants to launch a missile at Buckingham Palace! Can you believe that?"

"I know what he wants. The question is, what did he want with *you*?"

"I need to sit down. Let's go into the study."

Raven followed him.

———

"WHAT DOES HE WANT?"

Wallace leaned back on a couch. Raven sat on the edge of a chair close by. The study was loaded with books and model Navy ships, with awards from his Navy service adorning the walls. A ticking clock filled the silence when they weren't speaking. Raven didn't want to push the obviously tired minister, but he'd have to if the man didn't get a grip and push away the effects of the drug Rahmil's people had slipped him.

The defense minister repeated the conversation he had with Rahmil, leaving out no detail. Raven listened without comment until Wallace finished.

"Do you have access to what he wants?"

"I do."

"If he turns off the system, what happens?"

"The palace is vulnerable. But how far away does he

intend to shoot from? Security extends far from the palace grounds, there's no way—"

"I know it, and you know, he, Rahmil knows it, too. But he must have figured out what to do." Raven thought back to his conversation with Ana Gray about the rockets stolen in the United States. Nothing on the material taken from Barnaby's Electronic Shop pinpointed where they might be fired from, but he knew the answers were there, somewhere.

Raven explained the missile theft in the US and how he assumed Rahmil would use the stolen rockets.

"What we have to do now," he added, "is figure out how to handle this."

"I will not betray my country, Mr. Raven. I'd rather take my chances with a scandal. Even if it ends my career."

"Do what he says."

"Are you mad?"

"Probably," Raven said. "Rahmil has used this technique before to get information out of somebody. I think I know what we can do to thwart this, at least long enough to intercept the missiles, wherever he plans to launch them from."

"That means—"

"Getting your superiors involved. Maybe even talking to King Charles himself."

"Oh, no."

"It's the only way, minister. We need to stop Rahmil, and fast. The best way to do so is make him think he has exactly what he wants."

"I hope you're right."

"Me too," Raven said.

———

LONDON ASSAULT   263

ANA CALLED HER MI5 CONTACT, DECLAN BARLOW, AND HIS supervisor, Lewis Doyle, to her home the next day. The way she explained it to Raven, they had been the pair who came to her asking to make a quiet inquiry into Thomas Granton's affairs. And if they wanted to continue to keep the matter quiet until MI5 said otherwise, they had to learn about the latest—from her. She set up a spread of cold cuts, snacks and water in the kitchen and they gathered at the corner table to discuss the latest.

Raven sat without talking as Ana went over the material found at Barnaby's and what happened at the Embassy of Denmark during Granton's party the night before. Barlow and his boss sat beside each other, and each listened intently, with the elder Doyle growing more irritated with each passing moment.

Finally, he stopped Ana in mid-sentence. He said, "What kind of ego does Rahmil have that he thinks he can lob missiles at Buckingham Palace?"

Ana gestured at Raven. "He's the expert. Raven?"

"When Rahmil and I last confronted each other, he'd done something similar with a NATO colonel and a list of spies. This is his usual MO The more I look at it, the more I see he hasn't refined his plans in the last ten years and sticks to what works. If we didn't know about the missiles stolen from the US, I'd say he wanted defense plans to sell to the highest bidder."

"But you're convinced," Doyle said, "he plans to attack the palace as soon as he gets them?"

"Or soon after," Raven said. "With US agents looking for those missiles, he can't sit on them for long. Eventually somebody will talk, or want to cash in on the reward money

—the US always offers rewards because they seem to work well."

"We can't give him the plans!" Doyle said. He looked around for support. Declan Barlow nodded. Ana Gray did as well. Raven remained stoic.

"We *can* give him fakes," Raven said. "Same as we did in Naples years ago. But let's make sure Wallace doesn't swap them for the real thing."

"Did such a swap happen in the Naples case?"

"Almost ruined the whole operation, yes."

"My goodness...we have to tell His Majesty as well."

Ana asked, "What will he do? Evacuate?"

"Are you kidding? With *his* sense of adventure? He'll march out on the green if it means showing Rahmil he's not afraid of anything. No, he'll make sure the place is cleared of anybody not absolutely necessary for day-to-day function, and keep his regular tea time."

"What about the leak?" Ana said. "I know it was primarily concerned with the White case, but—"

Declan Barlow finally spoke. "The leak is plugged."

Ana raised an eyebrow.

Barlow filled her in on how he discovered Mick Taylor, and how they'd quietly arrested the (now former) MI5 man and had him in custody for questioning. They were learning a lot from Tammy as well, Barlow explained further. The White case may have taken a grim turn, but he assured both Ana and Raven that neither James White or Tammy Granton would see the sun again anytime soon. No jury in the country would let them off with reasonable doubt after seeing the government's case.

Raven thought it was all well and good, but didn't help their current situation. They'd solved one problem only to smash head-first into another and one with significantly greater chances of mass casualties.

He brought them back to the main topic, forging the defense system plans of Buckingham Palace. Barlow said he knew of one or two people familiar with the systems who could alter copies of the specifications enough to make them useless. Raven thought it was a good start.

Nobody touched any of the snacks or cold cuts. When the MI5 men departed, Raven and Ana enjoyed a quiet lunch and she wrapped up the leftovers for later.

CHAPTER THIRTY-NINE

DEFENSE MINISTER GORDON WALLACE RECEIVED THE doctored plans within four hours of the deadline. He waited till he left his office at the end of the day and proceeded to the dead drop as indicated in his instructions. Neither Raven, Ana, nor Piper Shaw watched him. Raven figured Rahmil wouldn't be far away, and if the terrorist saw anybody keeping Wallace under surveillance, they'd know the plan was exposed.

Rahmil and two of his operatives watched Wallace, however, as they had since the party, making sure he spoke to nobody about what happened. His home phones were tapped, listening devices placed inside his home—but they'd been a little late, not having had a chance to install the listening devices until *after* Raven made his appearance at Wallace's home. It was a mistake Rahmil wouldn't realize he'd made. As far as he knew, Wallace was doing everything required of him, with no wandering outside the established routine.

Once Wallace dropped the plans and departed, Rahmil left the car he sat in and collected the dropped package before anybody else found it. Hurrying back to the car, he examined the folded sheets of paper as his driver merged into traffic. For all he knew, the plans were fake. It didn't matter. When Wallace finally broke down and talked about what happened, in an attempt to warn his people, they'd be so busy trying to protect the palace they'd never think twice about a different target being part of Rahmil's true agenda. The palace was a wild goose chase. It didn't matter if the plans were fake. He had no intention of ever finding out. Try and hack Buckingham Palace? Good heavens, not even the most experienced and daring black hat hacker would try.

But Wallace had come through as ordered. Rahmil began tearing the sheets into strips, the strips into smaller pieces, and stuffing the results into an empty envelope he extracted from his jacket. This way, he could set fire to it all and watch it go up in smoke.

Now he only needed to make his diversion look good. The two brothers who ran the electronics shop had done well, accommodating Rahmil's request for a boat, rigging the missiles to a proper launching platform. The people who worked at GCHQ were going to have a very bad day. When the smoke settled, the British wouldn't know what hit them.

———

LATER IN THE EVENING, WHEN IT WAS MORNING IN Washington, D.C., Raven called his buddy at the CIA. Clark Wilson, a Senior Staff Operations Officer for the CIA's Special Activities Center, knew Raven from the old days. From his time in the military to his exit from the CIA, the pair had worked together often and forged a strong friendship. Wilson now acted as Raven's main point of contact at the Agency. Raven sat in Ana's guest bedroom with the door shut. He wanted privacy.

"I hear you lost some missiles," Raven said after they greeted each other and caught up on the latest in their personal lives. Wilson had a wife and two children in college. Raven always made a point to ask about them.

"You know where they are?" Wilson asked. "Everybody's going batshit. Those rockets were lifted straight from the truck in the middle of the highway. They had a helicopter with a machine gun and everything, Sam. Very organized. Somebody wanted those missiles *very* badly."

"And I think I know who."

"Can you tell me where as well?"

"London. A man named Rahmil. Ring any bells?"

"Naples, right?"

"Exactly."

"He comes across the radar now and then, yeah. He has them? You're sure?"

"I'll be sure enough in a day or two," Raven said. He went on to explain the situation in London, leaving out no details so Wilson had the clear picture. At this point, with US weapons involved, the CIA needed to know everything.

"I'll get this to my boss and we'll see if the Brits want any help," Wilson said. "It would be nice to nail Rahmil, that's for sure."

"I'd like a rematch, too," Raven said. "I owe him for Naples."

"Did he make the pickup at the dead drop?"

"He did. But—"

"What?"

"It's been awfully easy."

"You think it smells?" Wilson said.

"Something about it smells, yeah."

"Run with it till further notice," Wilson said. "You've wanted another shot at that punk for a long time. Don't screw it up now."

"Read you loud and clear," Raven said.

———

PIPER SHAW WANTED NOTHING TO DO WITH RAVEN'S elaborate bait and switch which was sure to cost lives.

She was going to end Rahmil's life *tonight*.

Rahmil might have collected the phony plans, but they still had no idea when he planned to make use of them. Ana put Piper back on surveillance duty, which suited her plans well. Simple enough job. But to Piper, Rahmil was the head of the snake. Cut off the head, and the rest of the body died, too. If they wanted to end the threat quickly, the best course of action was to shoot Rahmil dead in the street. Let the other jihadists know they'd discovered the plot and weren't going to let it get any further. Ana, Raven, MI5, all of them, were risking innocent lives for the sake of a sleight-of-hand game for all the marbles.

Well, she wanted no more of it. The small fry operatives weren't worth as much as a dead leader.

Dressed in black with a watch cap over her head and smears of dark combat cosmetics on her face, Piper waited in her car across from Rahmil's hotel. He might have been up in his suite; she wasn't sure. But if he was out late finalizing plans, he had to come back and sleep sometime, right? Holstered under her left arm was a Beretta 9mm Model 92FS equipped with a suppressor. The subsonic rounds in the magazine would be whisper-quiet when she worked the trigger. The cosmetics would obscure her face in any cameras catching the action. London was full of surveillance cameras. The UK was a surveillance state, but sometimes she wasn't sure who the government was watching for. The government made a habit of going after its own people more than foreign invaders intent on creating chaos.

She waited, growing more and more restless and bored as time ticked away. Her plan wouldn't work if he was tucked into bed already. She decided to give him another half hour. And fifteen minutes later, he pulled up in front of the hotel. A valet ran out to greet him.

Piper left the car. She pulled the watch cap further down her forehead. A long, tan overcoat concealed the rest of her body. She crossed the street, her eyes locked on target. Rahmil gave the valet his keys and a tip. The young man jumped into the car and ran it into the garage, while Rahmil approached the doorman.

Piper took out the Beretta.

She heard doors opening and closing behind her. A man shouted, "Rahmil!"

Piper watched Rahmil turn as another sound reached her ears. The *click-clack* of somebody cocking a submachine gun.

He had a backup team.

They were watching you watching him! Move!

Piper, in the middle of the street, with no cover to run to, ignored Rahmil and pivoted to face the threat at her back. She brought up the Beretta and sighted down the slide. Three men ran into the street from their car parked curbside; two had SMGs ready and a third held a pistol. She fired twice. One of the gunners fell in the street, his weapons skidding across the blacktop. As she shifted her aim, the second gunner with the SMG let rip with a controlled burst. The impact of the rounds knocked Piper back, and she landed with a choking gasp and blood filling her lungs. The other two shooters ran to her. Her vision faded as they stood above, and she had one last sense of another shot echoing along the street, but by then everything faded to black.

———

RAHMIL DIVED FOR COVER BEHIND A CAR PARKED IN FRONT OF the hotel. The doorman yelled for him to get inside. Rahmil retreated as another shot rang out, both he and the doorman crawling along the floor and out of view. One of the clerks at the front desk was on the phone with emergency services, while another suggested guests in the lobby either head back to their rooms or find another way out of the hotel. The front and street outside were going to be crowded for a while.

CHAPTER FORTY

ANA SHIVERED FROM THE CHILL, BUT MORE THAN THAT—SHE knew who was in the morgue drawer before the attendant pulled it open. The wheels on the track squealed a little. The attendant unzipped part of the top of the body bag and let Ana and Raven see the face of the dead woman.

Ana sighed. "It's Piper."

Raven concurred.

The attendant nodded and pulled the zipper up with a quick yank; he pushed the door shut. They left the chilly room and signed papers in the front office. Piper had no family Ana was aware of, but she'd try to find somebody. Worst case, she'd take care of the burial. Piper had left instructions for such an emergency in her work file, so Ana knew what she wanted. Raven took her hand, and they walked out of the building onto the street. It was cold outside, too. Ana wanted to head for a warmer climate as soon as possible, but not until the current job was finished. They stood on the sidewalk.

"What happened, Raven?" she said.

"She tried to kill Rahmil."

"Why would she do that? Why risk everything?"

"She thought she was doing the right thing."

"Do you think he'll run?"

"No," Raven said. "Not with everything in motion. He'll hide. We won't be able to find him again. But he won't run."

"Isn't that—"

"No, not the same thing. We won't be able to find him; I didn't say *I* won't be able to find him."

A car pulled up at the curb, and Declan Barlow exited. He looked alarmed.

"Is it what you thought, Ana?" he said with a nod to Raven.

"Piper's dead, yes."

"I'm sorry."

"Me too."

"What can we do?"

"He'll leave the hotel," she said, "but we know about the electronics shop. You can start there."

———

It only took a few hours for MI5 surveillance crews to pick up the trail of the brothers who owned Barnaby's Electronics—Faraj and Sakeen al-Zakaria. Rahmil didn't show up at the shop again, but the brothers behaved as if they were in charge of the operation and MI5 let them carry the ball.

The brothers closed shop in the middle of the afternoon. They traveled to a warehouse south of the city, near Brixton.

The surveillance crew stayed well back as other cars joined the brothers' vehicle inside. Quietly, and advising severe caution, the MI5 team called for backup. They expected the terrorists planning to attack Buckingham Palace were gathering for final preparations.

Inside the warehouse, the brothers and the rest of Rahmil's crew were indeed preparing. But they weren't loading missiles into the van previously selected for the job. The van was empty, and Faraj and Sakeen briefed the crew on their alternate mission. Another crew, Faraj explained, had the missiles, and as they spoke were on a boat chugging up the Severn River within range of GCHQ. That was the real target. They were a diversion. Their job was to get attention fixed on the palace and show the British a thing or two about guerrilla warfare.

They were to go through the motions, Faraj explained. The crew would proceed to the launch point on Piccadilly, with gun crews standing by in back to open fire on authorities when they came within range. The mission wasn't a total fabrication; Rahmil wanted casualties and as many as possible.

While the terrorists made their final equipment checks and climbed into the van, the MI5 team outside prepared to blast their way inside. When a heavily armed special weapons team blew the side door out with a pack of C4, tossing in smoke and tear gas grenades, along with flash bangs for added effect, they raced inside with submachine guns. The terrorists were not ready, having had their weapons "on safe" in preparation for a drive through the city. They didn't want to accidentally fire a gun while in traffic. As the British unit triggered precision bursts from their weapons, Faraj fell, his brother going for a handgun before a line of slugs slapped across his chest and put him on the ground for good.

Gunmen poured out of the van, four total, each attempting to get off a string of shots, but through the thick smoke and the eye-stinging tear gas, they had no chance. They put up a good fight, running for cover, knowing the nooks and crannies of the warehouse, heading for areas not affected by the tear gas. It didn't matter—the strike team advanced without mercy, in full breathing gear; the gas didn't affect them. Presently, the gunfire faded, the team opened more doors to let the smoke out, and emergency personnel rushed in to tend to the wounded and the dead.

When the team leader looked inside the van, he expected to see the stolen US missiles. He expected to be the one who secured the deadly payload and received the appropriate commendations for doing so; he was disappointed. The back of the van was empty. A search of the warehouse turned up only the remains of the crates the missiles had arrived in; the sense of victory, having "saved the palace," vanished as the team called in the update.

The missiles were still out there.

Headquarters ordered all available units to converge on Buckingham Palace. They had no idea what kind of vehicles they were looking for, but it had to be another van or truck with an enclosed trailer where the terrorists could fit the missiles and the launcher. The alert went far and wide and everybody hoped they weren't too late.

———

DEFENSE MINISTER GORDON WALLACE OBEYED ORDERS AND stayed home. Unofficial leave, they said. He had a feeling his unofficial leave would turn into permanent retirement shortly.

He was out in front of his home tending to his roses when he heard brakes squeak at the curb. It was early evening; he'd not bothered with the radio or television all day. He couldn't stand not knowing what was happening, waiting for *something* to happen, not knowing if anything *would* because terrorists followed their own schedule. With his shears in one hand and a few roses in the other, he turned, and any happiness provided by working on his prized roses vanished. Rahmil stepped out of the car and onto the stone path leading to the porch. He carried an envelope in his right hand.

"Good evening, Mr. Wallace."

"What do you want?"

Rahmil grinned. "For you to put those shears down, please." The grin didn't hide the threat behind the request. Wallace either put the shears down, or Rahmil would escalate. And Wallace had no other weapon with which to defend himself. He dropped the shears on the grass to his right.

"Want me to drop the roses, too?"

"No jokes, Mr. Wallace." Rahmil held the envelope out to Wallace. "Your pictures."

Frowning, Wallace took the envelope, set the roses down, and slit the envelope open with a nail. He found inside an SD card. He looked at Rahmil. "What's the meaning of this?"

"The SD card from my camera, sir," Rahmil said. "I am a man of my word. You did what I asked. There are your pictures."

Wallace, stunned, watched Rahmil turn around and return to his car. Every muscle in his body screamed for him to act, but what did he have to fight with? Nobody from the security service was watching his house; he hadn't thought to ask anybody to do so. And here he was, alone with the terrorist planning to attack Buckingham Palace, and all he had to show for it was an envelope with a plastic card inside and garden shears. Wallace had never felt so powerless.

Rahmil's car started with the first twist of the key, and he drove away. All Wallace could do was watch.

CHAPTER FORTY-ONE

Rahmil laughed. He saw the defense minister in his rearview mirror, standing impotently in his front garden, probably wishing he had a bazooka.

He checked his watch. No more time for frivolity. He had one more stop to make, one more task, and then it was time to get out of London. And never come back. Very soon the strike against GCHQ would put his name at the top of the most wanted list and make him a superstar among those engaged in the jihad.

———

"Tell me what's happening!"

Declan Barlow shouted the order into his phone. He was at Ana Gray's house, pacing in the living room. He'd placed a communication set and computer on one of her glass-topped tables. He wasn't directing the operation in the field but instead staying in close contact with those at the front. And the news from the warehouse was not good.

Raven and Ana watched the MI5 man; they watched his face tighten in frustration, then concern, then—dread? Or fear? Raven gave the MI5 man the benefit of the doubt. He wasn't afraid, but the answer to his question added a new layer of trouble to an already complex situation.

Barlow ended the cell phone call and turned to Raven and Ana. He gave them the highlights of the warehouse raid and the punch line. No missiles.

Raven said, "What now?"

"The palace is on high alert; we have patrols doubled up on each other. If they think they can launch from a roadway or some similar point, we'll find them."

Barlow took a seat in front of the computer and began scrolling through incoming messages and data points. He frowned again.

"This is odd," he said. "The security team at the palace isn't reporting any attempt at a breach."

"How fake was the information Wallace gave them?" Raven said.

"Passwords were fake. Router names and network IDs were correct, just to give them something to check against what they might already know."

Raven smiled. He remembered thinking the same thing in Naples when he first clashed with Rahmil.

"But there's been no attempt at breaching the network," Barlow said.

"Almost as if they never wanted the palace data to begin with," Raven said.

Ana gasped. "You mean—"

"The palace is a diversion. Those missiles are somewhere else. And we won't know until they hit what they're aimed at."

THE SEVERN RIVER IS GREAT BRITAIN'S LONGEST RIVER. Total length: 354 kilometers (or 220 miles if you're a Yank). The medium-sized boat with no name on the hull chugged up the river, making the painfully long trip through countryside and urban areas, following the twists and turns extending forever and seemingly leading to nowhere. But the crew on the boat had a destination and a purpose for their short voyage. They were heading for the end of the line, near Gloucester, where they'd anchor and remove the tarp covering sensitive equipment mounted mid-ship. Under the tarp sat the missile launching platform with two large pods containing the sixteen missiles appropriated from the United States. Target: GCHQ.

From Gloucester, the missiles only had to travel eight miles to the headquarters building of Government Communications Headquarters, one of the major intelligence and information centers of the UK government. The missile warheads had been programmed with the appropriate longitude and latitude coordinates, and Rahmil had a specific portion of the building he wanted to hit. The east side, where the counter-terror section housed most of their staff and computers. He wanted the east side of the building pummeled into pieces. He knew the data wouldn't be harmed. They had multiple backups in other locations. But the attack would send a message. The message was important.

The boat continued chugging. Nothing stood in its way.

RAHMIL MADE A RIGHT TURN OFF THE MAIN ROAD AND started up the winding two-lane route to Granton's estate. The radio played at low volume, Rahmil only passively listening to the current affairs chat show in progress. What the pair on the air spoke about hardly mattered. He waited for the BBC to interrupt with news of a "shocking" attack on GCHQ in Gloucester.

By now, the crew on the boat should be within firing range. Any minute now…

He followed the twisty road at five miles under the posted limit. Rahmil refused to rush this last task. His anxious heart-beat was something he had to deal with. He needed to keep cool, remain methodical, focus on the goal. He'd come this far. Now was not the time to mess up.

It was time to sever ties with Thomas Granton.

Rahmil would miss the flow of money, but the man was far too compromised because of his daughter. And once British authorities dug into the GCHQ attack, he was surely to crack once they found a thread leading to him. It was time to exit the partnership. There would be other sources of money in the future.

Halfway up to the main gate, Rahmil phoned Granton to announce his unscheduled visit. Granton promised to have the guard at the gate let him through and made no comment about the surprise.

Rahmil passed through the gate with a wave and continued along the access road. As the estate house grew in size with his approach, Rahmil saw Granton emerge to stand on the porch. *As is his habit,* Rahmil thought. *He makes it so easy. Remain alert for witnesses.*

Rahmil examined the grounds. No yard crew tending the grass and trees. Granton didn't have sentries roaming, either.

Servants would be inside. Granton was all smiles when Rahmil stopped the car in front of the porch steps. But the smile turned to a frown when Rahmil exited without shutting off the car. He stood with the car between him and Granton.

"I wasn't expecting you today," Granton said.

"I know."

With his right hand, Rahmil reached for the gun holstered cross draw on his left hip. Granton didn't recognize the motion; he waited for Rahmil to further explain his visit. He wasn't going to be rude and press for an answer.

But the Brit shuffled back in fright, his hands up and forward, when Rahmil lifted the gun over the roof of the car and aimed at Granton's face.

"What are you—"

Rahmil fired once. The crack of the shot echoed across the estate field.

Rahmil dropped the gun in a jacket pocket and slid back into the car. Minus his seat belt, he steered for the main gate, the guard rushing out, Rahmil turning the car slightly to strike him with the right side of the front bumper. The impact flung the guard's body to the side, where it bounced off the shack before landing on the grass. Rahmil rushed out, ran into the shack, and found the switch to open the gate.

He left the estate and traveled back the way he'd come, at a much greater speed than before.

CHAPTER FORTY-TWO

THE EMERGENCY ALERT FLASHED ON BARLOW'S LAPTOP screen, a square box with a yellow ALERT on top and white text below. He sat at the glass-topped table, watching the online exchanges from the field, the radio chatter from the com set blending into the background. The emergency message brought him to fast attention.

"Oh, no," he said. He turned shocked eyes on Raven and Ana as they joined him.

"Is this—" Raven began.

"I'm afraid so."

The message advised of a "missile strike" on GCHQ. More messages popped onto the screen, more details of the attack. Missiles fired from a boat eight miles away. Teams were heading to the Severn to try and catch the boat. Part of the headquarters building was on fire; multiple missiles fired, no exact count. Raven wondered if it mattered how many had been fired. They'd all landed on target.

"This is terrible," Barlow said. "A direct assault on the anti-terror section in the east wing."

"Now we can tell the CIA what happened to their missiles," Raven said.

Before Barlow replied, his cell phone rang. He answered, and Raven watched another look of shock wash over his features. He glanced at Ana, who had the same question on her face. What worse news could there be? Rahmil had won; outmaneuvered British intelligence; Raven himself. He would have been impressed if the event hadn't come with a death toll.

The MI5 ended his call. His face was pale.

"What's wrong?" Raven asked.

"Granton is dead. Shot in front of his house."

————

TAMMY GRANTON HAD LOST TRACK OF THE DATE AND TIME and had no idea how much longer they'd hold her "for questioning." Every day, more questions. They'd yet to formally charge her, and her lawyer was beginning to make noise about filing charges or letting her go until they made up their minds.

When the usual guard collected her from the holding cell and snapped her wrists into handcuffs, she figured it was going to be more of the same. They traveled down a long and brightly lit hallway once more, same as always. At least she spotted a hint of sunlight through the barred and ground-glass windows they passed.

The guard nudged her into an interview room on the left. Usually they entered on the right, and she stumbled making the correction. The guard tried to intervene to keep her from falling but she shook him off.

The small room with its bright light and white walls

didn't make an impression any longer. She was numb to the proceedings. But today was going to be different after all. On all other days, she had no idea who her questioner was. They gave their names, but she forgot them. But she knew the man waiting for her in the interview room.

Declan Barlow.

His face looked grim.

The guard sat her in the chair, and Barlow took his seat across from her. Bare table between them, same as always. Tammy already felt bored. But she also had a sense of hope. If Barlow looked unhappy, perhaps her lawyer had finally sprung her loose.

She smiled a little.

———

BARLOW WAS ABOUT TO WIPE THE SMILE STRAIGHT OFF HER face.

But he didn't feel good about it.

"Agent Barlow," she said.

"You remembered."

"Why wouldn't I?"

He still didn't smile. He had to tell the young woman her father was dead. This had nothing to do with her case, and he hated to bear the bad news. But as the agent in overall charge of the investigation related to her arrest, he felt it was his responsibility. Telling Tammy her father was dead was one thing; explaining *why* he died was another, and Barlow wasn't sure he knew how to handle the second part.

"I have bad news, Miss Granton."

Her face changed. If she'd been hoping for better news, it wasn't coming.

"Your father is dead."

She didn't believe him and said so with a desperate pitch behind the words. For proof, Barlow handed her a copy of The Guardian from his briefcase. The front-page headline announced the murder. She read the story and slumped into stunned silence.

"I'm so sorry, Miss Granton."

Her eyes pleaded an unasked question. Barlow had to do his best now.

"He was murdered by an associate named Rahmil, a man connected to the jihadist networks," he explained. Then he switched back to detective mode. "Did your father ever mention—"

"No. He told me he went to the Middle East for work and because he joined their religion."

"So you knew nothing—"

She leaned forward with fierce determination replacing grief.

"Stop talking! I need my lawyer. I have instructions."

"Miss Granton—"

"Don't you get it? Dad told me if anything ever happened, I had to get an envelope from the lawyer. Then I have to hand it to you. Well, not you *specifically*, but MI5 for sure."

Barlow frowned. He felt excited.

Had Granton left a dead man's switch?

What did it contain?

"Goddammit, Barlow!" Tammy shouted. "*Call my lawyer!*"

———

LONDON ASSAULT 287

RAVEN DIDN'T WANT TO GET IN THE CAR. BUT THE CHIEF OF the Secret Intelligence Service, SIS; or, MI6; wanted a conversation with him and Ana. So, he had to climb into the armored black Bentley which collected the pair in front of Ana's Notting Hill home.

The older man sat on the reverse rear seat, his back to the driver, facing Raven and Ana. He wore a thick coat. Full head of gray hair, plenty of wrinkles. His eye remained sharp and vibrant in contrast to his jowly and dour expression.

"Mr. Raven."

"Sir Reginald."

"I suppose you're wondering why I asked to see you."

"After the last thirty-six hours, it's not hard to guess."

The chief of SIS only nodded in agreement. Sir Reginald August was a career civil servant, having previously held several ambassador roles overseas. His appointment to the big chair at SIS had surprised him. He'd remarked publicly he had not expected to come back to the UK until he retired.

"The situation with GCHQ, and Thomas Granton," Sir Reginald said, "has left us all reeling. The King himself—"

"Expressed his grief very eloquently, I thought," Raven said, "while keeping mum on the dead man's switch."

"Yes indeed. Miss Gray, I'd like to extend my appreciation for what I know was an unpleasant task."

"We wanted hard proof," she said, "yet we only got it after Granton died. Seems like—"

"He got away with it?"

"Sort of," she said.

"Hardly. Now, Rahmil—he's another story. If we don't move fast, he stands a *chance* of getting away."

The treasure trove of information in the "envelope" left for Tammy Granton provided more than enough data to finish the mission. Granton wrote out a full confession. He detailed every account where the money marked for the jihad had gone. He named contacts, their locations, everything needed to close Rahmil's money network. The cherry on top was the location of Rahmil's private retreat in the Swiss Alps. Because of the envelope, the British government decided to give Granton a hero's tribute, hide all the dirty laundry, and treat his murder as a ghastly attack instead of the fallout of terrorist conspiracy. They were instead blaming the same as-yet-undiscovered terrorist who attacked GCHQ. They needed to keep Rahmil from realizing he'd cut his own throat when he decided to murder Thomas Granton.

"You have all you need," Raven said. "SAS can turn Rahmil into swiss cheese—my presence isn't required."

"Stop it, Mr. Raven. I know your reputation. If I tell you to stand down, you'll go to Switzerland on your own. I know you have a personal interest in seeing this through to the end. I'm not going to take that from you."

"Okay."

"You're waiting for the *catch*, aren't you?"

"What do you want me to do, Sir Reginald?"

"Piper Shaw was my granddaughter."

Ana sucked in a sharp breath. Raven remained unmoved.

Sir Reginald continued, "I want you to go with the SAS team. While they take care of the gunmen around Rahmil, I want *you* to *personally* finish him off. End his existence, Mr. Raven."

"What's happening at his hideout that will keep the strike team occupied?" Raven asked.

"He's called his associates for a meeting. We figure he wants to talk about the attack. Pat his men on the back. Many of the names Granton mentioned have left their current places of hiding—from Cairo, Tripoli, others—to head for Switzerland. They are all under heavy surveillance. Our best people. The *ghosts*, Mr. Raven. The ones nobody ever sees."

"I know many like them," Raven said. "How long do we have?"

"Wheels up at three a.m. tomorrow. You have today to prepare and meet the rest of the team."

"The SAS usually don't appreciate stragglers, Sir Reginald."

"They know this is a personal request from me. They *will* offer you a seat on the helicopter."

"I'll go, certainly," Raven told him.

"Finish this once and for all," the SIS boss said. "For all of us."

CHAPTER FORTY-THREE

ANA NEXT DROVE RAVEN TO THE HEADQUARTERS OF THE Special Air Service in Hereford. The briefing began right away with Raven seated in the back row while the British commandos filled chairs in front of him. He was the odd man out in his civilian clothes, but Raven refused to let the difference bother him. He'd get his fighting gear soon enough.

Images of Rahmil's chalet were shown on large monitors and a physical model of the house and surrounding terrain occupied a large table. There was no time to build a mock-up and practice. Nobody had any idea how long Rahmil and his people would be staying. Surveillance reported the last man to arrive had done so that morning, so they figured less than twenty-four hours unless Rahmil planned to go longer. They expected the opposite, that Rahmil would gather his crew for an "atta boy" session, and then send them scattering to new hiding places till further notice.

They'd have to improvise the attack when they arrived, but the mission goal was clear. *Kill them all. No prisoners.*

Two forty a.m. Time to load up. Raven had his own gear

now, black fatigues and SAS-issued weapons. Five large helicopters would carry them to the target, and the SAS team worked together getting men and equipment aboard.

Ana Gray walked with Raven to the third chopper, the one in which he was assigned to ride with the team commanders. She grabbed his right arm to stop him within a few feet of the open cabin door.

"Come and see me when you get back," she said. "We'll have a drink or two."

"I never turn down free booze," he said.

"You just turn down everything else I offer." She laughed. He smiled. Ana stood on her toes and kissed his left cheek. "Good hunting."

"We'll need it."

He turned and walked to the chopper, climbing aboard to take a seat with the other eight commandos and two squad leaders. He gave Ana a final eave, and she turned to walk back to the building at the edge of the airfield.

Raven watched her till the crew chief pulled the cabin door closed. Then the engine started.

Liftoff at 3:02 a.m. A ninety-minute flight.

They'd attack while the enemy slept.

————

RAHMIL HAD GONE FOR SOMETHING MODEST IN HIS ALPS hideaway. A two-story spread over 1800 square feet, it sat on a low slope backed by a forest and tall green grass in front. Beside the house was a fenced patio with furniture, tables, and cooking space—all one needed for outdoor entertaining. Around back, a path led into the forest; a corner-to-corner balcony on the second floor overlooked the natural splendor.

His five close advisers arrived in separate vehicles, off-roaders which handled the rough terrain and lack of roads without complaint. He greeted each one and showed them their guest rooms.

Two days only. Rahmil didn't want to go longer, and he'd send them off early if possible. They needed to talk about the success of the GCHQ attack and what it would do for their standing in the jihadi world. They needed to drain Granton's accounts and launder the millions of dollars still available to them. Rahmil didn't expect every man to agree with eliminating Granton, but he planned to state he had no choice. A small security force worked around the clock, and as Rahmil and his men slept, the guards remained in the shadows watching for danger. There were no neighbors for miles. If anybody wandered into the area, they were hostiles. Rahmil ordered they be treated as such without hesitation.

———

THE CRICKETS CEASED AS THE SAS TEAM NEARED THE chalet. Raven hoped the guards on duty weren't counting on night sounds to stay steady—but, were he in their shoes, he'd notice the sudden silence and immediately go to yellow alert. It didn't mean there was an enemy lurking. Night critters went quiet for a variety of reasons, and the simplest reason was another, larger critter in the area. But it would be too much of a maybe for Raven, and he expected Rahmil's security force to feel the same way.

It had not been an easy march from the landing site five miles away, but the commandos made it. The roving sentries a half mile from the target didn't surprise them; they'd been easily dispatched with quick and silent knife work. They'd left the bodies behind and continued to the objective.

The thirty-two SAS operators—thirty-three if one counted Raven—spread out in a J around the house. The plan was to shoot out the windows, fire grenades, and then fill the house with sustained machine-gun fire. Once the terrorists inside had been sufficiently subdued, Raven and a handful of operatives would enter and look for the prize.

Raven waited in the open grass, the blades tall enough to conceal their forms in the dead of night but not a hiding place he'd consider for a second during daylight. Rahmil had chosen well—all the cover was in the back of the house, where, presumably, he'd placed electronic sensors to warn of intruders approaching from the rear. It would have been the go-to decision of anybody planning to hit the place. The ground around them appeared undisturbed by such electronic emplacements; didn't mean they weren't there, though. The fact nobody in the house was stirring—guard or otherwise—proved Raven right. They counted on the open area to dissuade a frontal attack.

Raven carried the same equipment as the other SAS men, with the exception of the heavy-machine gunners. Head weapon was the C8 CQB with a ten-inch barrel. Based on the AR platform and the M-4 specifically, it was a weapon Raven needed no familiarization with. It felt as natural to him as any other AR-type rifle. Body armor, a set of three grenades, and a combat knife made up the rest of his fighting kit. He did keep his personal pistol. Sidearms for everybody else consisted of ubiquitous Glock 9 mm autoloaders—Models 17 and 19, depending on the individual's preference. Every member of the assault team wore Kevlar helmets with night vision goggles attached.

Raven scanned the house through the green hue of the night vision device in front of his eyes. He registered at least three bodies around the patio. They used the furniture and posts holding up the cross-beam overhead for cover. The windows offered no view of what went on inside the house, if anything—the drapes were drawn across every pane of glass.

The man to Raven's left was in charge of the SAS crew. His name was Tomkins. He didn't have a rank visible on his uniform, nor had he shared it with Raven during the flight from London. Didn't matter. He'd be going into the house with Raven when the time came, and he leaned close to Raven's right ear to talk.

"Ready for the show?"

"Take 'em down," Raven said. He turned off his night vision and raised the goggles to the top of his helmet. He didn't want his eyes affected when the explosions started going off.

Tomkins communicated to his men through their com link. Acknowledgments weren't verbal, but a series of clicks and beeps. Raven braced the C8 CQB carbine against his shoulder. Chugging machine gun fire from a trio of squad automatic weapons shook the ground. One concentrated on the sentries in the patio; resulting screams indicated hits, but Raven couldn't tell how many were permanently off the playing field. The other full-auto streams shattered glass and punched holes in the solid wall of the chalet. Belches from HK M320 grenade launchers mounted under the barrels of C8 carbines sent high-explosive projectiles through the now-open windows. Thumps and bright flashes accompanied the detonation; a second set followed, three belches one after the other, more explosions inside.

The machine gunners started up again, filling the chalet

with steel-core projectiles. The operators at the curved point of the J fired into the side and rear of the house. Raven shoved the night vision goggles over his eyes again and watched. No movement from anywhere inside or out. Nobody returning fire. Was the place empty? The set of Land Rover off-roaders said otherwise. But how could there only be three sentries visible yet nobody else tried to defend the place?

Tomkins called a cease-fire. He tapped Raven on the right shoulder. No more time for questions. Time to go in and find out for himself what was happening inside. Raven and Tomkins broke free of the firing line and rushed toward the house; two more SAS shooters followed along Raven's left.

Tomkins used a 12-gauge Remington shotgun to blow the hinges off the front door. He ducked back as Raven entered first behind the falling front door, shoulder-rolling to the right to clear the entryway for the others. The heavy door landed on the hardwood floor with a loud smack. Up in a crouch, C8 ready, scanning. He moved the muzzle with his eyes. No targets. He raised the goggles once again and turned on the mini-light mounted on the C8's handguards. The bright beam swung back and forth with Raven's movements. Dust particles and debris filled the air; the beam highlighted the particles, resembling a continuous laser ray. No hostiles. Zip. Zilch. Nada.

"Clear!" Raven shouted. He stayed low, covered partially by a sofa and end table, more furniture to his right, but hard to identify outside the beam of the flashlight. The other three SAS personnel entered and went in separate directions.

A floorboard creaked.

Raven snapped his muzzle up, following the steps to the second-floor landing. Part of the walkway was visible from the first floor, a wooden railing at the edge, connecting wall-to-stairs, and then a hallway continued to the other end of the house. At the corner of the hallway stood a man with a Kalashnikov. It wasn't Rahmil. The man was older with long hair going gray with a thin and bony face. As Raven's light struck him, the man opened fire with a full-auto burst.

CHAPTER FORTY-FOUR

No way out!

Rahmil hugged the floor as machine gun fire tore into his chalet and wreaked havoc on the interior. None of the heavy gunfire came near him. His bedroom was at the back of the house, upper floor; the shooting seemed concentrated at the front. The grenades had entered through the front, too. The first blast had shaken him from the bed.

He had weapons but no way out. Unless he wanted to jump off the balcony and certainly break a leg on landing.

How had they found him?

The chalet wasn't known to anybody but—

Had Granton survived?

The thought sent a chill through Rahmil's body despite the commotion outside, the continued slamming of heavy-caliber rounds into his home. Yes, Granton knew; he'd visited. Rahmil had *invited* him to visit. And there was no way he'd survived a point-blank gunshot to the head. It was a stupid question to consider. What Granton had done was something more insidious, something Rahmil should have taken into consideration. Granton had left behind a confession and details. It was the only way the British could have found him in the Alps. *Too many years of getting away with it, dummy,* he decided, gritting his teeth. *You got soft and now you're finished unless you get creative quick.*

Men grunted and breathed heavily. They crawled on hands and knees into his bedroom, all in their pajamas, all with sleep still in their eyes as they attempted to comprehend the commotion happening around them. His men. His close associates. How long had it been since most of them had last fired a gun in anger?

Too long.

"I hope you're ready to fight!" he shouted, rising, running to a cabinet on the forward wall facing his bed. He swung both thick doors open. Inside, on a metal rack, hung automatic weapons with full magazines. He didn't have to ask his men a second time to get ready for action. They swarmed the weapons, grabbing spare magazines, dropping the spares into pajama pants pockets and checking actions in the dark. Rahmil smiled. Maybe they weren't rusty after all.

"If we don't hold them off, we're all dead," Rahmil said. "Unless you want to jump off the balcony, but I promise there are people waiting for you below. If you survive. We make a stand *here*."

Five faces looked back at him in the dark. He could barely make them out, but it didn't matter. He began directing them to positions. The hallway would be critical. There may not be any way out, but there was only one way *up*, too.

Well, two ways.

They could climb over the balcony from below.

He grabbed the arm of Borja Elim, his old friend, the man

who ran things for him in Cairo. He'd been with Rahmil from the beginning, and he'd be there for the end, too.

"My friend," Rahmil said, "I need you to take point. Cover the stairs. Don't let them get up here."

"We will beat them together," Elim said, "or die together."

They clasped hands once more, and Borja Elim was out the door heading down the hall. Another of Rahmil's associates, Yousef, followed for backup. Rahmil told the other three to spread out around the room, watch the balcony, and he'd watch the bedroom door in case Elim failed.

Or, rather, *when* Elim failed.

Rahmil was under no illusion of surviving the night.

But if he was going down, he wanted to take Sam Raven with him.

———

Borja Elim always knew he'd die in battle. Once he left the field to handle Rahmil's Cairo headquarters and watched his hair go gray and the wrinkles arrive, he thought perhaps his goal wouldn't happen. He'd die in bed after all, despite his best efforts to fight the infidel until the end. Now, he had his wish. And he wasn't going down easy, either. The enemy was going to pay dearly before he fired his last shot.

He clutched the AKM to his body as he waited at the hallway corner. He peered around the edge at the steps and into the entryway below. Movement behind him—one of the others, Yousef, based on the bald head Elim briefly glimpsed. Yousef clutched his own AKM and ran along the rail to the far end, where he effectively set up a crossfire. The shooting outside stopped. The grenades ceased. The attack force would be coming. A small number at first, per protocol, but the rest would be ready.

Three shotgun blasts shook the house. The hinges on the door exploded inward, the metal pieces sliding across the hardwood floor. The door fell inward, landing with a flat smack, the shadowy outlines of men in the doorway. One ran inside, dodged to his right, and found cover. Elim tucked the AKM to his shoulder. His finger caressed the trigger. But he barely registered the man's outline. He wanted a clear shot. The man turned on a flashlight and began waving it around, looking for targets. But he didn't look up until Borja Elim began to squeeze his trigger. Elim had him dead to rights. The AKM blazed to life with a bright flash and jolting recoil— had the kick always been that strong? Elim adjusted his aim and flinched as the bright light hit him in the face.

———

TOMKINS SHOUTED ORDERS, BUT RAVEN BARELY DISCERNED his voice. He rolled right, knocking over the end table, a lamp falling onto his left shoulder; he shook it off, the beam of his flashlight pinpointing him like a moving bullseye. The gunner at the top of the stairs was taking full advantage. The gunman paused to adjust his aim, and Raven took his chance. Laying on his side, he aimed the C8 carbine up, highlighting the old man behind the gun. He saw the man flinch, but before he fired again, Raven tagged him with a pair of 5.56mm man shredders. The slugs entered between his stomach and chest, turning his flinch into a scream. He started to fall back with his support hand leaving the handguard of his rifle; Raven fired twice more, through the man's neck and face. The body hit the floor.

Then the second shooter fired from the opposite end of the stairs, but his target wasn't Raven. He fired on the SAS men. Raven swung his weapon left, highlighting the second shooter. He didn't get a chance to fire. Tomkins blasted him with his C8; the man's body jerked with hits before he slumped in the corner.

Raven turned off his light. He stayed on the ground. The lamp had fallen from his shoulder and now sat against his back. He couldn't go backward, so he slithered forward until another sofa provided partial cover.

Tomkins told his men to use their grenades. One each. The three men flung the high-explosive orbs toward the top floor landing, the grenades bouncing off the facing wall to deflect deeper down the hall. *Boom!*—one, two, three. The house shook. Raven left the sofa and ran closer to Tomkins, squatting beside the SAS leader.

"Rahmil's up there," Raven said.

"You want to go?"

"Get ready to come and get me if it goes bad."

Tomkins said nothing more as Raven advanced to the stairs, taking the first flight carefully, turning left for the second, keeping his back to the wall as he ascended to the second-floor landing. He plucked a grenade from his web belt, pulled the pin, and pitched it around the corner at the top of the stairs. He heard it bounce off the wall and hit the floor and roll. The hardwood motif continued on the second level, too. He waited until the *thump* of the grenade blast—this time, somebody screamed and kept screaming. A gunshot. The screaming stopped.

Raven grinned. Rahmil was still alive. And waiting.

Raven left the stairs and stayed low, stepping over body in front of him. The hallway was dark. The floor creaked. They knew he was coming. Doors along the hall remained shut. The only open door was at the end of the hall, probably the master bedroom; was Rahmil hiding within? Another body. Raven briefly flashed his light over the fallen figure. Not Rahmil. The grenade had chewed up the lower part of his body and the bullet hole in the back of the head took care of the rest. Raven turned off the light and reached for another grenade.

"Raven!"

The voice was familiar. He remembered it from ten years ago in Naples.

"It's only you and me, Raven!"

Raven slowly pulled the pin from the grenade and held on tight.

"No ticking time bombs, no saving the world, only two gladiators fighting to the death! Tonight, we finish this!"

Sure, Raven thought. He pitched the grenade through the doorway. The pink flash of the explosion filled the room. Raven hustled forward with the C8 tucked to his shoulder. Through the doorway, he pivoted left, probing for targets, the mounted light shining at its brightest setting. Two figures near the balcony doorway. Raven fired. Bullets spit from the muzzle and cut down the two shooters. Neither was Rahmil. *Where the hell—*

The blur of motion came from his right, outside of the beam of light. Raven dropped and slid across the floor as the full-auto burst from Rahmi's weapon chopped into the wall, shattering the dresser mirror. Raven stayed low and raised the C8 to fire blindly, one-handed, in the hopes of striking his target. Nothing. He brought the weapon back to reload, but Rahmil sprang from the other side of the bed, not holding a rifle this time, but a knife. The outer edge of the flashlight glinted off the sharpened steel. Raven braced, bringing up his right elbow. He was going to smash it into Rahmil's throat. But he missed, the tip of the elbow whooshing through air instead, and Rahmil collided with him and pushed Raven into a dresser. The light flashed off the steel edge of the knife in Rahmil's fist. The hard thumps against Raven's back told him only his body armor prevented the cutting edge from slicing him to ribbons. Raven swung his right elbow again. *Crack!* He felt a solid impact with Rahmil's jaw, which made the terrorist step back far enough for Raven to pivot and bash him in the head with the buttstock of the C8. Rahmil tumbled but executed a shoulder roll. He gained his feet but was unsteady as he launched another attack with a forward rush.

Raven let the C8 dangle on its sling and grabbed his pistol. He ran back to put more distance between himself and Rahmil, then his feet stopped. He'd struck one of the dead bodies on the floor. Falling back, Raven gasped. He hit the floor on the other side of the body, and Rahmil raised the knife above his head. Raven lifted the .45 and fired point-blank into Rahmil's stomach and chest. Rahmil landed on top of him, Raven shoving the heavy body aside. He rose to his feet. Rahmil lay on his back, his eyes still open, staring blankly at the ceiling. A gurgling noise came from Rahmil's throat. He was still alive, but barely. Raven fired a last single round through Rahmil's head. The gurgle stopped.

Raven stepped back and took a few seconds to catch his breath. He knew he was talking to a corpse, but he spoke anyway.

"*Now* we're finished."

IF YOU LIKED THIS, YOU MAY ENJOY:
SKILLS TO KILL
A STEVE DANE THRILLER BOOK ONE

International adventurer Steve Dane never should have set foot in Italy.

Witnessing a young woman's kidnapping, he is drawn into the decades-old vendetta behind the crime. Hired by the girl's father, racing against time as her life hangs in the balance, Dane battles the mafia who want him dead and the police and international agents who want him out of the way.

With the help of his lover, Nina Talikova, Dane plunges along a path leading him past a mere kidnapping and into an ever-more complex world of high stakes, ruled by a powerful and mysterious woman known only as The Duchess. Life, it seems, is getting cheaper than Dane could ever imagine and The Duchess has put a price on the ultimate weapon that will make it worthless. Only he and Nina have the power to stop a clock ticking away the life of both the girl and the world.

Steve Dane & Nina Talikova race around the world delivering justice one bullet at a time.

AVAILABLE NOW

ABOUT THE AUTHOR

A twenty-five year veteran of radio and television broadcasting, Brian Drake has spent his career in San Francisco where he's filled writing, producing, and reporting duties with stations such as KPIX-TV, KCBS, KQED, among many others. Currently carrying out sports and traffic reporting duties for Bloomberg 960, Brian Drake spends time between reports and carefully guarded morning and evening hours cranking out action/adventure tales.

A love of reading when he was younger inspired him to create his own stories, and he sold his first short story, "The Desperate Minutes," to an obscure webzine when he was 25 (more years ago than he cares to remember, so don't ask). Many more short story sales followed before he expanded to novels, entering the self-publishing field in 2010, and quickly building enough of a following to attract the attention of several publishers and other writing professionals.

Brian Drake lives in California with his wife and two cats, and when he's not writing he is usually blasting along the back roads in his Corvette with his wife telling him not to drive so fast, but the engine is so loud he usually can't hear her.

Printed in Great Britain
by Amazon